Secret Society

GIRL

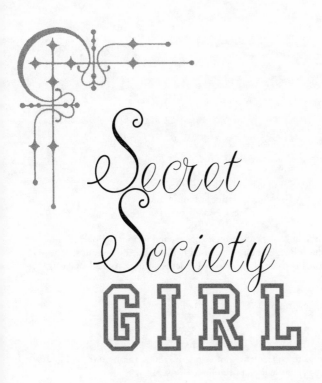

Secret Society GIRL

AN IVY LEAGUE NOVEL

Diana Peterfreund

DELACORTE PRESS

SECRET SOCIETY GIRL
A Delacorte Press Book / July 2006

Published by Bantam Dell
A Division of Random House, Inc.
New York, New York

Book design by Carol Malcolm Russo

Library of Congress Cataloging-in-Publication Data

Peterfreund, Diana.
Secret society girl : an Ivy League novel / Diana Peterfreund.
p.   cm.
ISBN-13: 978-0-385-34002-1
ISBN-10: 0-385-34002-8
1. Women college students—Fiction.   2. Greek letter societies—
Fiction.   I. Title.

PS3616.E835S43 2006
813'.6—dc22   2006040663

Printed in the United States of America
Published simultaneously in Canada

www.bantamdell.com

10 9 8 7 6 5 4 3 2
BVG

For the sons and daughters of Eli

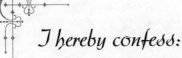

I hereby confess:
I am a member of one of the most
infamous secret societies in the world.

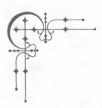

You've heard the legends, I'm sure. We're the Ivy League's dirty little secret. We run the country, even the states you wouldn't think we'd care about, like Nebraska. We start wars, we coordinate coups, and we have a hand in writing the constitution of every new nation. Every presidential candidate is a member—that way, whoever wins, they'll always be under our thumb.

The media fears us, which is silly, since the CEO of every newspaper and television network in the country is already a member of our brotherhood. We've been controlling every aspect of the media for more than a century, from deciding which movies get greenlighted to choosing the next American Idol. (Do you actually think your text-message votes count?)

We own most of the buildings of the university, as well as most of the land in the city, and we've got a good proportion of it bugged. The local police work for us. The mayor lives in our pocket. There's not a student on campus who isn't afraid to walk past our imposing stone tomb.

Election to our society is a ticket into a life beyond anyone's wildest dreams. Success is our birthright from the moment we emerge from our initiation coffins into our new lives as members of the society. Any job we want is within our reach, and any job we don't want our enemies to have is out of theirs. We are given enormous monetary gifts upon graduation, as well as sports cars, valuable antiques, and a mansion on a private luxury island. We will never be arrested. We will never be impoverished. The society will see to that.

Our loyalty to the society supercedes everything else in our life—our families, our friendships, even our love lives. If anyone, even someone we care about with all our heart, mentions the name of our society in our presence, we must leave the room immediately and never speak to them again.

We can never tell anyone that we are members. We can never let anyone who is not a member into our tomb, or they'll be killed.

We can never quit the society or reveal any of its secrets, or *we'll* be killed.

———

Which of these rumors are true and which are overblown conspiracy theories?

I'd tell you, but then I'd have to kill you.

Don't believe me? Fine, then turn the page. But don't say I didn't warn you....

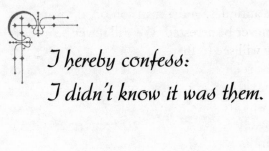

I hereby confess:
I didn't know it was them.

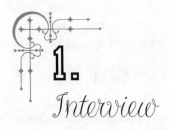

1.
Interview

It all began on a day in late April of my junior year. I was in my dorm room, for once, trying to squeeze in a load of laundry between a tuna salad sandwich in the dining hall and my afternoon lecture on *War and Peace*, or as I like to think of it, WAP. (That's not an acronym, by the way, but onomatopoeia. It's the sound the hefty volume makes when I drop it on my desk.) Professor Muravcek's* lectures tended toward the impenetrable side and I wanted to spend some time brushing up on my notes. I was tilting toward a B in that class, which was unacceptable if I wanted to graduate with honors in the major. However, it was either laundry or rushing out that night to buy a new package of underwear. You know you're desperate when trekking downtown to GAP Body is easier than waiting for a free dryer.

But neither Tide nor Tolstoy was in the cards for me that afternoon. I'd just finished disentangling my fuchsia lace thong

---

* Names of people, places, and organizations have been changed to protect the confessor from litigation or, you know, assassination.

(Friday night date panties) from the legs of my "going out jeans" and was on my way out the door with a load of darks when the phone rang.

Crap. It was probably my mom. She seemed to have a divine sense of when I'd be in my room.

I balanced the basket on my hip and picked up the phone. "Hello?"

"Amy Maureen Haskel?"

"You got her," I said, shaking one of my balled-up gym socks free.

"Your presence is required at 750 College Street, room 400, at two o'clock this afternoon."

Two o'clock was in fifteen minutes. "Who is this?"

"750 College Street, room 400. Two P.M." And then the line went dead.

I plopped back onto the faded couch, strewing tank tops and pj bottoms across the floor. Talk about rotten timing.

There was no question in my mind who it was on the other end of the phone. Quill & Ink was the "literary" senior society on campus, the usual refuge for scribblers of all varieties. It boasted several well-known writers amongst its alumni, and as the current editor-in-chief of the campus literary magazine, I knew I was a shoo-in, just like my predecessor Glenda Foster had been before me. That is, I would be if I made it to the afternoon's impromptu interview.

I was going to have to have a long talk with Glenda. She was in the Russian Novel class, too, and knew I was struggling, yet still scheduled my society interview during lecture time!

Society interviews were always arranged on super-short notice. Part of the test was to see if you could get there. I hadn't yet figured out what they did if the prospective tap didn't answer her phone—if she was busy, for example, enduring both the crime and the punishment of Professor Muravcek's soporific speaking voice.

Laundry all but forgotten, I hurried back into my room. Though the interview would be merely a formality, I fully intended to follow along with society pomp and circumstance and dress up. (Societies are all about the spectacle.) My suit was crammed in the back of my closet behind my ski jacket and the flared velvet getup I'd worn to February's seventies-themed Boogie Night. I hadn't worn my suit since January's spate of internship interviews, during which I'd landed a posh (insert eye roll here) summer job xeroxing form rejections at Horton. It needed a good lint brushing, but otherwise, it was okay. I paired it with a fresh cotton shell, and went spelunking for a pair of panty hose sans runs. On the third dip into my underwear drawer, I found one. When, oh, when will I learn to throw away unusable nylons? (Not today, apparently.) I stuffed the other two pairs back in the drawer and wrestled the third onto my legs. I needed to shave, but the nylons would cover that.

In January, I'd gotten my light brown hair cut into one of those shoulder-length, multilayered bobs I was positive was the height of fashion for the Manhattan literati. (It wasn't.) The downside of the cut was that, even with three months' growth, it took twenty minutes with a blow dryer and a big round brush to make it look halfway decent. I didn't have that kind of time right now, so I was relegated to ponytail-ville.

I slipped into my black pumps and clopped through my suite's early Gothic—complete with lead-veined windows—common room. We have one of the sweetest setups in the whole residential college—two sizeable singles connected by a wood-lined common room that featured a non-working, but darn pretty, fireplace. Only downside is the slightly pockmarked hardwood floor. Have I mentioned how much I hate heels?

The door to the suite opened before I could turn the knob. My suitemate and best friend, Lydia Travinecek, entered, balancing an armload of dusty library books, a travel mug of coffee, and her dry cleaning. Lydia is always more organized than I am. She has time for lunch, homework, and trouser pleats. It's like she's a lawyer already.

She looked me up and down. "Quill?"

I shrugged. "Who else?" Quill & Ink wasn't a secret society in the traditional sense. Heck, they didn't even have one of those giant stone tombs like the big societies used to hold their meetings—just a one-bedroom apartment above Starbucks.

She nodded curtly, and flopped the dry-cleaning bags over the back of our couch. Two days ago, Lydia had hurried out of here in her own carefully pressed suit. "Good luck, not that you'll need it. Hasn't every Lit Mag editor gotten into Quill & Ink since, like, the Stone Age?"

Pretty much. I pushed back the tiny thread of annoyance that Lydia hadn't yet told me what society had been courting her. It was silly; I knew that when Tap Night came around and she was picked by her society (whatever one it was), Lydia would drop the secrecy routine.

She took a paper sack out of her messenger bag and held up a bottle of Finlandia Mango in triumph. "Check it out. I thought we'd go tropical with our Gumdrop Drops tomorrow." Gumdrop Drops had become a weekly ritual in our suite since Lydia turned twenty-one last August (I didn't go legal until December). A bottle of vodka, two shot glasses, and a bag of Brach's Spice Drops to use as chasers were all we needed for a party. I wondered briefly what would happen to the tradition once we were both in our respective societies and had other obligations on Thursday nights (all the secret societies meet on Thursdays and Sundays).

"Awesome! Can't wait. Gotta run." I waved good-bye and clopped out of the suite, down the stairs, and into the sunny

April afternoon. Connecticut had finally decided to get with the program and realize it was spring.

I just knew Lydia would be tapped. She'd been vying for election into one of the more prestigious societies since the moment she'd stepped on campus as a freshman. She honestly felt that it was the only way to get anywhere at this school. I thought the attitude was a bit out-of-date, myself. This wasn't the twenties, when you were tapped into a society straight out of graduating from Andover or one of the other elite prep schools, and every student on campus was white, male, and rich beyond the dreams of avarice.

In those days, failure to receive election into one of the big secret societies was tantamount to permanent social ostracizing. Forget the leather-furnished office on Wall Street, forget the vacation home in Newport. Your kids probably wouldn't even get into Exeter!

But the world didn't work like that anymore. Now most of the societies had diverse membership rosters that reflected a modern student body composed of kids from every walk of life. There was no doubt in my mind that come Tap Night, even without the benefit of blue blood, Lydia would be elected into one of the best societies on campus—Dragon's Head, perhaps, or Book & Key. In fact, the only secret society I knew she would not get into was Rose & Grave, the oldest and most notorious society in the country. But that was because all the members—known as "Diggers"—were men.

As for me, I was joining Quill & Ink for the same reason that I did everything else—it would look good on my resume. I was already well acquainted with the other literary types on campus. They were all my nearest and dearest. We didn't need the formality of a society like Quill & Ink to cement our bond. What we did need was the networking and resume puffing it would provide us. You know how it goes. If there's an organization to head, an award to win, a connection to pursue—you've got to do it. Otherwise everyone would wonder why you didn't, and your whole carefully constructed C.V. of success would topple like a ninety-eight pound freshman at a kegger.

This was it, 750 College Street. And, according to my watch, I had a little over ninety seconds to make it into the room. And yet, when at last I arrived, slightly puffing, at the darkened classroom on the fourth floor, the first words out of the mouth of the person who laser-pointed me to my seat were: "You're late."

I looked at my watch again, though I couldn't see the hands in the dark. "I—"

The shadowed man sitting at the nearest table pointed something at me that glowed with a green 2:01 in digital numbers. "This is an atomic clock. You were forty-eight seconds late."

"Are you joking?" I squinted, trying in vain to see his face through the gloom. Since all of our classrooms are equipped with motion-detecting lights, I was surprised that they managed to pull this off. They'd draped the windows with black hangings, and though each of the dozen people seated about the room appeared to have a book light in front of their place, the most I could make out was a jawline here, the curve of a nose there. Wow, they'd gone all out. Must be the writers' creative juices at work.

"Are we *joking*, Ms. Haskel?" Shadow Guy #2 said with what I swear was a sneer. I didn't even need to see it. "Do you believe there is anything about this process that is a joke?"

Not until now. But come on, what was this, *Eyes Wide Shut*? "No, sir."

I strained my neck to see if I could recognize Glenda's features amongst the group, but I couldn't make her out. Where was she? Oh, let me guess. *War and Peace*. I was so going to swipe her lecture notes!

"Let me assure you, Ms. Haskel," Shadow Guy #2 went on,

"that we take our election procedure very seriously. Punctuality is of utmost importance to us. So is electing a person who can be trusted to obey the mandates of the society, no matter how minor they might seem."

Whoa. So forty-eight seconds and I'd screwed the pooch? I sat up in my seat. "I understand that, sir, and can assure you that I will take my position in the society very seriously." I paused, weighing the advisability of my next words. "I didn't know I was supposed to invest in an atomic watch. Do I get one of those when I join?"

No answer.

I giggled nervously. "What about a grandfather clock? I heard every member of Rose & Grave gets one at graduation." Quill, however, didn't quite have the endowment for such lavish presents. Maybe they could swing a Timex.

Still nothing. Um, was this thing on? "Though I suppose that a grandfather clock would be hard to lug around." Lame, lame, lame. "And probably not atomic." Shut up, Amy. Man, I was crashing and burning here.

We sat in silence for a full ten seconds. And then someone three rows back spoke up. "Ms. Haskel, if you could answer a few questions for us." I saw a shuffling of papers. "I have here your transcript. It states that sophomore year you received a B– in Dust Pages: Ethiopian Immigrant Narrative of the Mid-20th Century West."

"Yes."

"Do you have an explanation for that performance?"

Yeah, beware of classes bearing colons. In this case, the prof was a prick who thought that everything in the text that was even remotely cylindrical was some sort of phallic representation, and unless our term papers explored the ongoing problem of feminine penis envy, we'd completely missed the mark.

I think he had bedroom issues.

The B– was my single black mark in my English major, or would be as long as I kicked all 1,472 pages of WAP ass in my Russian Novel final.

"I'm more of a New Critic than a Freudian analyst," I began, choosing the time-honored liberal arts tradition of obfuscation. If you can't beat 'em, confuse 'em. "The signifiers of the primary texts in the class"—man, even *I* didn't know what I was saying by this point—"lent themselves to readings more in keeping with the works of Said, Levi-Strauss, and ..." Crap. I ran out of steam. Okay, pick an old standby. "... Aristotle's theories as laid out in *Poetics*."

Ha, question that! I was an English major. I could bullshit with the best of them.

The third-row shadow smiled, and I could see that someone had a very talented orthodontist. His choppers were as bright and even as a movie star's. "Good answer." Then he cleared his throat.

All the lights blinked on and off. Twice.

Shadow-Who-Smiles shuffled a few more papers. "Do you remember Beverly Campbell?"

"My third-grade teacher?" I'd had to think about that one for a minute. Glenda had not warned me of any of this. No doubt she was sitting pretty right now, taking notes about the bleak Siberian winter in her usual purple gel pen. And here I was, getting grilled by Quill & Ink for heaven knew what reason. Wasn't I supposed to be a sure thing?

Furthermore, it was official: I didn't recognize any of these people's voices. Had they brought in alumni to conduct the interviews?

"If we asked Beverly Campbell about you, what would she say?"

"That I was good with phonics." Enough of this. "Come on, it was third grade."

"What about Janine Harper?" Fourth grade. "Marilyn Mahan." Fifth. "James Field, Tracy Cole, Debra Blumenthal." Shadow-Who-Smiles proceeded to name every homeroom teacher I'd ever had. It was more than a little freaky.

"Can I ask you a question?" I said, interrupting his recitation in tenth grade.

"Go ahead."

"Congressional confirmation hearings wouldn't care this much about my early childhood. Why do you?"

Quill was a second-rate society at best, more concerned with getting its members into J-school than taking over the world—the reported purpose of *real* secret societies. What was up with the *Da Vinci Code* act?

Shadow Guy #2 spoke up. "What are your ambitions, Ms. Haskel?"

I kinda wanted to write the Great American Novel. But not even Quill & Ink would find that a satisfactory answer. Not goal-oriented enough. Not feasible. There aren't enough Nobel Prizes in Literature to go around. Plus, I wasn't sure I had any Great American Ideas. So, once again, with the fall-back plan. "To be a media magnate." There, that should hold them.

"You're lying." Shadow-Who-Smiles was no longer showing me his pearly whites.

"What makes you say that?" I folded my hands in my lap. And why did they care? I'd have bet each and every one of these people had a frustrated novelist buried deep inside.

Shadow-Who-Smiles (though he wasn't right now) picked up another piece of paper and began to read aloud. It was the first page of my unfinished novel—the one that no one but Lydia and I knew about. The one that existed only on my laptop's hard drive, back in my room.

"Hey!" I shouted, and he stopped. "Where did you get that? Did you hack my computer or something?"

Everything got really quiet. I thought I could hear the atomic clock whirring away. Who were these people?

"We have everything you've ever done, Ms. Haskel," Shadow Guy #2 said. He lifted a manila envelope from the table in front of him. "This is your FBI file."

My mouth dropped open. I have an FBI file? Why would I have an FBI file? I'd never done a summer internship at the White House or the Pentagon. My dad is an accountant, not a politician. I didn't need security clearance. And even if I did, how the heck did these people get their hands on it?

There was only one answer. They were playing me. I shook my head, leaned back in my chair, and laughed. "Right, my FBI file. The Federal Bureau of *I-Don't-Think-So*. Look, I'm glad I've given you guys a good laugh, but since you aren't the Men in Black, can we please get back to the interview now?"

There was a long pause, then all the lights on the tables blinked again. This time, most of them blinked once, except for the one in front of Shadow-Who-Smiles.

"I think," said Shadow Guy #2, "that the interview is over."

"No!" said Shadow-Who-Smiles.

"She's not what we're looking for."

"I don't agree."

Hold the phone. I sat forward. "Guys, I'm not quite clear what's going on here. Where's Glenda?"

Shadow Guy #2 tilted his head until I got a glimpse of pale cheekbone. "Glenda?"

"Yeah, Glenda. Glenda Foster, the old Lit Mag editor? The girl who is sponsoring me for this society? The girl who is too taken with Russian literature to show up this afternoon?"

Again with the silence, though this one was punctuated with a few snickers. Finally, Shadow-Who-Smiles (and he was definitely doing it again!) spoke up. "Glenda Foster is not a member of this organization."

Holy shitzu.

Who were these people?!?

Okay, to be fair, there was still one little corner in my mind that was shouting that Glenda had been lying to me all year, and that she wasn't a member of Quill & Ink after all. But it was a pretty minuscule corner, the one where all of my most paranoid tendencies live. The rest of my head was busy spinning. I'd been taking this process rather lightly because, hey, it was Quill & Ink. Not a big deal, and I was a sure bet anyway.

But they obviously weren't Quill & Ink. I was out of my depth, for one of the first times in my life. And I didn't have a clue what I was supposed to do.

"I think we're done here," Shadow Guy #2 said.

"No, we're not," insisted Shadow-Who-Smiles.

Shadow Guy #2 turned around and I caught a glimpse of perfectly shaved neck. "She's not what we want. We have to be serious about this."

"I can be serious!" I leaned forward and smacked my hand down on Shadow Guy #2's notes. I saw his mouth drop open. Oops. "Sorry," I said, sitting back and folding my hands demurely. "I was a little—confused."

"Clearly."

"Can I ask who you people are?"

This time, they all laughed, before Shadow Guy #2 said, "No."

"So you get a list of my middle-school study-hall proctors and I get squat?"

"That's why we call it a *secret* society." Shadow-Who-Smiles cleared his throat.

"Fair enough."

Shadow-Who-Smiles flicked his light on and off a few times, and all the members began shuffling the papers on their desks. I wondered what the signal meant.

Okey-doke. I figured I'd humiliated myself enough for one afternoon. I rose from my seat. "Am I free to go?"

"One moment, Ms. Haskel." Shadow-Who-Smiles put his hand out, and I was surprised that I could see it. Apparently, my eyes were adjusting to the dark. "Tell us. What do you have to offer this organization?"

I bit my tongue to keep from snapping back with, *And what organization is that?* Okay, so they weren't Quill & Ink. Someone else was courting me, and I'd royally screwed up any chance I might have had to impress—whoever. The real question was, did I care? After all, this wasn't my thing. Lydia was the one who wanted to get into a secret society—any prestigious secret society. I just wanted to be in Quill & Ink, so I could keep tabs on which literary agents were hiring assistants and whether or not *Cosmopolitan* needed interns.

And finally, the absurdity of the whole situation hit me. All the juniors who, like me, had spent an hour in a darkened classroom, answering vague questions about their ambitions and accomplishments for a bunch of shadowy strangers—they hadn't the foggiest clue to whom they were spilling their guts. Lydia, for all her secretive, superior smugness, didn't know if she was being courted by Dragon's Head or punk'd by a bunch of rowdy frat boys. And neither did I.

What did I have to offer this mysterious, unidentified organization? Aside from the finger, which I lifted, to little effect in the darkness.

I straightened my skirt, stuck out my chin, and laughed. "You already know what I have to offer. Straight As in the major, except for that little snafu with Ethiopian Immigrant Narrative; the editorship of the Lit Magazine; participation and leadership in any number of other small campus publications; and thirty pages of a badly written novel. I don't do drugs, I've never been arrested, and from what I hear, I'm not too shabby in bed. Not that any of you people will ever have the opportunity to discover that firsthand." (Though, to be honest, I'd have no way of knowing, now would I?)

Then I turned on my heel and marched out. And as I exited into the hall, head held high, I thought I caught the flicker of a dozen tiny booklights.

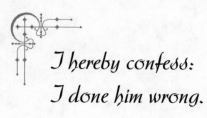

I hereby confess:
I done him wrong.

2.
Tap Night

The fun part about humiliating yourself in front of a cadre of shadowy figures is that you get to spend the next two days wondering if everyone you pass on campus saw you at your worst. I was in line at the dining hall last night and I swear I saw this trustafarian girl sniggering behind her bulgur-wheat pilaf. I spent the next two hours (WAP forgotten!) trying to figure out which secret society was most likely to tap vegan Environmental Science majors who wear designer dreadlocks and hundred-dollar hemp necklaces—well, other than joke organizations like Joint & Bong.

Cute name, huh? That's how things go at Eli University. Everyone copies everyone else. Rose & Grave set the trend back in the 1800s, and now anyone with a yen to start a social club has followed their illustrious lead: Book & Key, Sword & Mace, Quill & Ink. There are a few holdouts among the major societies—Dragon's Head, Serpent, St. Linus Hall—but nothing gives a proposed clandestine organization the Eli air like an ampersand. Lydia and I used to joke that they were in practice for joining law firms—they're all Blank & Blank as well, right?

That was before Lydia lost her sense of humor when it came to all things secret society. Seriously. I tried to talk to her about my interview that night at dinner, and she responded like my mom whenever I brought up sex. Which is to say, not at all.

The conversation went like this:

Me: So you want to hear what happened at my interview?

Lydia: *(fork paused halfway to her mouth)* Are you supposed to talk about that?

Me: Why not? I haven't taken any vows of silence. I don't even know who they were. Why, did yours tell you not to talk about it?

Lydia: ...

Me: They did? Did they tell you who they were?

Lydia: ...

Me: They did! Wow, I must have screwed up worse than I thought.

Lydia: *(glancing around furtively)* Amy, I really, really don't think we're supposed to talk about this.

Me: I can talk about anything I want. They're a bunch of strangers, and they were really rude to me, to boot.

Lydia: Amy! You're going to ruin your chances.

Me: I don't think I *have* any chances. And please. They didn't bug the tables or anything.

Lydia: Rose & Grave would.

Me: Rose & Grave doesn't tap women. Just future Presidents.

Lydia: *(standing and lifting her tray)* I'm not going to keep talking about this here.

Me: *(following)* Fine, let's do it in the suite.

But Lydia didn't go back to the suite. She went to the gym to swim laps, which, considering my long-standing aversion to deep water (my cousin threw me off a dock when I was a kid— don't like to talk about it), was a downright slap in the face. And as if the Chlorine Defense wasn't enough, whenever I saw her at all over the following two days, she rushed off before I had a chance to bring up the subject again.

Not that I was sitting around. With commencement just around the corner, I was super-busy with the literary magazine's commencement issue. Since I wasn't going to be tapped by Quill & Ink—or any other secret society—I couldn't afford any more missteps. This was my penultimate issue, and it needed to kick ass.

So, to be blunt, the theme of "Ambition" was not going to cut it.

"Been there, done that," I informed my second-in-command, managing editor Brandon Weare. "At Eli, Ambition is the new black."

"What a lovely pull quote for your intro page," Brandon said, putting the finishing touches on his fifth paper airplane.

"If we pick a good enough theme, I won't need to jazz it up with taglines."

"Ah, but then, what sort of *Cosmo* girl would you be? It seems to be all about the cutesy tagline there. It's certainly not about actual content." He launched the plane, and I watched it swoop and dive directly into the smudgy linoleum floor of the magazine office. A nose-heavy dart.

"You read *Cosmo*?"

"Female sex tips?" He toed the plane. "You betcha."

Brandon was an expert in the art of "Aerogami," and since we'd started working together in October, I learned that his chosen designs possessed a direct correlation with his opinion of the manuscript from which he drew his construction materials. Woe betide the writer whose submission merited a four-fold stinger...but if he sailed a square-nosed glider (Ken Blackburn's Guinness World Record design, I'd learned) past my nose, I should drop everything and read the story.

I'm pretty sure this was not how things worked at Horton.

Not that Brandon would care. He was one of those true geniuses that dotted the campus population, the kind that could compose concertos on breaks from discovering the cure for cancer. His raison d'être was applied math, but he spared enough time to fit in his knack for writing appallingly good short stories, and to compete with me for magazine editorships (I'd only just barely beat him out for this one). No scrambling for internships or resume stuffers for Brandon. He just went around being quietly brilliant, unapologetically dorky, and universally well liked.

And he had a point about the theme's potential. Ninety percent of the graduating class already had ambition oozing from their pores. The other ten had daddies that would pound it into them by the time they were thirty. The theme possessed a broad scope, as well as the possibility of incorporating some sort of existentialist statement about the futility of desire, the impossibility of purpose, all the stuff that made future Master's-in-Creative-Writing-from-Iowa candidates hot.

(Iowa, if you didn't know, is *the* place to go to graduate school to learn how to be a novelist. Don't ask me why. Must be the chemicals in the corn.)

The problem was, I was having enough troubles with ambition myself. Sure, my resume and GPA were in order, but if my snafu of a society interview proved anything, it was that all that accomplishment needed to add up to a plan, or it didn't count. Did I really want to spend the next month reading achingly bitter or brilliantly acerbic or sensationally snarky stories that would tell me to settle for a life of comfortable mediocrity or risk getting squashed into the pavement by the bigger rats in the race? Would that somehow prod me into picking an attainable yet still suitably lofty path, or would it simply convince me it wasn't worth trying?

"Okay," I said slowly, gauging his reaction, "but are we going to present said Ambition in a positive or negative light?"

Brandon, damn him, threw back his head and laughed. "Touched a nerve, Ames?"

Sometimes I suspected Genius-boy over there could read my mind. I shrugged, retrieved the airplane from where it had slid beneath my chair, and lobbed it back at him. "Fine. *Ambition* it is. It sounds like a Calvin Klein perfume, but let's run with it." I shuffled the papers on my desk, and started rearranging the thumbtacks in the side of the worn canvas cubicle according to rainbow color order.

He smoothed out the creases of the plane and studied me carefully. "What's up with you tonight? You're not in your usual take-over-the-world mode." Brandon was cute, in a kind of sidekick-on-a-WB-show way. He was only an inch or two taller than me, and had plain brown hair that was overgrown into an unruly shag, light olive skin, and big, soulful puppy-dog eyes with just the slightest tilt at the corners to hint at his Asian-American ("twenty-five percent and counting!") heritage.

Yeah, it was the eyes that got me, every time.

I shrugged again. "I don't know. End of year stress. Seven hundred pages of *War and Peace* to read before exams."

"Ah, The Russian Novel." Brandon nodded in sympathy. "Two hundred and thirty-two cubic inches of sheer torture. I hear just lifting the class texts put some guy in traction." He winked. "Don't worry. In two weeks, you'll be in Quill & Ink, and they've got to have an in with Lit exams. You'll rock it."

I bit my lip. "I'm . . . not getting tapped by Quill & Ink."

"What?" He pointed at the EDITOR-IN-CHIEF sign on my desk, at me, at the writing on the door that read ELI LITERARY MAGAZINE, a look of mock incredulity on his face. "How is that possible?"

Finally, someone to talk to about this! Lydia was doing her best *Tommy!* impression and Glenda Foster was MIA (probably out interviewing the real Quill & Ink taps). "I don't know! But I went to my interview, and it was all this crap about FBI files and my third-grade teacher and—other stuff—and then they told me they weren't Quill...."

"Maybe they were lying?"

"Either way, they couldn't stop talking about how I wasn't right for them. They were being pretty mean, so I told them off, gave them the finger—not that they could see it, the way the room was all dark—and walked out."

"Wow." Brandon grinned, and those puppy-dog eyes of his began to take on a very particular gleam. One that I knew well, after working in such close quarters with him on the magazine since October. One that I'd been curiously susceptible to ever since he'd plied me with flowers and Godiva on February 14th. "I think," he said, in a tone that betrayed how little of his interest truly lay in the subject of my society interview, "that we should continue this conversation over dinner. How about Thai? We've got half a dozen choices on Chapel Street alone." New Haven is replete with houses of curry.

I gave him a hairy eyeball. Brandon never asked for dates, he sprung them on you like a bear trap. You see, Brandon Weare wanted me to be his girlfriend. Friends-with-benefits wasn't cutting it for him anymore (though there'd been no complaints while he was receiving those benefits, let me tell you!).

Oh, yeah. I'd slept with Brandon. Six times, to be precise. Maybe I should back it up a bit:

Amy Haskel's Hit List

1) Jacob Allbrecker. 12th Grade. Prom Night. I dated Jacob for four months my senior year in high school, and he broke up with me two weeks before prom because I wouldn't go all the way. But since we'd already bought the tickets, and I'd made my hair appointment, we went to prom together anyway, where despite my earlier protests, I ended up losing my virginity in Colleen Morrison's little sister's bedroom at the after-party. Glamorous, huh? Jacob and I slept together twice more before graduation and then he started Duke in the summer session. I hooked up with him on Thanksgiving Break freshman year, but we didn't get past second base because I was already in heavy lust with

2) Galen Twilo. Freshman Year. Reading Week, first semester. Omigod, this guy was gorgeous! And an artist, the kind that a scant two years later I'd laugh at for thinking he was deep with all his black sweaters and cigarettes and dog-eared copies of *Naked Lunch* (which isn't half as sexy as it sounds). I spent all of Reading Week (the week without classes just before exams, when we're supposed to study but really just party) in his bed, where I learned all kinds of nifty facts about the male anatomy and everything I needed to rock my Twentieth Century American Poetry final. When I came back after Winter Break, though, he pretended he didn't know me.

3) Alan Albertson. Summer-Fall-Winter. Sophomore Year. We met at a summer job at the Eli University Press, and he was two years older than me. We spent the whole summer together avoiding beach trips and pool parties (I don't swim, c.f. unfortunate dockside incident, and he burns like a crab in the sun). It was love. And then he got a Fulbright and went to London (where there aren't any UV rays) and broke my heart, which put me on a dark path that led directly to

4) Ben...Somebody. Sophomore Year. Spring Break at Myrtle Beach. And that's all I know, except that I remember that his dick had a funny bend in the middle.

5) Brandon Weare. Junior Year. February 14th. All girls are notoriously weak-willed on Valentine's Day—it's like some sort of cosmic alignment of the Pathetic Planet and the Couples-Everywhere-You-Look Constellation in the seventh house of Loneliness. All I know is that every February 14th, even the most independent and academically focused girl on campus can be wooed with a dozen drugstore roses and a Hallmark card.

I've always been completely honest with him about the fact that I wasn't exactly girlfriend material (see above list if you don't believe me). Even on that Valentine's Day, somewhere between the removal of the tops and the removal of the bottoms, I told him, "This can't be serious, okay?"

And of course he said, "Okay." It doesn't matter how many articles of clothing you're still wearing. As soon as a guy thinks there's sex on the table, he'll agree to anything.

The five times I slept with him after Valentine's Day... well, what can I say? I'm a pushover. Now, at least, I knew what he'd been getting at with all the paper airplane–throwing and origami leapfrogs he'd been shooting my way since we'd met sophomore year. (Geeky boys flirt in random-access ways.) Brandon has been steadily campaigning for clarification on our "status" since February, and I've been putting off the conversation with notably more success than I've had resisting the temptations of the flesh.

Or the possibility of free crab rangoon. Forty-five minutes later, I had a belly full of pad Thai and an earful of Brandon's theories about how worthless the archaic tradition of the Eli secret society was to the modern meritocracy of the college, how he was quite sure that we'd done a bang-up job of networking and such without the benefit of black robes and secret handshakes, and how he liked me just the way I was, Quill & Ink be damned. Altogether a very heady speech for an impressionable young girl, especially given how many polysyllabic words he used. Man, Brandon must have rocked his SATs. If I wasn't careful, tonight might be Number Seven.

It wasn't until after the fried bananas that he started giving me the hard sell. "The problem with you, Haskel, is that you overanalyze everything."

"If you're looking to get laid, Weare," I snapped back, "you shouldn't start sentences with 'The problem with you...'"

"Ooh, is that a possibility?"

I threw my chopstick wrapper at him. "What do you mean, overanalyze?"

"I assume you're familiar with the definition of the word." He waited for confirmation, then continued. "You think that your life has to be a stack of bricks, and if you put down one bad brick, the whole tower will fall over."

That or I'd keep stacking bricks that never became a building.

"So you agonize over every single decision, terrified that you're going to screw up."

Ha! I *had* screwed up with this whole Quill thing. And let's not forget Ben Somebody. I was an old hand at making mistakes. I just wasn't a big fan of the process.

He waved his chopstick at me, his eyes flickering darkly by

the glow of the tableside tea lights, and started ticking off my supposed bricks. "Summer internship, position on the magazine staff, commencement issue theme, secret society membership. When was the last time you did something just because it was fun?"

"Lydia and I went dancing at Froggie's last weekend."

"Something big."

I raised my eyebrow. "Something like . . . getting into a relationship with you?"

"For example."

"Brandon, I think we have a great friendship. I don't want to mess it up."

He rolled his eyes. "Cliché alert."

The waitress came by with the check. I made feeble motions toward my handbag, but Brandon shook his head and pulled out his wallet.

"I'll get the next one," I offered, though I knew he wouldn't let me. Brandon did things like hold open doors and pull out chairs and pay for dinners. He also had the ability to engineer a type of smile that I knew was just for me. The Amy-smile. It was intoxicating. And I knew if I let myself fall for him, I'd crash like a four-fold stinger.

"Look, we've talked about this." I slipped my arms back into my coat. "You're one of my best friends, and I'm afraid that if I get involved with you, and it doesn't work out, I'll lose that."

Brandon signed his name across the receipt in a frustrated scrawl. "Amy," he said slowly, not looking up. "We *are* involved. And it's *not* working out."

"You know what I mean." I ducked my head.

He sighed. "Let's get out of here." We stood, and headed to the door, but before we got to the pink plaster Buddha at the entrance, he turned to me and looked me square in the eye. "Just promise me one thing. Just once in your life, just for kicks, don't overthink, okay? See how it goes."

I nodded. "Okay."

Brandon walked me back to my dorm entryway, and I, in defiance of the promise I'd just made, brainstormed ways to leave him at the door of my suite without hurting his feelings.

Which, as it turns out, was unnecessary. The door to my suite stood open, and Lydia sat on the couch inside our common room. She still wore her jacket, her lap was full of books, and she was staring fixedly at a small, square piece of paper sitting in the middle of the floor.

"Lydia?" I said, waving a hand in front of her face. "Are you all right?"

She didn't look up at me, didn't even blink, just whispered, "It's yours."

Brandon furrowed his brow and swiped the paper off the floor. "Sure is," he said, handing me a small white envelope edged in glossy black and sealed with a dollop of dark wax. "They must have slipped it under the door."

I turned the envelope over in my hands. It was made of heavy, luxurious linen paper, and my name had been printed on the front in an odd, angular font.

But it was the back that truly held my interest, for into the solid black wax was pressed the unmistakable imprint of a rose inside an elongated hexagon.

The seal of Rose & Grave.

I stuffed the envelope into my jacket pocket quicker than a jock with a cheat sheet, and then turned to my friends.

"So Quill came through after all?" Brandon said with a wry smile.

"Quill & Ink," Lydia said in that same strange, flat voice, "gives out blue-and-silver edged envelopes."

Brandon and I exchanged looks at Lydia's display of society obsession. "So who gives out black ones?" he asked her.

Lydia's eyes met mine, but she said nothing, and I knew then that she'd gotten a very good look at that seal. If she was knowledgeable about random society-stationery factoids, then she sure as hell knew what that seal meant.

I turned to Brandon. "Thanks so much for dinner. I wish I could hang out more, but it's getting late, and I have a lot of work to do tonight—"

"No way." He crossed his arms over his sweatshirt and planted his feet on my parquet. "Not until I get to see that envelope again."

Lydia appeared to have finally found her tongue, for she leapt to her feet and began ushering him out the door. "The lady says she's busy, Weare," she said, crowding up on him. "And much as we both like you, that means out. Now."

"But—" Brandon said, looking over his shoulder at me as Lydia hustled him out. I would have spoken up about the way she was manhandling my—well, my friend-with-bennies—but my mind was too busy doing round-off back handsprings and I was caressing that wax seal in my pocket like I was Frodo and it was the One Ring.

"Good night, Brandon!" I called as Lydia shoved him over the threshold and shut the door in his face. "I'll call you tomorrow, I promise!"

She threw the lock and turned to me. "Open it."

I drew back, protecting my pocket. "In front of you?"

"I'm your best friend!" she argued.

I snorted. "You've been pulling a disappearing act all week! You won't tell me a thing about your society interview, and yet you think you get dibs on reading my letter?"

She thought about it for a second, then nodded. "Yes!"

"You show me yours, I'll show you mine." I put my hands on my hips, realizing even as I did that I was leaving the envelope wide open for pickpockets.

"Fine," Lydia said, stepping back. "Be that way. I'll leave you alone with your precious envelope." And then she turned, walked into her room, and shut the door, leaving me blinking at her whiteboard in surprise.

That's not how I expected that to go at all. But I recovered a few seconds later, remembering that I still hadn't opened the envelope.

I spent a good long time just staring at the seal. Would it crack when I opened it? I turned the paper over and over in my hands. Yep, that was my name, and yep, that was the Rose & Grave seal. And that was still my name.

But Rose & Grave did not tap women.

What the hell was going on?

Finally, I carefully slipped my fingertips beneath the wax and popped it open in one piece. The envelope split on irregular lines, and unfolded into an odd, distorted hexagon. The words were written on the diagonal in a heavy, angular script, and this is what they said:

> *B. S. C.* Amy Maureen Haskel:*
> *You have been judged and found worthy. Be in your room tonight at five minutes past eight o'clock and await further instructions.*

And then beneath that was the mark of Rose & Grave.

I was being tapped by Rose & Grave!

Oh wow. Oh wow, oh wow, oh wow. (As missives go, it wasn't too groundbreaking, but at the time I was over the moon.)

I ran toward Lydia's bedroom, then skidded to a stop. Wait a second, I wasn't going to tell her anything until she shared with me.

Brandon! I bet he'd be back to his room by now. I could call— No, he'd just finished telling me how Paleolithic he

---

* The confessor later discovered this stood for Barbarian-So-Called.

thought secret societies were, and Rose & Grave was the undisputed T-Rex of the country. They were old school and blue blood and their pedigreed members grew up to be Supreme Court Justices and CEOs and founders of major media conglomerates like AOL Time-Warner. Male ones.

Could all of those rumors be wrong? Or worse, could this be someone's idea of a sick joke? Poor little Amy Haskel, didn't get an election, let's mess with her head. Such things had been known to happen before—of course, they tended to happen to gullible freshmen who didn't know any better. Every few years you heard stories about college pranksters dressing up in robes, kidnapping a gaggle of frosh, and putting them through all manner of humiliations in the guise of "initiation."

But really, wouldn't it be just as easy to fool an upperclassman? It wasn't as if I could ask a bunch of black-robed figures for ID when they showed up. As that Shadow-Who-Smiles guy had said to me at the interview, that's why they called it *secret*.

I stabbed my hands into my hair in frustration. Why was there no information session on this? Why wasn't it covered in the student handbook? Why had the paranoid corner of my brain hog-tied and gagged the rational part?

Okay, Amy, think. Think. I checked my watch, and amended my mantra. *Think quicker.* I had ten minutes before the boys in black arrived.

Should I accept? Should I accept, even if I suspected this was nothing but a mean prank—because what if this *was* Rose & Grave? And if this invitation was what it appeared to be, what would membership in the society mean to me?

I was still considering this nine and a half minutes later, when there was a knock on my door. I froze, clutching the envelope tightly in my hands and staring at the door as if it were the only thing standing between me and Armageddon.

There was another knock.

Lydia cracked her bedroom door, stuck her head out, and glanced from the entrance to me and back again. "Gonna get that?"

"I'm deciding."

"Oh, is that what you're doing?" She quirked an eyebrow at me. " 'Cause you don't look particularly decisive."

Another knock, this one very insistent. Lydia rolled her eyes, crossed to the door, and opened it wide...and in they came, brushing right past a bemused Lydia and surrounding me.

I couldn't tell how many there were—at least, not before they swept me up in their arms and hustled me out the door, their black cloaks flapping in their wake. It was every bit as exciting as I'd always hoped it would be. But the trip ended abruptly about ten seconds later when we entered another dark room (they really go in for dark rooms) somewhere in my building. They deposited me right-side up and backed off.

After a second, I caught my breath. The room was lit by a single black taper candle, behind which I could see a man with his black hood pulled low over his eyes. I obviously hadn't been eating my carrots, because I couldn't see anything beyond the glow of the candle. There was an odd smell in the air, something familiar but unidentifiable, and definitely incongruous with the sight before me.

"Amy Maureen Haskel?"

"Yes," I said in a rather breathless voice.

"Rose & Grave: Accept or reject."

Here it was. No more time. And I had no idea what to think.

And then, Brandon's words came back to me: *Promise me, just once in your life, just for kicks, don't overthink.*

I opened my mouth. "Accept."

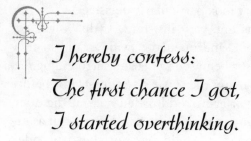

I hereby confess:
The first chance I got,
I started overthinking.

3.
Second Thoughts

As soon as I spoke the words, the light was extinguished, and judging by the bustle that followed, they weren't waiting around to relight it. Someone leaned in and hissed in my ear, "Remember well, but keep silent, concerning what you have heard here."

By the time I stumbled to the wall and felt cool tile beneath my fingers, everyone was gone. I flipped on the light. I was standing in a bathroom, alone, with nothing but condom dispensers and mildewy grout to keep me company. So that was the smell. And it wasn't even my entryway.

Um, hello? Weren't they supposed to spirit me off to their stone tomb and introduce me to a life beyond my wildest dreams? I frowned, opened the bathroom door, and stepped outside.

About half a dozen students milled around the hall, watching me. One of those guys—there's one in every dorm—who never did get used to the idea of Eli's unisex bathrooms hopped up and down on the balls of his feet as if waiting for the *girl* to

leave before he braved the toilet. "You done, or is there gonna
be another party in there?"

I schooled my features into a neutral expression. "Anyone
have a roll of toilet paper?"

See? I would be an expert at this secret stuff yet.

Ignoring the onlookers, I made my way back to my suite,
where I assumed Lydia would be waiting to receive her blow-
by-blow of the whole (truncated) experience. But Lydia was
gone—tapped, perhaps, by another society in my absence. She
wouldn't have left for any other reason, right? Not tonight.

I waited in the common room for fifteen minutes, figuring
that if her tap worked the way mine had, she'd be back in no
time. I drank a Coke and tried to read a three-month-old copy
of *Cosmo* that was lying on the coffee table. Brandon was right;
the taglines were much more intriguing than yet another recy-
cled article explaining that women have G-spots. I didn't make
it past the third perfume ad (none of which, I was chuffed to
see, hawked anything called "Ambition").

I got up and went to the window, but there was no sign of
Lydia or of a bunch of robed figures. Half an hour later, I de-
cided to calm my nerves by taking a nice stroll—down to High
Street.

Now, aside from being home to the English department
and the Art History lecture hall, High Street is also known for
hosting the Rose & Grave tomb. (These "tombs" dotted the
campus, their huge, mausoleum-like facades hiding interiors
that were supposedly more like mansions. Remember, the
Egyptian pyramids were tombs as well. But no one knew if
the society tombs held actual . . . bodies.) According to rumor,
there's an intricate code for members that can tell them exactly
what is going on inside the tomb based on the position of the
low, wrought-iron gates guarding the entrance. I didn't know
what the code was, but I assumed that I'd find out. Sometime.

I walked past the entrance to two residential colleges, and

then, as was common amongst all students, crossed to the other side of the street so I wouldn't be seen walking in front of the Rose & Grave tomb. It was an unwritten rule on campus— the college equivalent of refusing to walk in front of a haunted house in our childhood neighborhoods.

The tomb was made of sandstone blocks and seemed somehow darker than the surrounding stone and slate buildings. A fence surrounded an unkempt yard spotted with patches of grass and a few late, struggling daffodils. Strange that the Diggers didn't keep up the landscaping, though it added to the imposing nature of the property. The sodium streetlight nearest the tomb was perpetually out of order, meaning that the tomb itself stood in a pool of deep shade and long, sinister shadows. If I didn't know better, I'd think they did it on purpose.

Maybe I didn't know better. I sat down on the curb and rested my chin in my hands, regarding the building warily. The gate was half open. What did that mean? Someone was inside? Someone wasn't? Someone was lurking in the shadows, waiting to pounce on me the second I came near? I looked both ways down the street, but it was deserted.

The niggling fear in the back of my mind rose up to taunt me. *It wasn't Rose & Grave who carried you into the bathroom. It was a prank, and you fell for it, hook, line, and hooded robe. Stupid Amy Haskel, you'll be the laughingstock of Eli tomorrow.*

Why hadn't they taken me away with them? They'd tapped me, right? I was a member now, right? So if I wanted to go up to that gate, if I wanted to walk right through and pound on the door and demand to know what the hell they were doing— then I was entitled to. Right?

And if you're not a member, they'll cart you away to the dungeon.

I stood up, clenched my fists at my sides, and marched across the street, utterly determined for all of ten steps. As soon as I got to the gate, my resolve wavered and I stopped to check again. Still no one coming.

I held my breath and put my hand on the gate. Nothing. No one came to arrest me, or yell at me, or threaten to eradicate my existence from the planet for daring to infiltrate the society grounds without permission. I took a step inside. Then two. Somewhere around six steps, the gate clanged shut behind me. I yelped, jumped about two feet in the air, and rushed back to the fence.

The gate wouldn't open. I fumbled with the catches, but if there was a release mechanism, my fingers weren't finding it, and I couldn't see a thing in the dark. Oh, crap. I'd been a member for all of fifty minutes and I'd already broken the fence and messed with the secret code.

And trespassed. Don't forget how you trespassed. They're going to get you. Run! Run, before anyone catches you.

The voice won, and I climbed over the gate, catching the flare of my favorite jeans on one of the spikes protruding from the top. For several seconds, I acted like a hopscotch player on crack while trying to free my leg from its wrought-iron trap. Then I saw a group of three students exiting Calvin College and heading toward Old Campus. I stopped hopping. Maybe they wouldn't see me if I stayed perfectly still. Hey, it worked for those people in *Jurassic Park*.

Fortunately, the average college student has the environmental acuity of a beanbag chair. They don't even look both ways before crossing the street. So they didn't look down High Street at the girl who was stuck to the Rose & Grave gate.

I ripped my hem free, and then, torn denim flapping on the cement behind me, sprinted away from the tomb at a pace that would have easily earned me a spot on the Eli track team.

I didn't slow to a jog until I was back inside my residential college courtyard. Eli University, kind of like Harry Potter's Hogwarts, is arranged according to this British boarding school–style residential house system. We don't use a magical sorting hat or anything like that, but when you matriculate, you're assigned to one of twelve residential "colleges" that determines where you live, which dining hall you eat in, what allegiance you take during intramural sports, and which dean has the privilege of lowering the ax when you screw up. Every one of the twelve colleges comes supplied with resident faculty as well as its own dean, a sort of collegiate "principal" who serves as an academic advisor and resident disciplinarian, and a college master, who oversees our social scene and college-specific organizations. If you couldn't turn in a paper on time, you went to your dean for help. If you wanted some funds to hold a Prescott College chili cook-off, the master was the go-to guy (or girl).

The worst punishment you can get at Eli short of expulsion is called "rustication"—which means that after a fun-filled period of suspension, you are welcomed back into the bosom of Eli but stripped of your college identity. From that point on, the rusticated individual can't live on campus (all under-grad housing is based on college designation) and doesn't have a college master or dean to turn to in the rough times. You're merely marking time and classroom credits until the diploma. It's named after a type of banishment popular during the Roman Empire, which says a lot about these schools' puffed self-images. College identity is paramount, even to people with much more powerful affiliations—like Rose & Grave. If ever you meet another Eli grad, the very first question you'll be asked is, "What college were you in?"

I was a member of Prescott College, which was named after one of the school's founders. Other colleges are named after Connecticut towns (Hartford College, where Glenda lived) and famous historical figures, scientists, and religious leaders (such as Calvin College, next to the Rose & Grave tomb). Though nowadays your college assignment is mostly random (but you can choose to be in the same college as your sibling or parent was), it used to be that each college had a specific personality based on its members—kind of like secret societies. Prescott College was once known as the "legacy" college—it's where the President lived while he was at Eli, as well as his father before that. It still has a lot of money in trust from alumni donations, and really big rooms. So I lucked out there, since I'm neither a legacy nor richer than Trump.

I looked up at my suite; still dark, which meant Lydia hadn't come home yet. I thought about going to find some of my other friends, but knew that no conversation would last ten minutes before I blurted out, "Would a secret society tap a person then disappear? Hypothetically, of course."

Oh, I was pathetic. After a thorough inspection of the courtyard (during which I stumbled across one puddle of vomit, one pile of unidentified books, and one fellow junior making out with someone who was decidedly *not* her boyfriend—but no sign of robed figures), I headed back to my room, utterly defeated and more than a little pissed that I'd torn my jeans.

According to every legend I'd ever heard, this is not what Tap Night was supposed to be like. What a letdown. I changed into my pajamas and padded into the bathroom to brush my teeth. Flossing, fortunately, gave me the opportunity for a good long observation of myself in the mirror. I didn't *look* like a member of one of the most notorious secret societies in America. I didn't look like someone who could claim brotherhood with the head of the CIA, the President of the United States, or the new CEO of Fox.

"Faeth it," I garbled to my reflection through the floss. "Youffe been hadth."

———

I fully intended to be out of the suite before I saw Lydia and was forced to tell her all about what *hadn't* happened to me the night before. I even dressed for the part, in secret-mission dark jeans (not the ones I'd torn) and my fade-into-the-woodwork Eli University crest hoodie.

What I did not anticipate was that she'd be waiting for me in the dining hall, having staked out a spot right next to the cereal bar. This is the problem with best friends. They know exactly what breakfast you're going to go for. If I'd been in the mood for a bagel rather than a bowl of Frosted Flakes, she never would have caught me.

"Nice outfit," she murmured over her coffee cup. "You really look the part."

I splashed some skim milk into my bowl and plopped down across from her. "What's that supposed to mean?"

She gestured with her teaspoon at my outfit. "Dark colors, mysterious hoods...it's very subtle." She smirked.

"I've worn this sweatshirt a hundred times."

"Never when you were actually *in* a secret society." Lydia was dressed in a pale pink blouse and a pair of khakis, and looked about as mysterious as a church picnic.

Okay, maybe I didn't *look* coy, but I could sure as hell play the part. "What makes you think I'm in a secret society?" I asked, spooning up my flakes.

"The dozen robed figures who carried you bodily out of our suite last night."

Ha! I took a deep breath. "How do you know they were a secret society?"

She gave me a look that said, *I've got a 3.9 GPA, and you know it.*

But all of a sudden, I very much wanted to hear her thoughts on the matter. "Seriously, Lyds, how do you know? How would any of us know that they weren't a bunch of guys in hoods playing a practical joke?"

"I think the Rose & Grave letterhead is a good clue."

"You looked at the envelope."

"It's pretty hard to miss, Amy. Little flower, great big coffin?" She eyed me warily. "Are you going to get up and leave the room now?" By all accounts, secret society members had to leave the room if anyone mentioned the name of their organization. Supposedly it was to protect them from entering into discussion about the society, but it always seemed like a raw deal to me. Say you were at a rocking party and some chick wanted you out of the picture so she could mack on your man. All she had to do was start listing societies until she hit on yours. I suppose this is the kind of thing you have to think about when you join one.

"It depends," I said, setting down my spoon. "Dragon's Head. Book & Key. Serpent. You going anywhere?"

Lydia said nothing. We sat there, staring at each other. Either she wasn't following the rule, I hadn't named her society, or she was just as unsure of what was going on as I was.

I tried turning the tables. "I came back to the room not five minutes after I left it, and you weren't there anymore. And you didn't come back for the rest of the evening. Were you tapped by someone after I left?"

"You know I can't tell you that."

"No, I don't!" I noticed my raised voice had attracted some listeners from nearby tables, and leaned forward to talk to her more privately. Luckily, dining halls are mostly deserted during the breakfast hours—especially on Fridays. "I don't know anything about how this works. I don't even know if those guys in their robes were serious last night. As far as I know, I wasn't tapped by anyone, Diggers or otherwise."

At the word "Diggers," Lydia flinched.

A horrible thought then came to me. Maybe *Lydia* had been tapped by Rose & Grave—the *real* Rose & Grave—and the reason she wasn't talking was that telling me that my experience was a hoax meant revealing exactly how she knew. After all, she hadn't reacted to any of the society names I'd thrown out earlier, but I hadn't mentioned the Diggers. Still, *she* had, which she probably wouldn't if she'd been tapped...my head started to hurt.

Am I paranoid, or what? If I hadn't been tapped, they sure had missed out on a prime candidate. Smart, sexy, and neurotic enough to do any clandestine organization proud.

Lydia sat back and took another sip of her coffee. "It's true there have been hoaxes in the past. Do you think that's what happened to you?"

I shrugged. "How do I know? If it was a hoax, it wasn't too high on the personal humiliation scale. You'd think they'd have at least tried for a fake initiation of some sort."

She nodded thoughtfully. "So what did they do?"

I opened my mouth to tell her, but then shut it again. Why should I share anything with Lydia if she wasn't willing to reciprocate? Besides, what was I supposed to say and what wasn't I? On the off chance that this whole fiasco had been for real, what kind of trouble would I get in for reporting the experience? There were too many options to keep track of.

POSSIBILITIES

A) I was tapped by Rose & Grave, and so shouldn't tell anyone anything.

B) I was either tapped or tricked, and telling Lydia meant I could figure out which one it was.

C) I was the victim of a practical joke and Lydia was a member of Rose & Grave and was just toying with me.

D) None of the above.

Too bad Lydia was the one who'd spent the semester doing logic problems in preparation for the LSAT. Ugh. As if I wasn't under enough pressure. Why couldn't a girl just finish *War and*

Peace, rock her finals, whip out a kick-ass commencement issue of the Lit Mag, prepare for a summer in Manhattan, and enjoy a no-strings-attached relationship with a cute if slightly dorky boy who liked to buy her pad Thai? Was that too much to ask?

Actually, looking at it laid out like that, yeah. It was an awful lot. And now I may or may not have to add "join a notorious underground brotherhood" to the list.

"I don't know," I said. "Nothing like what happens in the movies, that's for sure."

"No pig's blood or sacrificed virgins?"

"Where would they find a virgin around here?"

Lydia spit out her coffee. After she finished composing herself, she set her cup back on her tray and regarded me. "You know, if you really think it's a hoax, I suggest you do some research."

"What kind of research?" I certainly hoped she wasn't about to propose another field trip to the Rose & Grave tomb. I was still scarred from last night, and I couldn't afford to lose another pair of jeans.

"At the library. They have lots and lots of info on secret societies."

"Really?" I raised my eyebrows. "But what about the 'secret' part?"

"A surprisingly recent development." She leaned in. "They used to publish the list of Rose & Grave taps every year in the *New York Times*."

"That can't be true."

"It is. Members put it on their resume. They were very open about it. Kind of at odds with the whole 'leaving the room' thing, huh?" She paused and looked down at her plate. "But that doesn't make it any less valid."

Her subtext was clear: She wasn't going to tell me anything

about her society. And it hurt me more than I expected. Lydia and I had always shared everything. We'd lived together for three years. I'd gone to visit her in London last summer. We'd rented that room in the beach house in Myrtle Beach our sophomore spring. She knew I had been dabbling in novel writing, I knew she'd had an affair with her sophomore year poli-sci T.A. Aside from the whole he's-her-teacher-eww factor, it's not as sketchy as it sounds. He was only twenty-four. Okay, you're right, it's sketchy, but I'm not one to judge— remember Ben Somebody? When I'd returned to our beach house the next morning, in equal parts mortified and terror-stricken—How could I have slept with someone I didn't know? What was wrong with me?—Lydia never lectured me, just encouraged me to remember as much as I could about the incident (like, for example, putting the condom on, thank God!) and for the rest of the week happily stayed home from the party scene and played sober and boy-free Scrabble with me on the beach. She was my best friend.

But this was turning out to be bigger than ill-conceived one-night stands. It might even be bigger than our friendship.

Lydia glanced at her watch and groaned. "I've got to get up to Rocks for Jocks lab." (All of the science courses, even the loser ones designed for history majors like Lydia who can't tell a covalent bond from a computer chip, are located on the other end of campus. Does Eli have its priorities straight, or what?) "If you go to the library, could you take back two books for me? They're sitting on the end of my bed."

I nodded and Lydia departed, leaving me alone with my Frosted Flakes and a quickly dwindling appetite. Did I really want to spend my morning combing through the Stacks, only to find out that my whole Tap Night experience had been a hoax?

I'm evidently a sucker for punishment. On my way to

Dwight Memorial Library, I swung by the suite to pick up Lydia's books, some dusty history tomes with titles I could barely make out on the disintegrating covers. A piece of paper stuck out from between the pages of one, covered in Lydia's careful, upright script. She'd forgotten her notes.

But when I pulled the paper out, I could see that it was a printout from the online card catalog, covered in check marks and other notations. I was about to drop it to the desk when one of the titles caught my eye:

Kellogg, H. L. *College Secret Societies: Their Customs, Character, and the Efforts for Their Suppression.* Chicago: Ezra A. Cook, 1874.

No wonder Lydia knew where to get the scoop.

———

As if to convince myself that I wasn't obsessing about this whole secret society thing (after all, at least ninety percent of every Eli class never joins one!), I brought WAP with me to read in the library. It took me two hours to track down the five titles listed on Lydia's printout. Dwight Library Stacks are about twelve stories tall, with enough hidden nooks and crannies for half the student body to hide in. It's an old Eli tradition to have sex in the Stacks at least once before graduation. (And, no, I've never done it, not even with the faux beatnik Galen Twilo.)

I finally found one of the books tucked away in between the ceiling and the top of the bookcase where it was supposed to be shelved. Another old library trick: If you don't want anyone to take out the books you need, you hide them. I often wondered how many volumes were forever lost in the morass of the Stacks because some student had decided to play nut-storing squirrel and lost track of his hiding places—or never bothered to undo the damage once the semester was over. (See, you'd think that Ivy League students were an honest, trustworthy bunch, but no. Some of the crap I've seen pulled on this campus is practically criminal. But I never thought Lydia was the type to engage in that type of behavior.)

I trekked down to the nearest reading room and set up shop at one of the carved wooden tables that ran from end to end. Giant burgundy leather wingback chairs and elegant reading lamps with green shades rounded out the décor, and the Friday morning sun shone in from the lead-veined windows and highlighted the Gothic stone arches vaulting high above my head. The Dwight Memorial reading rooms just reeked of high-class academia.

I immediately started to feel sleepy.

Which had more in common with the caffeinating qualities of a mochacchino: 1,472 pages of Russian historic literature extolling the exploits of the Napoleonic invasion, or dusty essays about 19th century collegiate frats?

Blecch. I decided to stave off boredom by switching back and forth on a regular basis. Natasha Rostov was up to her usual antics, but the society tome didn't gift me with any useful info. Seriously, do I care whether or not Phi Beta Kappa started at William & Mary? I want to know what's going on with Rose & Grave in the 21st century.

"Hi, Amy."

I looked up to see Malcolm Cabot standing over my table. A senior, a popular party boy, and the son of a state governor, Malcolm Cabot and I didn't run in the same social circles. My friends stocked up on popcorn and had *Sex and the City* marathons, while his crowd liked to drive down to "The City" for marathon sex weekends. He wasn't in my college, we'd never been in the same class, and as far as I knew, we hadn't exchanged so much as three words in my years at Eli. "Um, hi."

Okay, four words.

"What's up?" Malcolm craned his neck toward my reading material, which, luckily, was currently opened to page 834 of WAP. He was dressed in a spring green polo shirt with the letters "CC" printed in the corner, and a pair of very well-fitting blue jeans. His sandy hair looked like it had been ripped right out of an Abercrombie & Fitch catalog. He wore his messenger bag slung across his chest and was thrumming his fingers against the strap. "Russian Novel class, huh? Which one did you like best?"

"Crime and Punishment," I said. "It's only 500 pages long."

He laughed, which earned him dirty looks from at least three other people at my table.

Malcolm straightened then, but continued beating that tattoo on his shoulder strap. If you ask me, the rhythm, more than the whispered conversation, was what was distracting about his presence. And now we were up to two dozen words.

"The final's a breeze," he went on. "So don't worry about it."

"Thanks." I guess. *Thrum, thrum, thrum.*

"Just don't work too hard. You'll need your energy."

Huh? My eyes shot to his face. "What are you talking about?"

He grinned then, showing me a set of gorgeous white teeth. "Oh, I almost forgot." He stopped thrumming for a second, reached into his messenger bag, pulled out three books, and set them down on my desk. "This might help you out when you're stuck in class." He pointed at each of them in turn. "Said was a post-colonialist critic, Levi-Strauss advocated structuralism, and Aristotle...well, he's the *oldest* critic in the book. None of them is a New Critic. Get your facts straight, or I'll think you deserved that B– in Ethiopian Lit."

I stared up at that all-too-familiar smile, then down to his hands, which had started tapping on his shoulder strap again. Right next to the little gold pin stuck through the canvas that showed a rose inside an elongated hexagon.

Malcolm Cabot was the Shadow-Who-Smiles. And he was in Rose & Grave.

Which meant...

"Hey!" I said. Loudly.

"Shh!" The harsh rebuke came from a girl at the next table. I craned my neck around Malcolm's torso to see Clarissa Cuthbert glaring at me over the rim of her Louis Vuitton bag. Clarissa's gaze ping-ponged from me to Malcolm and back again, and then her ice blue eyes narrowed. Little wonder. She was probably wondering what Governor Cabot's son was doing talking to me. Like Malcolm, Clarissa was part of the school's über elite.

And Malcolm was taking advantage of my distraction. He ruffled my hair. "See you soon, babe." Then he turned on his heel and walked off.

Ignoring Clarissa, and completely forgetting about both the society books and Malcolm's favorite literary critics, I snatched up WAP (with both hands, of course, since the stupid thing weighs two hundred pounds) and dashed after him.

By the time I got into the main hall of the library, he was nowhere to be seen. Stacks? Exit? Ugh! I walked as quickly as possible to the front doors, all the while scanning down each bay for any sight of his green shirt or blond hair. No luck.

At the door, I went through the usual No-This-Is-My-Copy-of-*War-and-Peace*-That's-Why-It-Doesn't-Have-a-Library-Bar-Code-on-It rigmarole, then sprinted down the front steps onto the Cross Campus Green. No sign of him there, either.

What, did Rose & Grave members have a secret entrance to the library, too?

Fine, I'd beard the lion in his den. "CC" stood for Calvin College in Eli shorthand, and green was the college color. I'd follow him right back to his dorm room. I tried to look dignified as I power-walked across the Green and back onto High Street, but the weight of WAP kept throwing off my stride.

THOUGHTS THAT WENT THROUGH MY HEAD ON THE WAY

1) Malcolm Cabot knew I'd been bullshitting at my interview but tapped me anyway.
2) Must be convenient for Malcolm that Calvin College and the Rose & Grave tomb are right next door to each other.
3) I wonder if the Diggers have the Russian Novel final on file.

I swiped my keycard at the entrance to Calvin College, and opened the heavy gate. A few steps later and I was in their small, sunny courtyard, empty but for one guy in a green polo shirt booking it toward one of the far entryways.

"Malcolm!" I shouted, and he stopped in his tracks. I ran to meet him. "You're a Digger," I said when I arrived, panting slightly.

He grabbed my arm and maneuvered me to one of the stone benches positioned farther away from the windows. "And you," he hissed in my ear in a much lower tone than I'd been using, "are not exactly discreet."

I rolled my eyes as we sat. "How discreet is that pin of yours?"

He snorted. "It took you about ninety seconds to notice it, and I practically had to jab you in the eye with the pointy end."

"Thanks for restraining yourself."

"Think nothing of it."

I crossed my arms over my chest. "Now I want an explanation."

He narrowed his eyes. "For what?"

"For what!" I looked around the courtyard. Still empty. But I lowered my voice anyway. "For last night, of course."

"You seemed to understand the process at the time."

"Yeah, but then you just left me there. In the bathroom."

"Of course. We had to get to eleven other people, you know, Amy. We were busy."

I digested that point while he glanced around. "Look, this isn't the time to talk. Everything you need to know is in the—" He stopped and looked down at my hands, empty but for WAP. "Where are the books I gave you?"

"In the library, I suppose."

"WHAT!" Now it was Malcolm's turn to get loud. He jumped up from the bench and threw his hands in the air. "You just left them there?"

I blinked at him. "They were library books. And I already have a copy of *Poetics* back in my suite."

"There was—urgh!" He spiked his hands in his hair. "There was something in the Aristotle. For you. From us."

"Oh."

"*Oh?*" He paced back and forth in front of me. "Oh?!? That's all you have to say?"

"What am I supposed to say? Did you honestly think that after that little act of yours I'd be more interested in hunting you down or settling back for a little bit of Dead White Guy's take on literary criticism?"

"Well, I didn't think you'd just leave them there!" He plopped back down on the bench and put his head in his hands. "I told them we shouldn't get creative. I said, 'What's wrong with the Post Office?' But did anyone listen to me? No. And now look."

I patted him on the shoulder, because it seemed like the only appropriate response, but inside I was already plotting my course back to the reading room.

Malcolm whipped up and caught me by the shoulders. He

stared at me intently. "Listen, you can't let anyone else see the letter I put inside those books. It could ruin everything. You have to get back to the library and get them back. Now. Understand?"

I nodded, a bit taken aback, and put my hands on his chest to push him away. And, naturally, that's when the door to the nearest entryway opened and Brandon Weare walked out.

"Hey, Haskel," he said in a voice that was anything but casual. "What's up?"

Malcolm dropped his hands and stepped back and I tried to think of the least awkward way to respond.

Option One: "Whoa, Malcolm, be careful on those uneven flagstones, you don't want to trip!"

Option Two: "Hey, Brandon. Malcolm here was acting out this scene I missed on *The OC* last week."

Option Three: "Hi, Brandon. Malcolm and I can't talk right now. We have to go back to the library before anyone finds the top-secret Rose & Grave correspondence Agent Double-Oh-Cabot here left in a book I had no intention of checking out."

But Malcolm took over, going from Bobcat-Goldthwait-freaked-out to James-Dean-cool in a flash. "Hey, man, how's it going?" He held out his hand and slapped Brandon five before my friend-with-bennies could figure out what was going on. "I've been meaning to congratulate you on that last intramural badminton game. Have you thought about being team captain next year? I think Calvin is going to make a real play for the Tibbs Cup."

Brandon played badminton? Live and learn. Of course, considering the guy's obsession with paper airplanes, the aerodynamically designed shuttle used in badminton fit perfectly.

"Thanks," Brandon said, and stood a little taller. "I have been thinking about it."

Unbelievable. I looked at Malcolm with new appreciation. Brandon was completely distracted. "Are you doing anything right now?" Malcolm was asking him. "We can go talk to the Calvin Tibbs Coordinator about it."

"Well, I wanted to chat with Amy. . . ." Brandon cast me a quick glance, but before he could break out his Amy-smile, Malcolm stepped in.

"Oh, she's headed off to the library." Malcolm clapped Brandon on the shoulder and made some kind of complicated eyebrow gesture in my direction. "Let's go," he went on, guiding my Brandon away.

I stood there, alone in the Calvin courtyard, and began to question the veracity of Brandon's ongoing Hopelessly-Devoted-to-You act. The man had just ditched me for intramural badminton.

On the upside, I was definitely on my way to becoming a member of Rose & Grave. So, boy, did I need to reclaim those books!

I hurried back to the library, crossing my fingers that the shelving assistants hadn't made their rounds in the reading room yet.

But my luck didn't hold out. I got to the table where I'd been sitting, and it was completely cleared. No society tomes, no volumes of literary criticism, no missive from Rose & Grave.

Crap. The next freshman who had to read *Poetics* was sure in for a surprise. And I'd already screwed up my first objective as a member of a secret society—actually getting initiated. (Though, seriously, I don't think I'm entirely to blame for this snafu. How was I to know? It's not like there's a "So You Wanna Be in a Secret Society" brochure.) *Okay, Amy, think.* They wouldn't have had time to reshelve them yet, so they were probably sitting on one of the book carts behind the circulation desk. I could just go up to the people at the desk and tell them I needed it back.

So there I was, standing in line, practically hopping with impatience and straining my eyes to see past the counter to the book carts, hoping that I'd recognize at least one of the volumes. The petite girl working the computer had a nose ring and two green stripes in her hair, and when I told her I needed my Aristotle back, she just stared at me and blinked. "According to the system," she said, pulling the info up on the screen, "there are 215 copies of the collected writings of Aristotle in the Dwight Stacks alone."

"I know, but I need the one I was just looking at."

"And another 167 in the rest of the Eli University library system."

"Right," I said, pointing behind her. "But I need the one on that little cart back there."

She looked over her shoulder, then back at me. "You want me to go digging through the cart to find a particular book, another copy of which you can easily retrieve from the shelves in 382 different forms?"

Nice math, bitch. I was still carrying the one. But my momma always told me you catch more flies with honey.

"Pretty please." I leaned forward. "I left some rather *sensitive* health information in there, accidentally." I gestured vaguely at my lower regions and whispered, *"Test results."*

She retrieved the cart forthwith and started rummaging through the books. Unfortunately, *Poetics* was not among them, nor were any of the other books I'd had with me earlier.

"Sorry," she said, then reached into her pocket and pulled out a card. She slid it across the counter, then laid her hand softly over mine. "You know, I volunteer at the Eli Women's Center. If you need to talk about anything, we have a twenty-four-hour Crisis Help Line."

I did my best to look somber. "Thank you," I said, taking the card and stuffing it in my pocket. Okay, now what was I supposed to do?

"Hey! Psst, Amy. Amy Haskel."

I turned in the direction of the voice and saw Clarissa Cuthbert seated in a leather armchair in a little reading alcove. Her Louis Vuitton bag was on her lap, a pile of library books sat on the table beside her, and between two of her French manicured fingers, she dangled a white envelope with a black border and a black wax seal.

"Looking for this?"

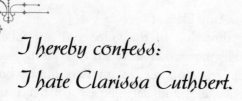

I hereby confess:
I hate Clarissa Cuthbert.

4.
Semper Paratus

And let me tell you why.

Remember Galen Twilo, *numero dos* on my Hit List? Well, soon after our Reading Week love-in, about two weeks into the second semester, when it was just penetrating my lust-addled brain that I would never again be treated to a post-coital discussion about existentialism and the incontrovertible nothingness of being (I know, strange thing to think right after an orgasm) in the arms of Mr. Twilo, I had a rather unfortunate encounter.

There's a sort of restaurant/club in New Haven called Tory's that caters to the very, very old-school factions of the student body. To eat there, you have to be a member, and the dress code is incredibly strict. They serve stuff like Welsh rarebit, and campus organizations who have Tory's members on their roster like to go and have what we call "Tory's Nights," where we sing songs and drink toasts out of giant silver trophy cups at the long tables in the restaurant's private banquet rooms, though we never actually eat anything. Clarissa Cuthbert is amongst the very oldest of the old school, and her father, some hotshot Wall Street guy, is the type of person who pays the steep post-graduate membership fee to Tory's just so he can eat toast points whenever he visits his daughter at his old alma mater.

I didn't know any of this then. I knew *of* Clarissa—she was beautiful in that "Bergdorf blonde" way, dressed like she was in a fashion show for every class, and had a dorm room on campus (as all freshmen are required to) as well as a swank penthouse on the corner of Chapel and College Streets, the town's ritziest student-friendly address. She held champagne-tasting parties. At eighteen.

I was still getting used to keggers.

My first Tory's Night with the Lit Mag had been going on for about an hour and a half when the almost-empty trophy cup was passed to me. "Finish it," Glenda Foster, then a sophomore, had whispered to me, and the whole table lifted their voices in song. Now, the rules of the Tory's Cup Game are a little bit complicated (especially considering it's a drinking game), but here's a short list.

TORY'S NIGHT RULES

1) The Tory's Cup can *never* touch the table.
2) The players pass the cup to the left, making a half turn every time, and everyone takes a sip.
3) When it gets down to a low enough level of mixed alcoholic beverage (identified only by color—i.e., a Red Tory's Cup, a Gold Tory's Cup, a Green Tory's Cup), the person holding it is obliged to chug the rest, wipe the inside of the cup out on her hair and/or clothes, and rest it, upside down, on a napkin. If there's any ring of moisture imprinted on the napkin, she has to pay for the next cup. (Tory's Cups are prohibitively expensive, hence the not ordering

food at Tory's Nights. We can't blow our budget on cucumber sandwiches.)

4) All this is done while the other people at the table sing "the Tory's Song," which is an incomprehensible mix of letters, hand-clapping, and general drunken revelry, into which they insert the unlucky drinker's name. Students aren't ever taught the Tory's Song, we just pick it up through osmosis as soon as we get on campus.

These cups probably hold more than a gallon, so even when they look nearly empty, there's still a highly deceptive amount of liquor, juice, and other people's backwash swishing around on the bottom of the polished-silver bowl. And I had to drink it—without drowning. For a second I thought I'd have as much luck trying to swim in it. But I rallied, and chugged, and did my best to dry the rim and interior off on my hair and clothing. The price of a Green Cup is about sixty bucks, which was my freshman-year spending money for a month, so I had to win the game.

And I did, but I paid the price. Woozy, sticky, and already regretting my future dry-cleaning bill, I excused myself right afterward to go to the restroom. I wobbled down the stairs into the main dining hall and practically tripped over a table containing Clarissa Cuthbert, her father, a few people I didn't recognize, and Galen Twilo, dressed unaccountably in khaki dress pants, a shirt and tie, and a blue blazer with gold buttons on the cuffs.

They looked up from their watercress salads at my sticky, green-stained outfit, and Galen's eyes (I will never forget this) showed absolutely no recognition. For a moment there, I thought maybe I was seeing things and it wasn't Galen after all. Galen wore black pants with chains hanging off them and Clash concert T-shirts he found at thrift stores in the Village.

Not blue blazers with gold buttons and—I looked down at his feet—brown loafers with little leather tassels.

Just then, that pint and a half of Tory's Cup in my stomach got the better of me and I rushed to the toilet. I was still in the stall, trying to erase the image of violent green alcoholic vomit from my mind, when the door to the ladies' room opened and in walked Clarissa and one of her friends. (I peeped through the crack in the stall door.)

"—he says they went out a few times," Clarissa was saying as she popped open a Chanel compact and brushed bronzer on her nose. "But he never thought she'd just show up here."

"Following him around like a devoted puppy, huh?" The other girl made a clucking sound with her tongue. "And what was that stuff in her hair?"

Clarissa shrugged. "You know how Galen likes slumming."

What I Learned That Night

1) There's a restroom near the private banquet halls that Tory's prefers its student Tory's Night guests to use so as not to disturb the people in the main dining hall with their sticky outfits.
2) Mr. Rebel-Without-a-Cause Twilo was actually a trust-fund baby from Manhattan who'd grown up on the Upper East Side and attended the same twee private school as Clarissa.
3) Never finish a Green Tory's Cup.

And I never did like Clarissa Cuthbert after that. *Slumming!*

So here I was, two and a half years later, watching Clarissa fondle my letter from Rose & Grave with a smug little smile plastered on her (probably plastic surgery–enhanced) face.

I swallowed. "Why, thanks," *bitch* "Clarissa!" I said in what I hoped was a tone of sincere gaiety, but probably came across as forced brittleness. "I was so wondering" *why you'd steal my books* "what I'd done with that" *secret society letter* "birthday party invitation."

"Can it," she said, and beckoned to me with the letter. "Come here."

I started to trot over, then remembered that, whatever Clarissa might have said freshman year, I am *not* an obedient little puppy, stopped, and held out my hand. "Please give me back my letter."

"As soon as we ascertain that it belongs to you."

That brought me fully into the alcove. "It belongs to me and you know it," I hissed.

She turned the envelope over in her hands, a look of serene innocence on her face. "No name on it."

I clenched my jaw. "Then let me describe it to you."

"Oh, please do!" She smiled sweetly. "Especially what's on the inside."

I sat down on the chair opposite her. "Clarissa, I'm not kidding around here. Give it back."

She hesitated, frowned, and handed it over. I snatched it out of her claws and, after ensuring the seal remained unbroken, shoved it between the covers of WAP. Well, that was easier than I thought it would be. Dude, if it were me, I'd have put up a real fight to get a look inside her letter.

All business between us seemingly at an end, I rose to go.

"Wait, Amy." She touched my arm, and I was quite proud of myself for not jerking away in revulsion. "We should talk."

"About what?" I said haughtily.

"You know about what." Her eyes softened for a second. "Please?"

What a crock. Like she'd be my friend now that I had won the approval of a group like Rose & Grave? I pulled out of her grip. "Sorry, Clarissa. I'm not into slumming."

The inside of the letter had been burned in places, and large charred blotches left black streaks on my hands as I tried to unfold it and read the writing. Like before, the print was lopsided on the page, which was folded into an irregular hexagon. This time, it smelled like smoke.

This is what it said:

> *Neophyte Haskel,*
> *At five minutes past eight this evening, wearing neither metal, nor sulfur, nor glass, leave the base of Whitney Tower and walk south on High Street. Look neither to the right nor to the left. Pass through the sacred pillars of Hercules and approach the Temple. Take the right Book in your left hand and knock thrice upon the sacred portals. Tell no one what you do.*
>
> *—Rex Grave*

Um, okaaaay. I knew what all those words meant, but the sum was still a mystery. Who wears sulfur? The glass restriction was okay, since I was blessed with 20/20 vision, but the metal thing would be a tough one. Jeans were out—what with all those copper rivets and the zipper and buttons. In fact, most of my pants had metal zippers in them, and even the button-fly ones had metal buttons. Was I supposed to wear a skirt? Sweatpants?

Lydia knocked on the door as I was ripping open the lining to one of my bras.

"What are you doing?" she asked, sticking her head in.

"Trying to find the underwire." Aha! I yanked it out, only to discover that "wire" was a relative term, and that Victoria's Secret apparently used some sort of hard, springy plastic.

"Ruined that one for nothing," I said, tossing the torn bra to the bed.

"What do you have against support?" Lydia sat down on the edge of the bed. I looked over in alarm, but the mountain of discarded clothes covered the Rose & Grave letter.

Shrugging, I pulled out another Vicky's bra—they're all plastic, right?—and shimmied into it. "Nothing. That one was just poking through." I glanced in the mirror over my dresser and pulled off my silver earrings.

"So I was thinking of going over to see that Pinter play Carol's putting up," Lydia said. "Wanna come?"

About as much as I wanted to dress in head-to-toe sulfur. "Pass." I made a face. "What would possess you to spend a beautiful Friday night watching something so depressing?"

"You have a better idea?"

I leaned against the counter, regarding my very best friend. Any other night, I would. We could pick up some smoothies and sneak them into the campus movie theater to avoid the overpriced refreshments they used to balance out the el cheapo entrance fees. We could order pizzas and spend the night watching the Meg Ryan oeuvre on Lydia's twelve-inch set. We could run down to the CVS, stock up on nail polish, and have a pedicure party. We could grab that Finlandia Mango bottle and a bag of gumdrops, get drunk, drop the weird tension that had permeated our friendship since Tap Night, stop acting like children, and tell each other exactly what was going on with these secret societies we were joining.

But I wanted Lydia to go first.

"Not really," I replied. And on a scale of 1 to maturity, I'd call that a 2.3.

Lydia held one of my shirts up to her chest and checked out her reflection. "Yellow does nothing for my complexion."

"Yeah, but you look great in that blue silk blouse of mine

that you've had for—what, five weeks?" It very much suited her Black Irish looks. I took off my watch, wondering if the Diggers were going to do something weird and magnetic to me. No metal? I was lucky I didn't wear braces. I had half a mind to call Malcolm Cabot and ask him for wardrobe advice.

Lydia flopped back across my clothes. "Look who's talking! I haven't seen my red ankle boots since Spring Break."

I ducked my head guiltily and unclasped my necklace. Those boots were at Brandon's.

With all vestiges of metal removed, I headed back to my closet to find a pair of pants that didn't need to fasten and still looked like something you'd wear outside the gym or the bedroom.

Lydia started rooting through my pile of discards. "What are you dressing for?"

Beats me. "I'm going out, and I'm not exactly sure where I'm going to end up, so I want to be prepared."

She sat up. "Prepared? Are we talking *society* here?"

I rustled my clothes and pretended I didn't hear her.

"Amy?"

Rustle, rustle, rustle. My velour loungewear? How come they never looked as good on me as they did on (a pre-pregnancy) Britney Spears?

"Amy?"

The corduroy skirt might work, but it was too short to do anything but sit or stand in. Somehow, I suspected the initiation would require a tad more.

"Neophyte Haskel?"

I snapped to attention and pulled out of the closet. Lydia had found my letter, and was reading it out loud. Appalled, I launched my body toward the bed. "Give me that!" Lydia rolled away and I landed with my face in a pile of winter sweaters.

She skipped across the room, giggling and reading in a

creepy, Vincent Price–esque singsong. " *'Pass through the sacred pillars of Hercules and approach the Temple.'* Oooooh... This thing reads like an online Role-Playing Game."

"Lydia, stop it!" I fought to untangle myself from the sleeves of my fleece.

Sighing, she tossed the letter in my direction. "Here, don't have a coronary."

I stuffed the letter in my desk and glared at her. "Are those like the instructions you got in your letter?" I asked with a sneer.

She looked away. "I can't talk about that."

"Oh, please! You've got to be joking!" I pointed at my desk drawer. "Is there any way on earth that *your* society could take things more seriously than *mine*?"

Oops. Her face turned hard. "And the true colors come out. Pardon me for intruding. I should have known a peon like me had no business invading the room of a high and mighty *Digger*." She practically spat the word. At the door, she paused. "Don't wear the velour," she said coldly. "It makes your butt look huge."

———

As luck would have it, I owned a pair of cargo pants with a drawstring waist and Velcro fastenings, and so, properly attired at last, I set forth to meet my destiny. At Whitney Tower, I hung out, periodically checking the time on the clock face and hoping I looked more casual than I felt. Five minutes after the Whitney Tower Carillon finished sounding off the eight o'clock hour, I did an about-face and marched toward the Rose & Grave tomb. I was determined not to repeat the mistakes of my interview—I wasn't going to be late for initiation.

As I approached the tomb, I caught sight of another figure walking toward me from the south side of the street. Dammit. I couldn't enter the Rose & Grave yard with someone standing right there watching me, could I? How did the members keep their secrets without a private entrance?

The figure passed beneath a sodium streetlight, and I could see it was a man. He wore a shiny black jacket festooned with more zippers than one reasonably expected to see on the average overcoat. I knew that jacket. It belonged to George Harrison Prescott.

"Heya, Amy!" he said as we met on the sidewalk directly in front of that hated wrought-iron gate. George rested his hand on it (as if it were just any gate and not the entrance to the Diggers' tomb) and planted his feet directly in my path. "Whatcha up to?"

"Um..." I flickered my eyes toward the tomb. "Not much. You?"

"Same." He winked at me, his gorgeous copper-penny eyes glinting even more from behind the shiny bronze rims of his glasses.

I clamped my thighs together, then prayed fervently that he didn't notice. George Harrison Prescott was not only the most beautiful man in my class in Prescott College (and no, that's not a coincidence about the names), he was also a Player with a capital "P." Remember Marissa Corrs, who played opposite Orlando Bloom in that costume drama last year? Well, she recently took a leave of absence from Eli to concentrate on her acting career, but while she was here, guess whose room she was seen exiting every Sunday morning?

Yep. Chick could have had Orlando, but she chose George Harrison Prescott. Of course, if you squint your eyes a tad, George and Orlando could be twins, but for George's glasses, which, as far as I'm concerned, make him ten times hotter.

Marissa was just one of many on what I'm sure is more like George Prescott's Hit Dictionary. From what I've heard, George has slept with half of the straight and/or available women in Prescott College, and from what I *know*, the other half are impatiently waiting their turn.

Not me, of course! George and I are just friends. Acquaintances. The kind that nod in recognition when we pass each other on the street, or sit together in the Prescott dining hall when none of our other friends are around, chitchatting with each other in honor of class- and college-affiliation solidarity.

And if a girl indulges in the occasional sexual fantasy about *accidentally* stumbling into George Harrison Prescott's bathroom while he's in the shower—well, that's no big deal, right?

"Headed home?" he asked, and I tried not to fixate on his mouth.

Since I was walking in the precise opposite direction of Prescott College, it struck me as a rather unusual question. "Nope."

"Okay." He smiled genially and neither of us moved an inch. At last, giving up, I sidestepped him and walked a few paces down the street.

George waved, but didn't budge. By the time I reached the far corner and turned around, he'd taken a book of matches from his pocket and began striking them, one by one, and letting them burn down to his fingers before flicking the nubs to the curb.

I shook my head. Boys! Is it like a caveman thing to have to play with fire every chance they get? He looked ready to stand there doing his Prometheus act all night. How many times was I going to have to walk around the block before I got a clear shot at the tomb?

At last, George seemed to come to a decision. He turned and loped off toward Prescott College. I wasted no time scurrying back to the gate. So what if I wasn't following the precise directions in the letter? I'd done every step, despite the delay, and I couldn't risk being late again. Who knew how many atomic clocks they had in there?

The giant double doors at the threshold of the Rose & Grave tomb were weathered to a dull bronze sheen. A large brass knocker shaped like an open book hung at face height; its aged brass pages were engraved with an "R" and a "G." I took a breath.

Here goes nothing.

No sooner had I lifted the knocker than the door flew open. I glimpsed a shadowed face, maybe a pair of hands, then someone threw a burlap hood over my head, grabbed me by both of my arms, and pulled me inside.

I screamed. Of course.

"Silence, Neophyte." More hands surrounded me and I was lifted off my feet. "You are treading on sacred ground," a man intoned from somewhere in the vicinity of my right knee.

I wiggled my useless legs. "I'm not *treading* on anything," I mumbled through the hood.

Someone actually had the gall to slap me on my butt. "Shush."

"That had better be someone I know, or I'm suing for harass—"

"I said, 'Shush!' "

"Hands off, hood hound." I bucked my body as my captors carried me down a short flight of stairs with a series of bone-jarring bumps.

I heard a chuckle near my left shoulder blade. "Tapped a live one here, Lancelot."

Lancelot?

All talk ceased as the team turned left, halted, then flipped me right-side-up and set me on my (understandably) unsteady feet. Two hands on my shoulders shoved me down onto what felt like a wooden bench, and a third whipped the hood off my head.

I opened my eyes and gasped.

Not from shock, I'd like to point out. The room was still too dark to see much of anything, but what it lacked in illumination, it more than made up for in choking clouds of smoke. I coughed and spluttered, recognizing on my second or third wheeze that the tiny orange sparks invading my field of vision were the lit ends of cigarettes. There were dozens of them. My eyes began to water and I heard a few muffled coughs at my back. Okay, so I was not alone here.

You indoor-smoking bans, look upon that which you have wrought: a generation of twenty-somethings with zero tolerance for secondhand smoke.

"Neophyte!" The sparks trembled for a second, then seemed to freeze in air. "You seek to be Initiated into the Sacred Mysteries of Rose & Grave, to devote the Resolve of your Bone, the Passion of your Blood, and the Power of your Mind"—

And the patience of my ears, I thought, to listen to this cheesy crap. Who writes this stuff?

—"to our Order. This be your wish?"

"You bet!"

Someone poked me. "Say 'Aye.' "

"Aye," I repeated, hoping I didn't sound like a pirate.

The sparks began dancing again. "Do not speak in haste, Neophyte. For after this night, there is no turning away from the Path of Rose & Grave. Your mere admittance into our Tomb, your presence here in the Firefly Room"—

So that's what those cigarettes were supposed to represent. Cute.

—"has shown you more than is permitted to any Barbarian, but even these Mysteries are but tiny sparks alongside the Lamp of Knowledge. Are you willing to Witness this Light and be brought into its Flame, though it may blind you?" (You could totally hear the capital letters in his voice, by the way.) "Choose carefully, Neophyte, for there is no turning back."

Um, okay, Morpheus... "Yeah, I'll take the red pill."

"Huh?" said the voice. Someone else sniggered.

"Sorry," I said. "I mean, 'Aye.' "

The fireflies all did a nosedive and were extinguished, and for a second, impossibly, the smoke in the room became thicker. Then a light bloomed in the room and an old-fashioned oil lamp floated toward me. "Then come with us, Neophyte Haskel, and be Reborn."

I stood up and walked toward the light. As I got closer, I saw it was being held by a figure entirely shrouded in his long black cape and hood, looking for all the world like the Ghost of Christmas Future. He withdrew his fist from his robe, and in slow motion opened his hand to reveal a shiny golden key lying in his palm. I reached for it.

Suddenly, several people grabbed me at once and dragged me away from the robed figure. I heard a door open, felt a blast of icy wind, and then I was being propelled roughly up a flight of stairs.

"Not for you!" they cried, following it up with an uneven chorus of, "You're not worthy! You're not ready! You can't come in! Get out, get out, get out!"

"What the hell...?" I kicked my legs furiously and wrenched out of their grip, flailing through the darkness until I fell to my knees on hardwood floor. Ow! Was this part of the initiation? If so, then I think I must have missed a step. I heard shuffling behind me, and then, as if from far away, a voice sounding the alarm.

"Quick, quick, catch her! She mustn't infiltrate the Inner Temple."

I blinked furiously and peered through the darkness, hoping to discern some shape, some path, some giant lit-up sign saying EXIT in large red letters. Inner Temple, huh? How about a nice, relaxing Outer Veranda?

No luck. I pushed to my feet and began walking, hands out in front of me so I didn't break my nose. A few faltering steps later I hit a wall. I kept my fingertips along the edge as I moved forward, feeling the delicate texture of silk wallpaper, the edge of carved picture frames, and then, at last, a hinge. A door, but did it lead out, or farther in? Carefully, I ran my hand along the inside wall, past the threshold, hoping to discover a light switch.

But instead, my fingers touched something smooth and round affixed to the wall. It felt like a ceramic ball beneath my palm. I let my hand glide down, over the front of the object, and felt a few bumps, some indentations, three holes, and a jagged edge—

Oh. My. God. A human skull.

A hand clamped down over my wrist.

I tried to scream, but before I drew breath, someone covered my mouth and dragged me into the room.

"Be quiet, Amy! Or they'll catch you."

He released me and I spun around to see my captor. Like the others, he wore a dark robe with a hood pulled low over his eyes. He carried a tiny penlight, which he was shining up to his face like kids do to tell ghost stories. I couldn't have recognized him, even if I'd been trying.

"Nice costume. Who are you?"

"You screwed up in there, Amy, and they aren't going to let you in."

What? Whoa! Why didn't Malcolm warn me about this? And what had I done to screw up? This whole Rose & Grave thing was turning into a bona fide fiasco. I didn't know who these people were, what was happening to me, or why. Quill would have been infinitely easier than this. Did the Diggers have anything to do with my failure to get tapped by the literary society? I hadn't considered it earlier. I was too excited by the prospect of Rose & Grave. But if the Diggers were going to spend the evening screwing with my head before kicking me out, then I'd want some answers from Glenda Foster about why I was wandering through a drafty stone tomb rather than sitting pretty right now in Quill & Ink's one-bedroom.

"Fine," I said, lifting my chin. "Then just show me the way out."

He shook his head. "I can't. I'm sorry. It's too late."

"What do you mean?"

"They will try to silence you."

My mouth went dry, and for a second I believed him. After all, I'd just had my digits inside a dead man's eye sockets. These people used human skulls as light fixtures; maybe they should be taken seriously. And then I remembered Malcolm and his clumsy letter delivery that afternoon. These weren't omnipotent officials, they were college kids. If something happened to me, they wouldn't get away with it. Lydia, at least, knew where I'd gone tonight.

"You people talk big, but you don't have anything to back it up."

"So you've always expressed." He smiled then, an ill-tempered grimace, and in the strange, angled light, he resembled the evil emperor from *Star Wars*.

Uh-oh, Amy. This guy doesn't want to help you.

"You gave us a challenge at your interview," he went on. "And Diggers don't take things lying down. You're here to learn a lesson, Amy Haskel." The door behind me flew open. "I got her, guys," I heard him say as both of my arms were twisted behind my back, firmly, but not uncomfortably, and the first figure prodded me between my shoulder blades to make me march.

"Time for the Grand Tour."

"This is assault," I said. "I'm going to scream."

"If anyone could hear you, which they can't, do you think they'd react to it? A scream coming from the Rose & Grave tomb on Initiation Night?" A few of the figures surrounding me laughed.

Fear skittered down my spine and my skin began to crawl everywhere my captors were touching me. This had to be a joke, right? Part of the initiation game. But then again, I'd heard stories about Diggers and their run-ins with the law. Somehow, the power of Rose & Grave prevailed and the members wormed their way out of all charges. Some people said the society owned the police.

"Where's Malcolm?" I asked, in a voice far more devoid of snark than I'd been using a few moments earlier. Malcolm Cabot was a governor's son—he wouldn't be party to anything too illegal, right? Unless you believed the legends that said the society owned the whole government as well.

"He'll be around...eventually. Now shut up and enjoy the ride."

With that, they shoved me forward into the waiting arms of another group, who spun me around, lifted me up, and deposited me not-so-gently onto a hard, flat surface.

"You're destined for a pauper's grave."

For a moment, I thought they were letting me go. Boy, was I wrong—a point that became clear a few seconds later when they closed a lid in my face. I tried to move, but the walls closed tight around me on all sides. I could feel sanded wood a few inches from my shoulders, above my head, and most noticeably, right beyond my nose.

They'd put me in a coffin.

I pounded on the lid, but it was closed shut. "Let me out! Let me out, you sons of bitches!" I screamed, kicking my legs. They responded by turning me over. I tumbled around, hoping at once that the movement would knock a few screws loose and also that it was sturdy enough not to spill me out without warning.

"You don't take us seriously enough, Neophyte Haskel," said Darth Digger. His voice was muffled through the coffin, but I recognized it now. He was the jerk from my interview. The one who kept arguing with Malcolm about not letting me in the society.

"I promise you, I've learned my lesson!" I pounded the coffin lid for emphasis.

"You belittle us," he went on, as if he didn't hear. "You ridicule us. You challenge us. You call our Sacred Vestments *costumes.…*"

"Well, you dress like extras at a D&D convention."

They shook the coffin, which shut me up.

"Before this night is over, Neophyte, you *will* learn respect for your Elders."

I bit my tongue to keep from pointing out that I didn't count a few months as a generation gap. They'd been carrying me for what seemed like ages, but it was difficult to tell how much of the jostling was actual forward motion and how much was cleverly designed to seem that way. At last they set me down. I thought I could hear splashing sounds all around. Another bathroom?

I could hear my captor's voice very clearly now, as if he'd leaned down to whisper directly into the coffin lid. "You are in our power now, and we hold your life in our hands. This is the pool room, Neophyte. If we wanted, we could drop you in. Do you think you'd escape from the coffin before you drowned?"

No. Something scraped against the bottom of the box—or perhaps it was the coffin itself, being shoved along the ground. I felt myself sliding forward, as if tipping, and then something wet splashed against my legs. Water, flowing through the seams in the coffin. Oh my God, they were doing it! They were submerging me in the pool!

"Stop! Stop, please!" I shrieked, kicking for all I was worth. The wooden walls of the coffin remained uncompromised.

Oh, God, I can't swim. I can't swim! Let me out, please, don't let me drown!

Pure terror washed through my body as I practically broke my hands pounding on the lid. I heard a rush of water above my head, and it started seeping in at the top of the coffin, wetting my hair and my shirt. Any second now, they'd let go and I'd sink to the bottom. Helpless. How long would it take? The coffin's seams didn't appear very tight. "Please, please, take me out! I beg of you!"

My cry broke on the last words into a sob. At last, I felt them lift me up and the hysteria ebbed.

"Well, that was quick," he commented dryly.

Hot tears ran down my face and mixed with the cold pool water. Now that the danger had passed, I felt nothing but anger at myself for having let them see me squirm. I vowed I'd have no reaction for the rest of this crazy ride, no matter what they did to me.

"Do you remember what you said to us at your interview, Neophyte?" my head captor asked. He was clearly the master of ceremonies here—everyone else was playing the part of muscle. My captors swung the coffin in earnest now, and the water inside sloshed around, drenching the legs of my metal-free pants.

"Speak!"

Not a chance. But when I didn't they began shaking me up and down. "Okay, okay," I capitulated. "Which part of my interview?"

"Your parting shot."

I struggled to recall. I remembered giving them the finger, but that was about it. "Not really," I said haltingly, wondering what else they could possibly have planned for me. Whatever it was, there was no way it could beat the pool.

"Then let us jog your memory," he said as his cohorts jogged my container. "Knights!"

And then, in unison: "*I don't do drugs, I've never been arrested, and from what I hear, I'm not too shabby in bed. Not that any of you people will ever have the opportunity to discover that first-hand!*" The cacophony of voices had a garish, military quality to it, and if possible, I was even more humiliated by their recitation than I had been when I'd first opened my big mouth in that interview room.

"Have you ever heard the story of the Diggers' Whore, Neophyte?"

I shuddered at the way he addressed me.

"I take it by your silence that's a 'no.' "

Ugh, I could almost hear the bastard's smug smile. "Either that or you've knocked me cold in here."

"She doesn't learn her lesson, does she, boys?" Someone, I assumed it was my Sith M.C., thumped loudly on the lid of the coffin. "Do we have to dump you in the water again?"

Oh, boy, was this jerk going to lose some parts of his anatomy when I finally got out of here.

"As I was saying, the Diggers' Whore is a very special woman, given the sacred trust to Initiate the Knights of our Order into the Mysteries of Connubial Bliss."

"Lovely," I said, with extraordinarily minimal sarcasm. But this is what I thought: *Initiate? Hardly—or at least, not in the last few decades. If a man like Malcolm Cabot was a virgin, then I was a nun.*

As if he heard my unspoken musings, the M.C. went on. "Though most of the Knights are already familiar with such Earthly Pleasures"—

And Purple Prose.

—"there are few who leave Eli without having tasted of her Delights." The coffin stopped moving, as if we'd reached our destination. "Have you heard such tales, Neophyte?"

No, not as such, but it didn't sound off-base. A prostitute on call at the Rose & Grave tomb? A little gross, but in keeping with every other tall tale I'd ever heard about the society. "Sure, why not?"

He leaned so close to the coffin, it was as if he hissed the following words directly into my ear. "And have you never wondered, Miss Not-Too-Shabby-in-Bed, from whence we recruit her?"

Uh-oh.

"Why don't you find out?"

And with that, they flipped a latch and turned the coffin on its end, tipping me out. Plunging forward, I braced myself for a crash that never came. I fell down and down, too shocked by the disappearance of the ground even to scream.

And when I finally landed, things got even worse.

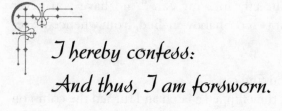

I hereby confess:

And thus, I am forsworn.

5.

Initiation

Blankets buffered my fall, and after the first bounce, I felt strong male arms close around my torso to keep me steady. But I was no one's whore. I lunged out with my fists.

"Help!" I clawed at my face, fighting to get my wet hair out of my eyes, and kicked to untangle my legs from the blankets. "Help! Rape! *Fire!*"

(I'd always been taught that people pay more attention when you yell "Fire" than when you yell "Rape" because fire endangers them as well. Fun world we live in, huh?)

"Help me, please!" My fist grazed someone's jaw.

"Ow! Amy, jeez, chill out." I paused in my flailing for a moment and peered through the ropy strands of my hair to see who was holding me. It was Malcolm, robed, but with his hood pushed back off his face.

"Get your hands off me, you political slime," I shouted, "or I swear to God I'll make sure your father never holds elected office again!"

These are the types of threats one makes at Eli.

He laughed then, and loosened his grip, setting me on my

feet. "You're preaching to the choir, girl." He brushed my hair back behind my ear. "And no one's going to touch you, least of all me. It was just a joke."

I looked around at the boys who stood there, holding the ends of the makeshift blanket parachute, and then up at the staircase landing, where the plywood coffin stood open. A few more robed figures were traipsing down the stairs to join us, pushing their hoods back as they went.

"Well, it wasn't funny," I said, straightening my clothes and glaring at Malcolm. "Especially the bit about the pool. I have a phobia about water."

"*What?*" Malcolm's voice betrayed genuine surprise.

"Oh, right. Like you know who my third-grade homeroom teacher was but not why I never joined the swim team?"

Malcolm's gaze flashed to the leader of the staircase crew, who merely lifted his chin in defiance. The guy was slim of build, with dark hair and very pale skin. I'd never seen him before, but knew instantly that this was my Sith M.C., Shadow Guy #2, he of the This-Is-Your-FBI-File line.

"Well, now you can add it to your fucking files." I wrung out my left pant leg and straightened. "Where's the exit?"

Malcolm's face fell. "You're not *leaving*?!?"

"You bet your GPA I am!" I pointed at Darth Digger. "I wouldn't join a tea party that asshole's at." I headed off, ignoring the squishing sound in my left sneaker and hoping that I was correct in my assessment that I was walking toward something vaguely exit-esque. The hallways were lined with dark red paper and lighted only intermittently by dim candles in skull-shaped sconces. With my luck, I would end up in their dungeon, and in seventy years, it would be *my* cranium lighting their way.

"Amy, wait!"

I turned, but it wasn't Malcolm who'd put his robed hand over mine.

"I'm sorry," the jerk said. His head was bowed as if in contrition, but the position just made him look like he was doing that evil looking-at-me-through-his-eyebrows thing so popular on horror movie posters. "Can we start again?" He stuck out his hand. "I'm Poe."

"Is that Korean?"

He blinked at me. "It's my society name." He pointed back at Malcolm. "Like Lancelot. We can't use any others while inside the tomb." He raised his eyebrow and gave me a wry smile. "And now that I've told you, you've got to join."

"Or what?"

"Or we'll have to kill you." Totally deadpan.

I nodded and opened the door. "Good luck with that. I'm going home."

No such luck. The door did not lead to High Street, but instead to a small, square courtyard ringed all around with towering walls of brown sandstone. *Crap.*

Poe chuckled softly. "Nice try, Neophyte." He leaned against the doorjamb and I could see Malcolm—I mean, *Lancelot*—join him on the other side.

Wait, what the hell was I thinking? I wasn't a Digger. I could call him whatever I wanted. Malcolm, Malcolm, Bo-Balcolm . . . I folded my arms across my chest.

"Come on, Amy," *Malcolm* said. "It's a little late to back out now. You accepted the tap."

"That was before the swimming lesson."

Malcolm tossed a look at Poe, who returned a smug smile. "I told you this would happen."

"Poe," Malcolm said in warning.

The guy sighed, then grumbled, "Okay. We don't have a pool."

My jaw forgot how to work. "But how—"

"Old trick," Poe said through clenched teeth. "Coolers

filled with water on either side of you, sloshing. Super Soakers for the leakage."

Genius. Malicious, but genius. And it was killing him to tell me. I loved it.

Malcolm stepped forward and took my hands in his. "I won't lie and say we're all nice, Amy, but we're good people to have on your side. Trust me. This is the best thing you'll ever do at Eli." His eyes were pleading, practically desperate, but he straightened then, and spoke in a much louder voice. "The life that we invite you to share in our society is based on such intangible factors that we cannot meaningfully convey to you either its nature or its quality. I'd ask you not to judge our worth by a few ill-advised jokes." And then, in a hushed whisper: "Come on, what do you say?"

I was so going to regret this.

"Aye."

————

I told *Lancelot* that I'd prefer they didn't carry me.

He said it couldn't be helped.

I wanted to know in advance where I would be taken.

He said all would become clear in time.

I was absolutely adamant that there would be no drinking of the blood of slaughtered virgins.

He said he'd see what he could do.

And that's how I found myself suspended in the arms of six hooded figures, blindfold loosened at last, poised over what looked for all the world like a skull full of blood. But in the plus column, how was I to know the sexual proclivities of the blood's previous owner?

"Drink it! Drink it! Drink it!" the figures chanted. The cup was lifted and placed in my hands, and the blindfold whisked away completely. The bone was smooth and almost slippery beneath my fingers, worn, perhaps, from almost two centuries of use. They'd plugged up the holes with the same clay that lined the interior, but that small nod to decency hardly swayed me. Drink it? This had been part of a *person* once.

And in all likelihood, it had also been a biology project, my rational side reasoned. Where else would college kids get their specimens? *Okay, Amy, time to get into the spirit of the proceedings. Skulls, schmulls.* I took a deep breath and Tory's Cupped it.

A fruit juice of some sort, perhaps mixed with Gatorade. There was a strange, tart current beneath the flavor, hinting at an additional ingredient—maybe dye to give it that dark red coloring?—but I'd bitten my tongue enough times in my life to know this wasn't blood. I finished it off, gave the skull a little rub on my shirt—no way in hell would I lick the bowl—and earned a few chuckles from my companions who recognized the act.

"Thatagirl," Lancelot said, as he tied the blindfold back on. "And away you go!"

Looking back, it's tough to define a chain of events for Initiation Night. Everything moved so quickly, with such chaotic visuals, and a cacophony of sounds, that I remember it mostly as a series of tableaux—a slide show of moments that all led up to the main event. They kept our blindfolds on as we moved from room to room, perhaps to make each vision all the more shocking by revealing it to us all at once, when we were already in the midst of the scenes. Indeed, with all the frenzy of the players, it took me several flashes of sight to even notice I was now in the company of other neophytes, two or three intersecting in any given room at a time.

This is what I remember:

Flash

A courtyard ringed in fire, in which a man dressed as a devil jumped around, letting out deep-throated shrieks. A group of men in rags stood before him, chained, and let out soft moans.

Flash

A tiny room lit by candlelight, with a figure dressed as
Quetzacoatl, in shimmering gold and colorful feathers. He
leaned over a stone slab, a golden knife poised ready to cut out
the heart of a maybe-naked woman who lay with her long
black hair splayed out behind her. As he brought the knife
down, the candle went out. The woman screamed.

Flash

Antony standing over the body of Cleopatra, holding a live
asp. Or maybe it was a boa constrictor. I don't know my snakes
as well as my Shakespeare. And I think Cleopatra was a man-
nequin in a black wig.

Flash

A room full of Puritans, standing watch over a gallows lit
by a spotlight. It looked as if we were back in the Firefly Room.
There were three women hanging with nooses around their
necks, black bags tied over their faces. I'd have thought they
were fakes, but their feet were twitching. . . .

Flash

There were hands on my shoulders, walking me down the
hall, but whoever placed the blindfold over my face after the
Salem room wasn't too careful. Out of the corner of my eye I
could see a tiny flash. Light, bouncing off metal zippers. They
removed the blindfold to view the next tableau—something
about a bowl full of fruit and the groaning of ghostly souls in
torment—but I was too interested in those zippers, and the
person wearing them. It was George Harrison Prescott in the
hall outside the room, and he was being stripped of his offen-
sive jacket and—yes, shoved into a smallish plywood coffin.
They'd clearly staggered our entrances and were amusing each
of us in turn with the various aspects of the initiation. I wondered what still lay in store.

Flash

They shoved me into a seat and secured my hands behind

my back. Something was placed over my face before the blindfold was yanked down. When I opened my eyes, I saw that I
was looking through tiny eyeholes in a mask. At first I thought
I'd been placed in front of a mirror, because before me I saw
another masked figure tied to a chair. Her mask was elaborate
and golden, with an elegant bird's beak and shimmering jewels
that suggested arched brows and a cruel, predatory mouth. But
she struggled against her bonds while I remained still. At last
her hands came free and she pulled her mask off her face.

Clarissa Cuthbert.

I gasped and she reached across to snatch my mask away. I
caught a glimpse out of the corner of my eye. A crone.

She frowned. "So you *are* here," she said, before they took
her away. My blindfold was replaced before my hands were released or my mouth remembered how to work.

Flash

A vampire rising from his coffin, blood dripping down his
chin.

Flash

A pale young man sat on a toilet seat in his underwear. He
had a gun pointed to his head, and he was repeating the same
phrase over and over again. In Latin.

Flash

George Harrison Prescott turned to me, in a room where
Othello was strangling Desdemona, and said in a tone entirely
unsuited to the bizarre situation, "The matches didn't work, by
the way. I had enough sulfur on me to bring down half a dozen
Diggers." I was hurried away before I had a chance to ask him
what he meant.

Flash

The scenes began to blur together after a while, and over
everything there were voices screaming phrases in other lan-
guages, shouting obscenities, chanting in gibberish, shrieking,
"The President Is Dead!" "The End Has Come!" "The Devil

Has Risen!" and other dire warnings. I felt a strange headiness, and wondered if there had been alcohol in the "blood" or if I was just succumbing to the magic of the evening. The downtimes seemed to float by as if in a dream and I stopped counting steps from room to room. I don't know how many times I made the circuit, or how many costume changes the players underwent. But at last I was shoved in a room, and I heard a door slam behind me as the racket was suddenly cut off.

By this point, I was so used to the tableaux being revealed that it was several heartbeats before I reached up to remove my own blindfold.

Before me stood the Grim Reaper in his black robe. He carried a scythe in his hand, and a grinning death's head hung with flaps of rotted flesh stared out at me from beneath the hood. I glanced around, but we were the only people in the room. The Reaper turned toward a cabinet that contained two skeletons.

"Wer war der Thor, wer Weiser, wer Bettler oder Kaiser?"

He pointed at each of the skeletons in turn, then handed me a crown. It was heavy in my hands, and I wondered for a moment if the jewels and gold around the red velvet base were real.

"Wer war der Thor, wer Weiser, wer Bettler oder Kaiser?" he said again, a little more insistently.

"I never took German," I replied helplessly.

He pointed at the crown, then at the two skeletons.

He wanted me to put the crown on one of their heads? Ah! *Kaiser.* "Kaiser" meant *king* in German. Enlightenment hit, and with it, another little lesson from history class. The Dance of Death from the Middle Ages. Alas, poor Yorick, and all that *Hamlet* jazz. The king was not either of the skeletons, but the force that had defeated them both.

I stepped forward and placed the crown on the head of the Reaper.

"*Gut! Ob Arm, ob Reich, im Tode gleich.*"* He captured my hands in his. "Nice move, Neophyte. You'll learn yet." He pulled me forward until my face was inches from his putrid one, and for a very scary moment, I was afraid the thing was going to kiss me, which was a little too Goth for my taste. I locked my elbows and resisted, and he released me, triumph glinting in his pale eyes.

I stumbled backward as the light went off, and I felt myself being whisked away once again.

This time, when the blindfold was removed, I was standing before a long wooden door, with two tall men flanking me. Before me was a knocker engraved with the Rose & Grave seal. The hooded figure to my right reached up and thumped the knocker three times, then once, then twice again.

"The Neophyte approaches!" someone inside yelled, and a bone-chilling din began beyond the doors. They screamed and shouted, hooted and groaned. Finally, beneath it, I could make out a chant that soon overwhelmed every other element of the noise. "Who is it? Who is it! *Who is it? WHO IS IT?*"

"Amy Maureen Haskel." I smiled. "Neophyte Haskel!"

The doors flew open and I blinked. This was by far the most elaborate of all of the tableaux. It looked like a carnival inside, and it was obvious I was the main attraction. The round room had a domed ceiling painted dark blue and dotted with tiny golden stars. Around me stood players, all masked, in the most outlandish costumes. They were all shouting my name.

The two hooded figures shoved me against a carved teak desk and pushed my head toward a piece of parchment.

A man in a gold, jewel-encrusted robe put down wizened hands on either side of the page. His half mask had hexagonal

---

* The confessor later learned the full text of the scene translated to: "Who was the fool, who the wise man, beggar or king?" and "Good. Whether rich or poor, all are equal in death."

eyeholes and was covered in real roses, and above it his hair was gray. "Read it! Read it! Read it now, or look your last upon the Inner Temple!"

This is the vow I took:

I, Amy Maureen Haskel, Barbarian-So-Called, do hereby most solemnly avow, within the Flame of Life and beneath the Shadow of Death, never to reveal, by commission or by omission, the existence of, the knowledge considered sacred by, or the names of the membership of the Order of Rose & Grave.

When I read it aloud, everyone cheered. They picked me up and whirled me around to face a tiny engraving of a woman in a Doric chiton, holding a skull in one hand and a flower in the other.

"Behold our goddess!" shouted one, and the others set up a chant.

"Persephone! Persephone! Persephone!"

Persephone, Goddess of Spring. Daughter of the Goddess of the Earth, Demeter, and wife of the King of the Underworld, Hades. According to what I remember from my World Mythology survey class, she was doomed to spend half of every year as the Queen of the Underworld—one month for each pomegranate seed she'd eaten in his gloom-filled garden. The other six months of the year, she was able to return home to her mother, who was so happy to see her daughter that she brought life back to the earth. Suddenly, the "rose" and "grave" of Rose & Grave made perfect sense.

I was yanked back to the desk bearing the oath, with another injunction to "Read! Read!"

"I, Amy Maureen Haskel, Barbarian-So-Called, do hereby most solemnly avow, within the Flame of Life and beneath the Shadow of Death, never to reveal, by commission or by omission, the existence of, the knowledge considered sacred by, or the names of the membership of the Order of Rose & Grave!" When I read the oath of secrecy this time, I was louder, more sure of myself.

And then back to the engraving, which was set by itself on an altar in a little wooden cabinet. The plaque shone with the patina of age and care.

"Persephone! Persephone! All hail Persephone!"

I pictured the scores of men who had come before me—raised in their fancy, rich boarding schools, destined to become captains of industry and leaders of nations. Good thing they took a vow of secrecy. Bunch of heathens. What would their constituents and boards of directors have thought had they known these guys had spent their senior year of college professing to worship a minor goddess of ancient Greece? *Persephone?* Please!

I read the oath one more time before they took me to another side of the room. On the wall hung a glorious oil painting of a nude with a come-hither look in her eye. A figure dressed as the pope and wearing a white bird's mask pumped his fist in the air. "Behold, Connubial Bliss!"

"Yeah, looks like it," I said, noting the woman's ample curves. God bless 19th century ideals of feminine beauty. If the men of today had commissioned that portrait, she'd have as much meat on her as one of the skeletons.

This time, when I was returned to the teak desk, there was a different parchment waiting for me.

"Read it! Read it! *Read it!*" the crowd yelled.

I, Amy Maureen Haskel, Barbarian-So-Called, do hereby most solemnly avow, within the Flame of Life and beneath the Shadow of Death, to bear the confidence and the confessions of my brothers, to support them in all their endeavors, and to keep

forever sacred whatsoever I may learn beneath the seal of the Order of Rose & Grave.

Aww, that's sweet.

The company cheered again after I read it, and they rushed me around the room three times. I began to feel dizzy and more than a little breathless, and they deposited me on the ground in front of another skull full of red liquid. This time, when I drank the sweet "blood," I recognized the flavor immediately. Pomegranate juice. How fitting.

Two more trips back to the oath of constancy—and in between, one trip around the room, then two—and they deposited me in front of the golden-robed man with the gray hair.

"Allow me to introduce myself," he said in a booming voice. "I am Uncle Tony Cthony Carnicks Carnage Carthage Parnassus Phinneas Philamagee Phimalarlico McPherson O'Phanel."

"Say it!" They all shouted at me. "Say it! Say it! *Say it!*"

So, not a student? But I bit back the smarm, for this didn't seem the time. "Uncle Tony...um, Carnage..."

"She can't say it! She can't! She can't!" A figure bounced up, dressed in red and painted to look like Lucifer. He swung his long, forked tail at me, whipping my face and arms playfully as he taunted me. Beneath the grease paint and prosthetic hooked nose, I noticed a set of sparkling white teeth.

They shoved me toward a guy dressed in 19th century garb, holding a leather-bound book marked all over with the Rose & Grave seal. He showed me the book—upside-down Greek. I think.

"Read it! Read it! Read it!"

Yeah, right! But this time, they hardly gave me a second before beginning to cry, "She can't read! The neophyte can't read!"

Their teasing seemed to have reached a crescendo, though, and I suspected it was because they were drawing to the end of the allotted time to issue such abuse. The golden-robed Uncle Tony propelled me back to the teak desk, where there stood a third and final oath. The oath of fidelity. "Let's see if she can read this!" he shouted.

> **I, Amy Maureen Haskel, Barbarian-So-Called, most solemnly pledge and avow my love and affection, everlasting loyalty and undying fealty. By the Flame of Life and the Shadow of Death, I swear to cleave wholly unto the principles of this ancient order, to further its friends and plight its enemies, and place above all others the causes of the Order of Rose & Grave.**

Ah, this was the oath that the conspiracy theorists loved to point at. This was the reason they attacked the President for being a member of Rose & Grave. I admit that even I, who was not a leader of men and had no intention of ever being so, faltered at the wording of the vow. Did I know these people enough to cleave wholly unto their principles? What *were* their principles? What if the causes of Rose & Grave were to destroy democracy, outlaw pizza, and overcome the knee-high leather boot industry? What if the enemies I was supposed to plight included the Dalai Lama, or Brad Pitt? I cast a furtive glance at the ridiculously dressed figures surrounding me.

Nah, probably not.

I spoke the oath of fidelity three times, and as the final words fell from my lips, the room seemed to crackle with the power of my promise.

(Although, in these pages, I have broken the first two vows, I have kept the third, and always shall, until the end of my days. Those of my brothers who believe my transgressions unforgivable, look again at my oath, and tell me if I am indeed forsworn.)

They lifted me up and placed me gently at the feet of a man dressed like Don Quixote. He wore a suit of ill-fitting armor and had scraggly gray whiskers beneath a long-handled saucepan hat. He lifted a rusty, ancient-looking sword and tapped me on the left shoulder. "From this moment on, you are no longer Barbarian-So-Called Amy Maureen Haskel. By the order of our Order, I dub thee Bugaboo, Knight of Persephone, Order of Rose & Grave."

Someone struck a tocsin thrice, once, and twice again, and everyone shouted, "Diggers!"

And that was it. I was a Digger.

Named *Bugaboo*.

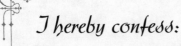 I hereby confess:
I eventually grew to like it.

6.
Party

When I stepped through the doors into the two-story Grand Library (room 311, since the Inner Temple had claimed the sacred designation of 312, according to the intelligence I gleaned from the two thirty-something alumni who showed me the way), everyone looked up and gave me a little toast with pomegranate juice–filled punch cups. There were already close to twenty people in the room—maybe ten college students and a handful of older men in suits.

"So you're number eleven," said a stocky black girl with hair the color of my Friday night date panties and a woven hemp shirt. "Welcome to our loony bin." I knew this girl by reputation—I'd seen her protests and her rallies—Demetria Robinson.

"You're Lydia's friend, right?" A guy with reddish-brown hair stepped up next and glad-handed me. "I think we met once, sophomore year."

I nodded in recognition. Leave it to Joshua Silver, political *wunderkind*, to never forget a face or a network connection. Only twenty-one and already the manager of several successful local election campaigns. To Lydia, he was both her hero and her rival in every Poli-Sci class they'd taken together. Joshua wore khaki pants and a rumpled white oxford liberally spattered with red juice. He gestured to the HELLO MY NAME IS sticker on his shirt. "I'm, uh, Keyser Soze."

"Now, there's a society name!" I wrinkled my nose. "I'm *Bugaboo*."

"Could be worse," Demetria said. "Some soon-to-be-dickless fuckwad thought it would be funny to christen me Thorndike."

Josh/Soze sniggered and Clarissa Cuthbert materialized by my side, holding two silver punch cups. She handed one to me. "It's a historical name. You should be proud of it. President Taft was a Thorndike."

"President Taft was a fat white fuck," Thorndike replied.

Clarissa clinked her glass against mine. Her HELLO MY NAME IS sticker read *Angel*. "Welcome, Bugaboo," she said. "Glad to see you *slumming* with us after all."

I flinched. Of all the secret societies in all the colleges in the world, Clarissa Cuthbert had to be tapped into mine. So that's what she'd wanted to discuss with me.

But Angel didn't seem interested in rehashing our earlier conversation. She turned to the others and said, "I guess there's just George Harrison Prescott left now, huh?"

"Yeah," said a short Asian guy joining the group. "But I hear they had to drag him into the tomb kicking and screaming." He stuck his hand out at me. "Hey there, I'm Frodo."

"At last, someone with a worse name than mine!" Thorndike sniffed.

"Do not go gently into that sweet night, GHP," said a young man with a completely edible English accent. "But rather... make your *daddy* force you." He winked at me. "I'm Bond... Barbarian-So-Called Greg Dorian. I hear you're the writer."

"Another creative type?" Frodo asked. "I'm a filmmaker.

And Little Demon is a...singer, of sorts. This is one artsy class."

I looked down into my punch cup. "I'm not really a writer." Thirty pages of a wretched novel does not count.

Soze shrugged. "Then what are you?"

"The editor of the Lit Mag."

They all exchanged glances.

"Why aren't you in Quill & Ink?" Thorndike asked. "My ex-girlfriend Glenda Foster is in that one."

TWO POINTS

1) Very good question.
2) Glenda Foster is a lesbian?!? You think you know someone....

" 'Girlfriend' is a relative term." A slender, stunning woman with waist-length red hair joined our group and extended a graceful hand toward me. Now, this chick I knew. But of course, you all know everything about Odile Dumas as well. She'd been tabloid fodder since she was 15. Her matriculation to Eli had been largely viewed by all to be an attempt to present herself as less Lindsay Lohan and more Natalie Portman. But to the media's shock, she'd taken to collegiate life with gusto and all but dropped out of public view. Odile hadn't had an album or movie out in three years, and the word around campus was that she was smarter (and less slutty) than anyone had expected (or hoped).

"Little Demon," she purred, "but if I end up pursuing that hip-hop career, I'll change it to Lil' Demon." The name rolled off her tongue with such ease that we all knew at once—hip-hop career or no—what we'd end up calling her.

"How droll." Thorndike rolled her eyes and Lil' Demon turned to her.

"Just because you get a poor girl drunk and seduce her once or twice does not make her your girlfriend. Bad as a man. Behavior like that is a disgrace to lesbians everywhere."

Thorndike narrowed her eyes. "Are you including yourself in that number?"

"I'm pansexual," Lil' Demon said, with a shake of her hair. "Why settle?"

Bond lifted his punch glass. "I'll drink to that."

But Thorndike wasn't finished. "And you, Odile, are a disgrace to *women* everywhere."

Angel clucked her tongue. "Watch the barbarian names in here, kiddies."

"Oh, get a room, you two," Frodo said. Thorndike and Lil' Demon looked at each other, sniffed in disdain, and turned in opposite directions.

This was one hell of a tap class.

Everyone chuckled, and I laughed uneasily to keep them company. Was it me, or did they all seem to know one another very well? I drained my glass and started back to the punch bowl, if only for something to do. I'd had my fill of pomegranate juice for one night.

Angel headed me off at the pass. "I looked it up," she whispered. "Little Demon is also a traditional name, given to the smallest tap every year." She cast a haughty glance back at the colorful Lil' Demon. "Don't you think I'm skinnier than she is?"

I ladled myself a glass of punch and resisted throwing it in her face. "I honestly"—*couldn't care less*—"wouldn't know."

She shook her head as if shrugging it off. "That was some piece of luck today in the library, huh?"

No. I was never *fortunate* to run into Clarissa. "How so?"

"Me being there to find that letter before someone else did. Pretty cool trick of Lancelot's—you know his society name is Lancelot, right?"

I nodded. Had Clarissa—*Angel*—already looked it up in one of the many leather-bound books lining the walls of the room? She had to be getting all her Rose & Grave trivia from somewhere. Man, she and Lydia were separated at birth!

I was about to ask her where she'd unearthed that bit of info when the doors opened and in shuffled George Harrison Prescott, sheepish grin plastered across his gorgeous face, zippered jacket and eyeglasses notably absent.

"Hey, guys. They got me." While everyone lifted their glasses in cheer, George crossed to a table I hadn't noticed before, scrawled something on a sticker, and slapped it against his chest. Then, with a flourish, he turned, presenting his society name sticker.

HELLO MY NAME IS

Puck

Angel's mouth dropped open.

"Yo, Amy!" George waved. "Another Prescotteer, thank God! What's your new handle?"

"Bugaboo." I looked down at my stickerless chest, glad that I'd been able to pull off underwire after all.

Angel looked at me. "Right, you need a sticker." A moment later she handed me one with *Bugaboo* printed in a curly, girly script. Good thing there were no "i"s in my name, or I was damn sure she would have dotted them with hearts.

"Thanks," I said as she leaned close to whisper in my ear, smelling of Chanel, vodka, and pomegranate juice.

"You know what 'Puck' is, right?"

Well, let's see....

Option One: The little black disk hockey players fight over.

Option Two: That annoying bicycle messenger from *Real World: San Francisco*.

Option Three:

"As an English major, I'm required by law to respond 'the head sprite in *Midsummer Night's Dream*,' " I said, sure she was about to give me another lesson in Digger lore. I was not disappointed.

"The name they give to the tap with the most sexual experience."

I rolled my eyes. "Well, there's a no-brainer. George Harrison Prescott probably has more sexual experience than the rest of us combined."

Angel threw back her head and laughed, giving me a great glimpse of what must have been two-carat sparklers in her ears. Guess the no-metal rule didn't apply to platinum earring backs. "I think we're going to get along great, girl."

Uh-oh. Certainly hadn't meant to deliver that impression. I moved closer to George. "Hey, what was the deal with the matches earlier?"

"They're tipped in sulfur," he responded. "Diggers aren't supposed to carry sulfur."

Oh, that's what they'd meant in the letter. Things a non-smoker never thinks about. Probably didn't want to accidentally ignite us in the Firefly Room.

He shrugged. "I was just screwing around with them. But look at you!" He beamed. "A Digger! What do you think?"

I glanced around the library, at the built-in bookshelves stuffed floor to two-story ceiling with leather-bound volumes, at the lead-veined windows overlooking a darkened courtyard. In one corner of the room, Frodo was giving an animated reenactment of his initiation to a knot of new taps, while in another, a group of half a dozen older men stood in stony silence, surveying the room as if grading us. A lone girl sat off to the side, fingering something around her neck.

"I'll tell you when I know." I cocked my head in the direction of the girl. "Let's go say hi to her."

She stood as we neared. "Hey," I said. "You new here, too? I'm Bugaboo."

"Jen—*Lucky*—Santos. Whatever." She took my hand, dropping the crucifix she'd been clutching against her throat.

"I'm Puck," George said, but the girl shot him a withering glance rather than take his proffered hand.

"I know who you are."

So, his reputation had preceded him. George opened his mouth, but before he could engineer a response, the huge double doors of the library were flung wide and in strode the rest of the Diggers in a five-deep pyramid formation. The most outlandish of their costumes had been traded out for a uniform of simple, black hooded cloaks, but traces of the makeup some had worn in the Inner Temple or the tableaux remained around their hairlines and jaws. I recognized the Devil, Othello, and one of the Puritans. They were followed into the room by another dozen men, all bearing similar remnants from their costumes.

The one I knew as Poe, standing at the apex, lowered his hood and spread his arms wide. "Welcome, Rose & Grave Tap Class *Anno Deae* 177."

My Latin was a bit rusty—okay, it was completely deplorable—but did he just say *The Year of the Goddess*? Everyone began clapping.

"Now that you have all been Initiated into our Brotherhood"—apparently, he hadn't gotten all his capital letters out during my torture session—"we will spend the rest of the evening teaching you the Secrets of the Tomb and the Ways of our Order."

"And partying," added Lancelot.

Poe shot him a glare. "And partying," he added with reluctance.

"Hear, hear," Puck said, lifting his glass.

"Will our newest Initiates please step forward and join hands?"

Twelve people threaded their way through the burgeoning crowd to stand before Poe. The Rose & Grave seniors fanned out until there was one standing behind each of us. Lancelot put his hand on my shoulder.

"Three of the taps are absent this evening, owing to the fact that they aren't currently on this continent."

I bit my lip. Clearly, nothing short of an ocean would be an acceptable excuse for Poe.

"However, they've been Tapped and, through the miracle of modern technology, we might actually be able to witness one going through his own Initiation Rites—Right, Barebones?"

One of the Diggers in the back gave him a thumbs-up. "We're a go."

Poe nodded. "And now, to introduce the newest Knights of the Order of Rose & Grave ..."

"Angel." Clarissa stepped up.

"Bond." Dorian took his place by her side.

"Little Demon." Odile sauntered over and struck a pose.

"Big Demon." A center from the Eli basketball team who'd been lurking in the corner with some of the suited alumni came forward.

"Bugaboo." My turn. I stepped into the forming circle. Lancelot met my eyes and grinned.

"Graverobber." Another man from the group of silent suits, looking like gold-plated Eurotrash.

"Frodo." Mr. Young Hollywood practically bounced into place.

"Kismet." A tall black man stepped up.

"Puck." George strolled into the circle, hands in pockets.

"Thorndike." Demetria rolled her eyes at Puck as she joined him.

"Lucky." Jennifer Santos shuffled in, keeping a safe distance between herself and her nearest neighbor.

"Keyser Soze." Josh completed the circle, taking Lucky's and Angel's hands in his own.

Poe lowered his head, as if in reverence. "Welcome, my brothers...and my first sisters. You have been granted a Sacred Trust. The Knights that stand before me will be legendary in the Annals of the Order, for you are the first to count women amongst your ranks. The five females before us are the only women ever to be Initiated into the Mysteries of Rose & Grave."

So that explained it. I *knew* that Rose & Grave didn't tap women. So, we were the first, huh? It's about time they caught up to the modern world. I glanced around the circle at the other four. And these are the women they chose. I wondered if there was any rhyme or reason to the choices.

The older man I knew as "Uncle Tony," now suited, stepped forward. "I would like to commend our departing seniors for having the strength and courage to drag this society into the 21st century. I know your path has not been an easy one, but I applaud your wills. You are truly a class of Brothers to be proud of." Then he turned away from the hooded knights and toward the circle of taps. "As the presiding Patriarch of the Initiation Ceremony, I am honored to welcome you into our Order. I would like to take this opportunity to remind the ladies in the group that these boys have taken a great risk and a big leap of faith letting you in here. We expect you to be model women...so don't blow it."

Some welcome, schmuck! From across the circle, I saw Thorndike roll her eyes. "Go blow *yourself*," she mouthed. Ha. Great minds think alike.

As if sensing that things were going downhill, Lancelot piped up. "I think we've got the hook up to Sarmast." He gestured to another Digger, who released a projector screen from the wall, while a third fiddled with his laptop and an overhead projector.

"Behold!" said Poe with a flourish. "The Initiation of Harun Sarmast."

"Right. Whatever." Lancelot clicked the projector on.

The picture was grainy, pixellated, but I could make out half a dozen men standing in a drab, corporate, pre-fab conference room lit by yellowish fluorescents. Some were in military uniforms, the rest in suits. They circled around a tall, gangly Middle Eastern young man, clapping and hooting undecipherable, static-filled phrases.

"Where is this?" Soze asked.

"U.S. embassy in Saudi Arabia."

Soze whistled through his teeth. "Wow! Who'd you have to kill to get *that* go-ahead?"

Poe was clearly an expert at the deadpan look.

The boy in the picture was blindfolded, and considering the current political climate, the scene would have made me very uncomfortable if I hadn't noted the enormous, shit-eating grin on his face. I wondered if that was the standard Rose & Grave M.O.—politically incorrect hazing scenes. After all, they'd done the whole "Diggers' Whore" act on me.

"Sarmast is doing language work for the government this semester. We pulled some major strings at the embassy to tap him before Dragon's Head could."

One of the hooded Diggers sniggered. "Their pockets just...aren't as deep."

"What about the other two?" I asked.

"They've been...secured."

"I thought you said they were tapped."

Poe shot me a look like a cobra ready to strike. "I've got it covered, Bugaboo."

"Don't mind him," Lancelot said. "He gets sore every time he's reminded that he's a mere mortal. Rest assured, if Poe couldn't track them down, no one else will, either. We'll get to them first. And you'll get to be in on the initiations."

"What if they reject the tap?" I asked, but Lancelot merely blinked at me as if such a predicament was inconceivable.

Poe pulled out a cell phone and began dialing. A moment later, one of the marines on-screen answered.

"Is this real-time streaming?" Lucky asked, joining in on the party at last.

The Digger manning the keyboard smiled and beckoned to her. "Yep. Come take a look."

Lucky took a place behind the computer, her look of fear replaced with one of rapture. Now I remembered—Jenny Santos, who at the tender age of seventeen developed some amazing software, sold it off, then donated every last cent of her eight-figure proceeds to her church. No wonder Rose & Grave wanted her on their team.

"Okay," Lancelot said to the man in Saudi Arabia. "Begin." He passed the phone to Uncle Tony and joined me.

"I knew we'd win her over eventually," he whispered in my ear, nodding his head at Lucky. "Just had to find the right apple with which to tempt her."

"Pomegranate."

"Huh?"

"Didn't you take the Bible as Literature class?" I asked, pleased I could get back at him for his literary critic crack. "No such thing as apples in the Cradle of Civilization. Closest modern translators can come is that Eve ate a pomegranate. Just like your Persephone."

Lancelot slipped his arm around my shoulders. "*Our* Persephone, Bugaboo."

I frowned. "And then they both got kicked out of Paradise."

He sighed. "Don't you get it yet, girl? This *is* Paradise."

"Shhh!" said Poe. "They're starting."

I turned back to the scene being beamed in from the Cradle of Civilization as Harun Sarmast was presented with his own pomegranate. The sound blipped in and out, but I caught enough to recognize that it was utterly incomprehensible.

"Are they speaking—German?" Angel asked, incredulous. Not surprising to me, though, considering my run-in with the Reaper. Hadn't Angel been subjected to that tableau as well?

Poe nodded. "Our Saudi contingent is a little old-school."

"And what are you?" I muttered under my breath. "A freakin' progressive?"

Lancelot leaned in. "By Digger standards? Hell, yeah. It was all in German prior to the Second Rose & Grave Council."

I laughed, earning yet another glare from Poe. What a killjoy.

Harun Sarmast proceeded along the path to initiation, and even without the wild costumes and the midnight-sky domed ceiling of the Inner Temple, it looked impressive. The Saudi-based alumni executed their roles with the type of military precision to be expected, considering their professions. Now that I was no longer the object of attention in the room, I could fully appreciate the earnest enthusiasm and joy the knights felt at showing the neophyte the overseas versions of the initiation players and paraphernalia. Even without the trappings of the tomb, the knights all raved about Persephone! Persephone! Persephone! (or at least a photocopy from a mythology book) Connubial Bliss! Connubial Bliss! Connubial Bliss! (crude reproduction) and Uncle Tony (whose Saudi incarnation was not wearing the elaborate rose mask) Cthony Carpathian...oh, bother. I forget the rest.

Every Digger in the room stood transfixed by the scene before us. They mouthed the words of the oaths as Harun took each one, they cheered along with the Saudi knights as he passed every stage of the initiation, they laughed when he spilled his third skull-full of pomegranate juice down the front of his shirt.

And then—here's the really strange part—something blossomed inside my chest. I know, I know, I'd spent the evening being carried around in a coffin, tricked into thinking I was drowning, forced to drink fruit juice out of human remains, vowing to worship an ancient Greek goddess and to never tell a living soul about the whole shebang, and *this* was the strange part? But yes, it was. The feeling was akin to an adrenaline rush, but not unlike that first swoop of pleasure when you jump in a hot tub. I watched the faces of the knights, laughed every time Lancelot gave me an encouraging nudge, and even managed to temper somewhat my hostility toward Angel. Now that I was on the inside, Rose & Grave seemed to hold little in common with its formidable and mysterious reputation. Okay, so there *were* dead bodies (skeletons, at least) in this tomb. So what? They had them in the biology lab as well. And divested of their hoods and freaky-ass makeup, the other knights looked less like a satanic cult and more like a bunch of college kids playing dress-up. Even the tomb itself seemed welcoming from within. The skull sconces were a little unnerving, but the light they cast upon the wood-paneled walls and towering bookshelves was rosy and inviting. I spotted a darling cushioned window seat in one corner, perfect for curling up with a novel. I might be able to get used to this. I might like it a lot. They picked me, out of all the students in the school, to join their ranks. To be one of the first women. This was way cooler than Quill & Ink!

As I watched another knight be brought within the Society of Rose & Grave, I could feel the circle being drawn, and I was inside of it. Camaraderie took over, and—dare I say it?—brotherhood. *They* became *we*.

Lucky ran her fingers across the keyboard and suddenly the picture got ten times better. I didn't even want to know what she'd just hacked to pull it off.

I watched Harun stumble over the oath of fidelity once, say it again with a strange, subtle flicker of his gaze toward something off-camera, and then, with a deep breath, capitulate and say it a third time with such sincerity in his eyes that it shone through even the pixellated, grainy image. Was that what we all looked like at that moment, when we promised to love, honor, and protect the society?

The Saudi Digger playing Uncle Tony lifted a scimitar. "From this moment on, you are no longer Barbarian-So-Called Harun Sarmast. By the order of our Order, I dub thee Tristram Shandy, Knight of Persephone, Order of Rose & Grave."

Someone off screen struck a drum thrice, once, and twice again.

And from deep inside it welled up, and all together, we shouted, "DIGGERS!"

———

What is there to say about the rest of the evening? What salacious, luxurious details can I confess? Should I reveal how we were herded into a fleet of white stretch SUVs and driven to a Connecticut country mansion (belonging to one of the alums, or "patriarchs")? How we drank champagne at midnight and feasted on broiled lobster at 2 A.M.? Even I was shocked that they had a chef up at three in the morning to caramelize the tops of the crème brûlée we had for dessert.

In between all of this, we had a crash course on the inner

workings of the society, and enough history lessons to qualify for half a credit. The lore of Rose & Grave stretched back almost two centuries. It's not particularly exciting (and it didn't help that we were all exhausted and tipsy). Seems this kid Russell Tobias got into a tizzy over not being invited to join Phi Beta Kappa, huffed off to Germany, met some Masonic or Templarian, or whatever kind of brotherhood folks, and got it into his head that, like the founder of every other Eli institution, including the university itself (which was started by a bunch of folks displeased with how they were running things at 17th century Harvard), if they wouldn't let him play in their club, he'd just start his own. So he did, and because he came from this ridiculously rich family with their fingers in every Victorian moneymaking scheme there was—agriculture, import-exports, early industry (here's where Soze leaned over and whispered, "Drugs")—he was able to devote a big chunk of change to his new little boys' club, and Rose & Grave was born, as was the Tobias Trust Association. The Tobias Trust Association (or TTA, as Poe proceeded to refer to it) is the closest thing to a ruling body that Rose & Grave has. It's presided over by a board voted in by the living members, and all monetary and other requests made by the seniors who comprise the active campus body of Rose & Grave have to be approved by this board of trustees.

"Like what?" Angel asked around a mouthful of champagne.

Poe exchanged careful looks with Lancelot. "Funding. Changes to the, um, bylaws."

Lancelot shrugged. "We had to do some art restoration work last year, and we had to get permission to pay for that."

One of the other knights cracked up. "Yeah. 'Art restoration.' You put a football through an oil painting, Lance."

He blushed and ducked his head.

All of the early 19th century brothers were similarly well

heeled, and the Tobias Trust grew in wealth. They invested in a chunk of prime campus real estate, built themselves a massive stone tomb, and filled it with a wealth of antiques, artwork, curiosities, and college knickknacks crooked from every other organization at Eli.

Aside from the property on High Street, the Tobias Trust (a tax-free non-profit, apparently) owned a lovely little set of suites at the Eli Club in midtown Manhattan and a private island down south, where the members went on retreats.

"How much is the trust worth?" Soze asked. I was quickly learning that Josh could always be counted on to get to the meat of any equation.

Poe quoted a number teetering on eight figures.

Personally? I was impressed, but a quick glance around the room showed a mixed bag of reactions. Angel looked like her last sip of champagne had gone to vinegar, and Soze appeared to be biting the inside of his cheek.

"Is that not...enough?" Lucky asked, speaking up for the first time. Small wonder. Her similarly large income had probably paid for a fleet of churches. But it most likely didn't equal Angel's trust fund.

Poe backpedaled. "Our actual operating budget's pretty large, so the cash value of the trust itself is not indicative—"

"We've got plenty of money," a patriarch interrupted, as if the discussion was closed.

I raised my eyebrows at him. "Are we still on a need-to-know basis?" I asked. "Even now that we've been initiated? Secrets within secrets?"

"Wrapped in riddles buried in enigmas, babe," Lancelot added, lifting his champagne glass in an impromptu toast.

"Look, Ms. Haskel—" the patriarch said, then bit his lip suddenly, his reproach forgotten. He dug into his pocket, pulled out his wallet, and handed two dollars to Poe.

"Barbarian names," Poe explained as he stuffed the money into the pocket of his robe. "Penalties go into our personal till."

"Two down, nine million to go," Soze said.

The point of this whole barbarian business was to separate our society lives from everything else. Inside the tomb and during official society events outside the tomb (like our lessons in the mansion), we used society names for each other, and society terms for various objects and events. We swore by Persephone rather than our professed religious figures. Time even ran differently; the Digger clocks were set five minutes ahead of the outside world and Diggers counted years from the time of the society's inception. Anything that happened in the normal world, even if it happened to society members, was referred to as "barbarian matters."

The party broke up soon afterward (and without any further elucidation on our financial standing, much to the new taps' chagrin), and we followed the seniors into the atrium, where there was an indoor swimming pool—a real one this time. I trailed along at a safe distance and watched them strip to their skivvies and splash around in the heated water. Mist rose from the surface and swirled toward the glass ceiling, and their shrieks and shouts echoed off the stone walls. My brothers, screaming their heads off in see-through BVDs and—oh, Lord, *Clarissa!*—lacy white thongs.

I collapsed on a cushioned lounge chair and poured myself another glass of champagne from the near-empty bottle of Veuve Cliquot I'd been toting around. My mind could not absorb the events of this evening. The crazy initiation, the new class of taps, the tour of the tomb, the history, the songs, the protocol—it was like cramming for a history exam and a lab practical all at once. There was no way I'd remember all the formulas, and they'd already outlawed crib sheets. There had been dozens of secret passwords and combinations and hiding places and handshakes—yes, we learned a secret handshake, too, can you believe it?

This is how it goes:

OFFICIAL ROSE & GRAVE SECRET HANDSHAKE

Step One: Giver extends hand as if giving a regular handshake, but before clutching, tucks index finger underneath and presses it against the other guy's palm. That's how you tell them you are in.

Step Two: Receiver taps thrice, once, and twice on the giver's ring, middle, and index finger knuckles, respectively. That's how you make sure you've separated a Rose & Grave member from some other organization that also uses the palm-tickle trick.

Apparently, it's derived from the Templars, or the Masons, or someone, and so a lot of other secret societies do similar things.

"Everyone copies us," Lancelot had said with his signature grin.

"Why don't you just do the part that's specifically Rose & Grave?" I had asked, and immediately regretted it, as I saw the other taps' eyes raise heavenward. Every time I opened my mouth, it seemed, I got myself in trouble.

Only Lancelot seemed immune to the annoyance. "Because, Bugaboo, some of these guys are eighty, and you can't teach an old dog new tricks."

"We've been using the shake for centuries," another Digger explained. "And we aren't about to change just because some idiots caught on and decided to copy."

I leaned back in my chair and practiced the secret hand-shake on myself, doing my best to make it look as subtle and unobtrusive as possible, so that nosy onlookers wouldn't notice all the fancy fingerwork. It was trickier than it looked, espe-cially given the fact that one of my hands was upside down.

Maybe there was someone else around here to practice with. I looked up, and sure enough, Jenny Santos was sitting by herself again, watching the swimmers with a mixture of amuse-ment and confusion on her face. She was the only one who hadn't been drinking tonight. In fact, of all the taps, she'd been acting the most aloof. Maybe it was time to break the ice.

"Don't you like swimming, either?" I asked, sitting down on the end of her chaise lounge.

She snapped out of her reverie. "I love it. But I'm not tak-ing my clothes off."

I checked out the various swimmers. And their underpants. Good point. "Want to try the secret handshake?"

I stuck out my hand and she proceeded to do the hand-shake with such ease and casual skill that my mouth dropped open. "Wow, how did you do that? Did you already know it?"

Jenny shrugged. "No."

Maybe it was a computer dork thing. Like she was so skill-ful at manipulating the keyboard, flitting her way around the finger work of a secret handshake was no problem. I felt around for another conversation topic, because it didn't seem like Jennifer here was going to introduce any. "So I hear you're a big-time computer genius. What did you invent?"

"It's complicated."

"I'm a smart girl. Try me." At least try with more than two words, honey.

She sighed, loudly, as if she was tired of explaining it. "I wrote the kernel for a desktop search program that avoids the repeating context search polling thread queries that invalidate the translation lookaside buffers and avoids the bogdown of

CPU resources. It got picked up by a software company, and they integrated it into their new operating system."

Okay, maybe I'm not that smart. But I'm sure I could understand the monetary part. "And they paid you a pile of money for it?"

"Not exactly. They didn't know how much they would like it until they started using it, so they made the mistake of paying me by commission instead of buying the program outright."

"That's awesome! So now you get a commission for every copy of their new operating system?"

"Yep."

"Which software company was it?"

"One of the big ones."

By this point, I was getting a little annoyed by her coy attitude. "We're Diggers now. We shouldn't have secrets."

Jenny looked at me, eyebrows raised. "Is that what you think? The Brotherhood of Death has many secrets, Amy. We've only just scratched the surface." She reached up to caress the cross around her neck. "Though, to tell you the truth, I think I was expecting something more"—she gestured weakly at the swimmers—"*devious.*"

I thought about what Malcolm had said about finding the right apple with which to tempt Jenny. Maybe she wasn't as tempted as they thought. I opened my mouth to ask her more about this "Brotherhood of Death" (because *I'd* certainly never heard the Diggers called that), when a bunch of soaking-wet Diggers descended upon us, trying to drag us to our feet.

"Come on!" they screamed, laughing, lifting Jenny in the air.

"Wait! Wait!" she yelled, giggling. "I have to get my BlackBerry off!" A few moments later, sans BlackBerry, they tossed her in the pool. She surfaced, splashing water on her captors and smiling so broadly, it was as if I'd just been talking to a different girl.

"You're next!" Thorndike yelled, grabbing my arm.

"No, wait!" I said, as the girl tugged me to my feet. "I don't swim."

She let go, and I fell back on the chaise. "At all?"

"Oh, please!" Josh said, grabbing my other arm. "She just doesn't want to get her clothes wet. Get her!"

Crap! Not again!

"Guys," said Malcolm. "Forget it. She's already had a dunk tonight." He put his hand on my shoulder and everyone let go. This is the effect that Malcolm Cabot has on people. They just *listen* to him.

"My hero," I said.

He shrugged. "Do me instead," he offered to the mob as he peeled off his shirt. A moment later, they picked him up and marched him to the water's edge. He didn't fight it, probably thinking that, if anything, it was good practice for when our class had to tap our own group next year.

I wondered how they went about choosing the class. High achievers, obviously—people like Josh, Jennifer, Demetria, and Harun didn't come around every day. Nothing I've ever done could hold a candle to those guys. From what I'd heard in the library, it was clear to me that George Harrison Prescott was a legacy (his daddy dragging him in, etc.), and I'd bet just about anything that Clarissa was, too. Mr. Cuthbert had just looked like the kind of guy who'd be in Rose & Grave. I didn't know the rest of them that well, but I bet their C.V.s were every bit as impressive from both a merit-based and a genetic perspective. And they all knew it. Except me.

Why aren't you in Quill & Ink?

Why indeed?

I started practicing the handshake on myself again. A few droplets of water dripped on my elbow. I looked up. Malcolm stood over me. His artfully tossed hair was slicked back from his face, and water dripped down his Abercrombie & Fitch abs and ran in rivulets from the legs of his clingy, soaked boxer shorts. He must have taken off his pants when I wasn't looking. Shame. Malcolm had clearly gotten into the poolside fun, though from what I could tell, Jenny was splashing around still hampered by her cargo pants and a white T-shirt that, sorry, girlfriend, ain't hiding nothing.

"You're kind of in my light," I said, squinting up at him.

"You really don't swim, do you?"

Malcolm Cabot was incredibly hot. And he'd been paying me a lot of attention all night. At first, I'd just been writing it off to his desire to make the new initiate feel welcome—especially after the way that Poe guy had treated me. But even after it was clear that I'd gotten over it and was more than ready to party, he stuck close. Uh-oh. Did Brandon have competition? If so, he'd better watch out—Malcolm was way out of his league.

(Oh my God, did I just think that? I'm such a bitch! Like it matters! How could I have entertained such a petty, worthless, small-minded thought? Was I already turning into a snob; I was in a secret society, therefore I was better than someone who wasn't? Was Lydia right? And to think it about Brandon, too—Brandon, who was so sweet to me, so good. *I liked him.* A lot. I wasn't in *love* with him, but...)

Actually, truth be told, Malcolm was way out of my league, too. So the idea that he was interested just didn't compute, even in my champagne-addled mind.

But, considering the above addling, I didn't really care if it made sense. He was here, wet and nearly naked.

"No, I really don't swim."

"Why?"

I winked at him. "It's a secret. I can still have secrets from you, can't I, Lance?"

He sat down beside me. "It's frowned upon, but technically,

yes. Come on, Bugaboo, tell me." He grabbed my thigh and jiggled it as if to shake the truth from me.

I blinked in what I hoped was a seductive manner, but the movement of my eyelids seemed to take much longer than strictly necessary. Note to self: When it looks like you might get the chance to hook up with a hot senior, go light on the bubbly. Then again, this probably wasn't all champagne knocking me for a loop. After all, it was near 5 A.M., and I'd never been good with all-nighters.

And I was sitting here, outclassed by an Adonis in a pair of wet boxer shorts.

Of course, "outclassed" had basically been the theme of the evening, hadn't it? I was wracking my Eli-educated brain trying to figure out where I fit in this world. Even the Christian computer nerd seemed a more appropriate ingredient.

"Please?" He batted his blond eyelashes at me. "I'll tell you a secret, too."

"Is it a big one?"

He smiled and leaned in. *"The biggest."*

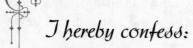

I hereby confess:
I woke up in a strange man's bed.

7.

Morning After

WAYS TO KNOW WITHOUT ROLLING OVER TO LOOK AT HIM

1) Instead of a thick, fluffy down duvet, boys have thin, cotton-fill bedspreads in black, navy, or forest green.
2) The stereo is huge.
3) There's a poster of one of the following on the wall: Angelina Jolie, the Beastie Boys, or *Star Wars*.
4) The pillow smells like hair gel.
5) There's a deep pit of dread in your stomach.

If your present surroundings fit at least three of these criteria, look forward to your upcoming Walk of Shame.

Mine fit four, but that fifth one was well on its way.

I rolled over to face my fate, dreading who I would find hogging the hair gel–scented pillow to my right. Had I really consumed so much champers last night that I couldn't remember? But the bed was empty. I sat up and took an in-depth survey of the room. No identifying features—family photos, a big sign saying: What's-His-Name's Room—and worse, no sign of my clothes.

Uh-oh.

I looked down at my body. Underwear, bra, long white boy's undershirt with a little gold pin stuck through the collar— Rose & Grave. As if that narrowed it down.

Think, Amy, think. Okay. Initiation, limo, mansion, lobster, swimming pool…do I remember the ride back to Eli? This was ridiculous! I had drunk half a bottle of champagne, tops, plus whatever may or may not have been in that Digger punch, and considering how many hours I was out there, there was no way I'd been drunk enough to hook up with someone and not remember…right?

The door opened like a reality-show reveal, and for one second, all I could see was a sneakered foot. Then in walked Malcolm Cabot in a pair of designer jeans and an Eli T-shirt, balancing a drink holder and a paper Starbucks bag in one hand and a stack of folded clothes in the other.

And then I remembered an image from last night: Malcolm Cabot, soaking wet, in a pair of boxer shorts and a smile.

Double uh-oh.

"Morning, sleepyhead!" He flopped the clothes on the bottom of the bed. "I tossed these in the wash for you. One thing you'll learn really quickly: Pomegranate juice stains."

I tucked the comforter up around my hips. "Thanks."

He sat down at my side and handed me one of the paper cups. "I hope you like mocha."

The sharp aroma of dark chocolate wafted up toward me and I folded my hands around the cup, grateful that he'd thought to bring me breakfast in bed. Brandon, for all his kindness, had never ducked out for mocha. Not even Alan Albertson, the great "love of my life" (and number three on the

Hit List, if you're still keeping track) had ever done that. I sipped the drink, and wondered what the protocol was. Do I kiss him? Act casual? Tell him that I have absolutely no memory of us hooking up?

Speaking of, how was I going to do the standard post-hook-up dissection with Lydia without breaking my oaths? There was no way I'd be able to explain this turn of events without letting her know that Malcolm Cabot was in Rose & Grave.

Malcolm was busy spreading vegetable cream cheese on a cinnamon raisin bagel that already bore a slab of sausage. Gross. "Sorry I brought you here last night," he said. "You zonked out back at the mansion, and my room was much closer to the limo drop-off than yours."

I choked on my mocha. "What?"

He looked up. "I know. I'm weak. These muscles are all for show." He flexed his biceps and grinned, then took a big bite of his disgusting breakfast.

"I—fell asleep?"

"Yeah. And it was only six-thirty, too. Don't you ever pull all-nighters?"

I shook my head. "No. It's been the bane of my college existence that I can't do it. But it helps in that I don't have the luxury to procrastinate. I have to get my work done in advance."

"Well, you'll have to learn to stay up now," Malcolm said. "Our meetings sometimes last all night."

This chitchat was all very well and good, but let's get to the point here. "Malcolm?" I asked. "Am I correct in assuming that"—I gestured to the bed—"nothing happened last night?"

He blinked at me. "Do you often wake up in strange boys' beds with no memory of what you're doing there?"

"No." I pursed my lips. "Which is why I feel a bit out of my depth here."

He leaned in, took me by the shoulders, and looked in my eyes, speaking very slowly and clearly, as one might to a lunatic or some other manner of unstable, amnesiac freak. "You were tired. You fell asleep. I carried you in."

"But my clothes..."

"I told you, pomegranate juice stains. And when I mentioned that last night, you were more than happy to let me throw your clothes in the wash."

"I don't remember that part."

"Little wonder, your eyes weren't open."

I collapsed back against the pillows, awash with relief and...okay, a small tinge of disappointment, too. Like I said, Malcolm is über-hot.

Malcolm scooted up by my side and propped his head on his arm. "Did you think we'd hooked up?"

"No," I lied.

He laughed. "No offense, babe, but you're not my type."

"Um, offense taken!" I stuck out my chin.

He shook his head again, eyes wide. "Dude, what *do* you remember about last night? You *do* recall joining Rose & Grave, right? That whole *most famous secret society at Eli* thing?"

"That whole oxymoronical thing? Yes." I started counting off on my hands. "You chased me around the tomb and shut me in a coffin and threatened to drown and/or rape me."

"That was a joke," he clarified.

"I took three oaths. We all got stupid nicknames. I ate lobster. I learned a secret handshake—look!" I did it to him, and he looked decently pleased with my progress. "Everyone went swimming. And then..."

Oh.

He started nodding at my slack-jawed face. "I think it's coming back to you."

"I told you about the pier."

"And?"

"And you told me that..." I took a good long look at Malcolm Cabot, at his stylish jeans, his fashionable hair, his shit-eating, aren't-you-an-idiot-Amy grin. Then I looked at the poster of the scantily-clad Angelina, who was hanging off an equally scantily-clad Brad Pitt. Then back at Malcolm. "You told me that you're gay."

He touched the tip of his nose. "Bingo."

"Offense no longer taken."

"I thought not." He returned to his cinnamon-veggie bagel horror.

"Remind me, though, how come no one knows this? I mean, it's not like we're prejudiced at Eli." If anything, the opposite was true. Eli had one of the highest percentages of gay men in the whole Ivy League system. *One in four, maybe more* was the slogan I'd been hearing since I first stepped on campus.

Malcolm sighed. "My dad, the big conservative. If he or his constituents knew my orientation, the shit would hit the fan."

I shook my head. "That doesn't make sense. If Dick Cheney can have a lesbian daughter and still be a good conservative, why can't Governor Cabot?"

"Dick Cheney never campaigned on the issue that homosexuals are the spawn of Satan and should all die writhing in the pits of hell," Malcolm said, a wealth of bitterness suddenly entering his tone. "He never went on record saying that AIDS was a curse from God sent to punish fags for their sins."

I looked down into my mocha cup. "Oh."

He shrugged. "I'm used to it," he said. "It was worse when I was younger, and insecure, and trying desperately to *fix* myself."

I looked at Malcolm, self-assured, charming, gift-of-gab Malcolm Cabot, and tried to picture how this guy could ever be insecure. Maybe he was very good at hiding it after so much practice bracing for his father's disapproval.

"Does your dad have any suspicion at all?"

Malcolm shook his head. "Tough to tell. I was the king of overcompensation in high school. I had quite the reputation as a player. Dad was so proud."

"You still do have a pretty decent rep, you know."

He shrugged. "Smoke and mirrors, mostly. And I've been really careful, really discreet. No one knows except the Diggers in my class. And now you." He smiled again. "But you're a Digger now, too!"

"That's right." But something still confused me. "You mean, your best friends don't know?"

He narrowed his eyes. "The Diggers know, and those are basically my closest friends. I don't even know if I would have told them if it weren't for the C.B.s."

"What are C.B.s?"

"Connubial Bliss reports," he replied. "One of the most important days in a Knight's Rose & Grave experience. You stand up in front of all your brothers and basically give them a rundown of your sexual experiences to date."

"A Hit List."

"Huh?"

I bit my lip. "Nothing. This is something that everybody does?"

"Yup. Rose & Grave tradition. You'll love it." He fixed me with a look. "Why? Do you have any deep, dark sexual secrets I should know about?"

I thought about Ben Somebody, but was pretty sure a large percentage of college girls had the same sort of embarrassing incident on their records. "No."

"Good," he said, copping a stern, fatherly sort of look. "Because I wouldn't want to have to issue a bad report to your boyfriend."

"A, you can't say a word—you took an oath, remember? And B, I don't have a boyfriend."

"What about Brandon Weare?"

Right. The badminton thing from Friday. Malcolm hadn't missed a beat of that interchange, had he? "Oh, well, he's . . ."

Malcolm laughed. "Say no more, Amy. I get it." He popped the last bite of bagel in his mouth. "I figured you weren't too crazy about him if you'd jump in the sack with me."

"I wouldn't!" Most likely.

"Now *I'm* offended." He frowned, adorably, and I threw my corner of the comforter over his face and got out of bed. I slipped into my cargo pants, pulled the T-shirt off, and yanked my shirt down over my head as quickly as possible. Not that I really cared if he saw me in my bra—after all, if he was gay, it didn't matter, right?

I came back to the bed. "Actually, I did want to ask you something about that."

He spread his arms wide. "Ask me anything you want. We have no more secrets."

I wondered how true that was. Jennifer didn't seem to believe it. "Why were you sticking so close to me last night if you weren't flirting with me?"

"I'm your big brother," Malcolm said, as if it were obvious. "Every new tap has one."

"Is there any rhyme or reason to the assignations? Like, who is Demetria Robinson's big brother?"

"Kevin Binder," he replied. "Can't you tell? Black, gay, extremely radical?"

"You mean they were paired up because they're so alike?"

"I mean she was *tapped* because they are so alike." Malcolm's brow wrinkled. "You do know that's how it works, right? We tap people to replace ourselves."

"And you picked me?"

"*Ja. Oui. Si. Hai.*" He shrugged. "Didn't you notice how the tap class is full of tokens? It's gotten pretty ridiculous the past few years, in my opinion. Everyone is so worried about choosing a representative that they don't really think about the intangibles. It's just—ethnicity, religion, political leaning, academic interest. We tap by genres, not souls. Everyone is turning into a walking stereotype."

Actually, I had noticed that, but figured it was just the usual extension of the Eli habit of wearing your heart on your sleeve. During those four years in college, whatever you were, you pushed it to the max. In order to carve out a niche for yourself, you needed to embody the image you were so desperately trying to create. I might not remember all the new taps' names (or code names) yet, but I recognized their "type." "So what stereotype are we?"

"Publishing, of course. And white."

"But not gay."

"Something you want to tell me?" He winked. "We don't have to be exact matches. Besides, we had to stretch a bit this year because our club decided we were tapping women."

In Diggers-speak, a "club" was the group of seniors that had been tapped together. The juniors were a club, but we'd be called the "tap class" until we took over the reins next fall.

"How did you choose which ones were tapping the women?"

"Do you really want to know?" He leaned in to whisper. "We drew straws."

"Did you lose or win?"

"Very funny." He paused for a second. "Look, it doesn't matter how we picked you. You're in now."

Yeah, but I didn't match up as well with Malcolm as I'm sure the other taps did with *their* big brothers. During his junior year, Malcolm Cabot had been the publisher of the daily newspaper—a snazzy business (not editorial, mind you) role at Eli's most shining and successful extracurricular program. The *Eli Daily News* (or *EDN*, as everyone called it) had a gothic castle of an office on campus that rivaled the tomb of any secret society. Their operating budget could have supported several dozen Lit Mags without breaking a sweat. And there were plenty of women on staff there.

"So I'm your replacement." I folded my hands in my lap. "That would make sense . . . if you were Glenda Foster."

He fell back against the pillow and threw his hand over his eyes. "I knew you were going to ask about that!"

"About Quill & Ink?" When he nodded, I continued. "I'm a smart girl. And I knew I was earmarked for that society."

"Well, I didn't. I had no idea we were poaching until that day at your interview where you thought that's who we were."

"I did wonder why there weren't any women in the room," I admitted, though what I was really wondering was how Malcolm had forgotten that Quill always took the Lit Mag editor. Was it some sort of society solipsism? He didn't concern himself with another society's wants?

"As soon as we decide to tap you we send a letter of intent out to the other societies," Malcolm explained.

"Doesn't that go against the whole 'secret' thing?"

"Honestly, you'll find a lot of the things we do go against it." He shrugged. "We're walking paradoxes. Required to wear the pins, yet instructed to leave the room if anyone dares to comment on them? How ridiculous is that?"

He said it, not me. Though, come to think of it, how prestigious can something be for you if you don't let *anyone* know about it? The Diggers must have some heretofore unknown method of exerting their influence while keeping their identities hidden. Pretty cool.

Malcolm was still explaining. "The other societies do the same thing to us, though, so if they want to be assholes and reveal our tap list, we have similar ammunition. And there's no guarantee that they'll back off, especially if they're a rival, like Book & Key or Dragon's Head."

"But Quill & Ink is no rival."

"Exactly." He smiled and lifted his hand off his face. "A letter from the Diggers scares the shit out of them."

I giggled. No wonder Glenda hadn't called me in a few days. She was probably afraid of being snuffed.

"You'll start to notice that a lot from your barbarian friends that suss out that you're a Digger," Malcolm went on. "It's no accident that all my closest buds are society members now."

Clarissa vs. Lydia? Not going to happen. "What happens if my friends...find out?" Since, you know, Brandon and Lydia already knew.

"We kill them." He grinned. "Nah, nothing. You're not supposed to talk about it, but it's going to be pretty much impossible to hide the fact that you disappear every Thursday and Sunday night from the people you're close to—from your roommate, Lydia, for example."

I crossed my arms. "Are you trying to do that Digger thing where you act like you know everything about me in order to freak me out?"

"Yeah."

"Well, cut it out. I'm not buying. You already screwed up by thinking I date Brandon."

"True. So, anything else you want to ask? I'm here to ease you into Digger life."

"Why did you really pick me?"

He stretched, easing his hands behind his head. "Sorry, kiddo, the annals of our deliberation sessions are destroyed. We burn them in a ritual pyre."

"Why?"

"Because fire is cool." What a man. "No, really, to save hurt feelings."

Made sense. I, for one, wouldn't want to know what kind of bad stuff Poe said about me after that interview. "Why am I named Bugaboo?"

"That will be two dollars for using the name outside of the confines of a society meeting, and I can't tell you that, either."

"Why not?"

"Part of the delib."

"If this is the name they're going to address me by for the rest of my society life, I have a right to know. Some of the other members know."

"Only the ones with the historical names. You can change it if you want, first thing next year. Don't you like it?" He looked hurt, as if I were rejecting a gift.

I shrugged. "It's okay, I guess. Just wish I knew why it was," I continued, slyly. I could guess, though. A bugaboo was a persistent problem, and if their little "lesson" during my initiation was anything to go by, I'd been a legendary pain in the ass during my interview.

"Little minx!" He poked me in the side until I squealed. "Maybe I should have given you that name!"

"Probably would have been preferable!"

He started tickling me in earnest then. "Come on, admit it. It's a cute name. Bugaboo, bugaboo, bugaboo!"

"Stop! Malcolm, please!"

"Bugaboo!" I rolled back, but he didn't relent. "Bugaboo!"

"That's...ten...bucks...." I gasped through the laughter.

He sat back and pulled a ten-spot out of his wallet, grinning. "True. But it was worth it."

I sat up, totally winded, flushed, and yes, a bit turned on. But come on, hot guy tickling me—what else can you expect? "Are you sure you're gay?"

He winked. "Shall I tell you how many of Hollywood's golden boys I've hooked up with?"

I raised an eyebrow with interest. "Are you going to name names?"

"No."

"Come on!" I batted my eyes. "I'm a Digger. We have no secrets."

He named a name.

"No!"

"Yes."

"How was he?"

Malcolm thought about it for a minute. "Not bad. Intense."

Figured. And closeted, just like Malcolm. But, as curious as I was about my big brother's Hit List, there were other, more pressing questions that took precedence. So I started asking, rapid-fire, like we were on a TV show and I had thirty seconds to find out everything there was to know about Rose & Grave.

EXCLUSIVE INTERVIEW WITH MALCOLM "LANCELOT" CABOT, DIGGER
by Amy "Bugaboo" Haskel

Do you really give us grandfather clocks?

When you marry—to our liking.

So I guess that leaves you out.

In most states.

How about the twenty thousand bucks upon graduation?

Negatory. To keep TTA in the black, that's more like what you'll end up contributing.

Wait. I've got dues?

Call them "Donations." Post-grad, of course.

Fuck. *(Probably have to edit that bit out for prime time.)* But I guess membership has its benefits, right?

Lots of them.

Like what?

Like you're going to ace that Russian Novel final, Amy.

Even if you don't finish the book. We have every exam on file since they stopped giving them in Latin.

And that's not cheating?

Why? The profs let you have the exams afterward. They should know that Elis are smart enough to catalog them for the benefit of future generations.

What else do we have squirreled away in that little tomb? I've heard a lot of rumors.

Let me debunk them.

Geronimo's skull?

Check.

Hitler's silverware?

Gross! No! *(leaning in to whisper)* But we've got some other weird Nazi paraphernalia.

(faltering) **Does that mean we have connections to the Nazis?** (*This goes on the top of my new list, Things to Find Out About Your Secret Society Before Taking an Oath of Fidelity. #1: Are we in league with any organized hate groups?*)

I hope not! I think some of our boys brought the junk back from World War II like battle spoils or something.

What else?

Some great first editions. A Shakespeare folio. A lot of swiped Eli memorabilia—winning crew boats and the like. Some of the treasures we've raided from other societies. Some decently valuable and butt-ugly art. More med school skeletons than you can shake a femur at.

Nuclear codes?

Out-of-date since the Cold War, but yeah.

On and on it went, until I'd amassed the kind of knowledge about my new secret society that conspiracy theorists from

here to Addis Ababa would have killed to discover. But eventually, we each realized that, stockpiled exams or not, we had
some work to do before the end of the semester. Besides, I
don't think you get a free pass to lounge around in bed all day
with a guy unless there's sex involved.

Before I left, Malcolm handed me my Rose & Grave pin.
"You have to keep this on you at all times," he said. "Pick
someplace discreet."

"What's the point?" I asked, as I pinned the little gold
hexagon to a belt loop and pulled the hem of my shirt back
down. "If no one is supposed to know it's there, why bother
wearing it at all?"

"*You'll* know it's there," he replied. He crossed to the door
and peeked out. "Just checking for Brandon Weare," he said,
grinning. "We wouldn't want him thinking you're cheating."

"Maybe you would," I said. "It would add to the ruse."
Malcolm merely shrugged a response with a sort of world-
weariness that made me wonder how much longer he'd be able
to keep it up.

I gave him a quick hug and headed out. Like most of the
entryways in an Eli dorm, this one had only one or two suites
on each floor. We didn't have "halls" like most university
dorms, but rather, many-storied entryways. Camaraderie due
to geographical proximity was arranged on a vertical—instead
of sharing bathrooms with the people next door, you shared it
with the people upstairs. Malcolm's digs were on the fourth
floor—a "garret" that when built had probably been home to a
poorer student who couldn't afford a "sitting room," but in
modern times would be a highly coveted "single" with a heap
of privacy. The landing was basically deserted—just a sophomore smoking out the second-story window and chatting on
his cell phone, and a junior girl with a long brown ponytail who opened her door and peeked out as I passed. I felt

the Rose & Grave pin burning like a brand against my hip. Malcolm was right. I did feel the difference.

I pushed open the heavy wooden doors guarding the entry- way and emerged into the sunny Calvin College courtyard. Brandon's entryway was on the other side of the building, so it was unlikely that I might have run into him while leaving Malcolm's room. And from what I could see, he wasn't in the courtyard, either. I glanced up at Brandon's suite window, wondering if I should drop by while I was on his side of the campus. No, I'd see him at the office later this weekend any- way, and there was a strong possibility that any aggressive move on my part (e.g., showing up unannounced at his dorm) would be taken as a signal to launch into The Talk. Or maybe Number Seven.

From the entrance of Calvin College, I could see the brown sandstone walls of the Rose & Grave tomb. My tomb. I fingered the little gold pin, and resisted the urge to head over and test out my memory of all the secret combinations and tricks it took to get inside (like, if you twist the knob the wrong way, you accidentally set off the doorbell, alerting anyone within that there's a non-member on the property). But there'd be plenty of time to play Digger. I was pretty sure Lydia was waiting for me back at the suite, just dying to see what a fully initiated member of Rose & Grave looked like.

Boy, was I wrong.

The doorknob to our suite had been smeared with a dark, reddish-brown substance. I opened it gingerly, only to see more of the liquid had dribbled a path across our thrift-store area rug and straight into Lydia's bedroom. Her torn wind- breaker lay in a heap by the entrance to her bedroom, and a pair of mud-caked shoes were overturned on the threshold. There were feathers everywhere, and the air smelled like burnt hair and bile. I immediately cracked a window and started fanning in a current with the help of Lydia's Rocks for Jocks binder. As soon as I could breathe again, I picked my way across the floor and peeked in her room. Her lavender duvet lay in a poufy heap on her bed, but Lydia herself was nowhere to be seen. There were more smeared, rust-colored finger-prints on her desk chair and closet door.

I swallowed. *Was it blood?*

One thing was certain: Whatever her society's initiation ritual, it made the staining power of pomegranate juice look pretty pale by comparison. At least Poe's coffin hadn't left any marks.

And where was Lydia? Her abandoned clothes made it clear that she wasn't napping the day away on *her* society big sibling's futon. Either she was out buying a can of Lysol, or... I dipped a finger in the puddle by the floor and took a whiff. An acrid, sour scent assaulted my nostrils. Yep, blood. Those bas-tards made my best friend bleed.

Maybe she'd gone to the health center to get...stitched up? I hoped she hadn't been forced to limp all the way out to the Department of University Health (DUH, and again, not so much an acronym as a philosophy, since whether you enter with the Hama virus or a hangnail, the first test they adminis-ter is invariably for pregnancy) while her roommate of three years had tickle fights in Calvin College with some guy she hadn't known before yesterday. Altogether, not a banner first day as a Digger. I thought about what Malcolm had said.

It's no accident that all my closest buds are society members now.

Well, it wouldn't happen to me! I don't care what kind of oath I took, my real friends came first. I surveyed the wreck of our suite.

Oh, God, Lydia, please be okay. I don't even care if you tell me what society you're in, as long as you're all right. *

---

* The confessor freely admits that this was a blatant lie.

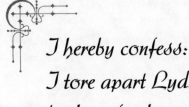 I hereby confess:
I tore apart Lydia's stuff
looking for her pin.

8.
Barbarians

For the first fifteen minutes, I blithely convinced myself that I was just cleaning up. Then I spent a good quarter of an hour under the happy self-delusion that such discovery would assist me in tracking down my roommate. After that, I simply admitted the truth: I was damn curious.

Are you wondering why I wasn't actively frantic?

THINGS I DISCOVERED
THAT CALMED ME DOWN

1) Lydia had taken the time to write down the phone messages before she left. Must not have been in too much of a hurry.
2) The first-aid kit we kept on the bookshelf hadn't been touched. Must not have been hurt.
3) In one of the little puddles of blood, I found a chunk of ground chuck.

That's right. Lydia's society peeps had scared me half to death with a splash of raw hamburger. And hell if I knew what it meant. My society liked pomegranates. Maybe hers liked meat loaf. Or maybe the members had spent too much time watching *The Ten Commandments* and had decided to borrow the Semitic symbolism of smearing blood on a door to indicate who was in-the-know. Either way, Lydia would be in for an earful when she came back. Rotting hamburger in the common room? So not cool.

Round about the forty-minute mark, I heard the door to our suite open. My pin quest had stranded me waist-deep in the back of Lydia's closet, methodically searching her winter coat pockets, where I knew Lydia kept her *real* valuables. But all I'd found were her emergency traveler's checks, her passport, and her spare P.O. Box key.

Drat.

"Welcome to my bedroom," she said dryly from the threshold.

"Lydia!" I launched myself at her. "Oh my God, girl, what have you been doing!"

She held up a plastic bag. "Mr. Clean."

Undaunted, I pressed forward. "What happened here?" I asked. "The feathers, the dirt, the mess on the doorknob?"

No answer.

"There's blood on the floor."

No answer.

"Lydia! Talk to me." I followed her back out to the common room. "I was so worried about you, when I came in and the common room..." I gestured weakly to the mess.

She mopped up one of the red pools with a wad of paper towels. "Well, I was worried about you when I came in and you were MIA." She kept her face to the floor. "Feel like telling me where you spent the night?"

"Calvin College."

She froze, there on the floor, then looked up at me. "Really?"

"Yes." Not a lie. Not really.

She stood up and looked at me, a blush spreading across her skin. "Oh, Amy, I feel like such an ass. I thought—I'm sorry." She shook her head. "What are you going to do about this? He's a nice guy, you know."

"Yeah." And I was no longer just using him for sex. Brandon had now become my alibi. "He is. I'm a jerk."

She hugged me, hard. "You're not. You care about him. It's not your fault that you're a mess when it comes to men."

"Hey!" I smacked her on the shoulder and she pulled away.

"Look, I feel awful that I've been letting all this society crap get in the way of our friendship."

"I think we both have," I replied, almost glad of the lie now, since it seemed to have broken whatever weird tension had blanketed our suite since that letter showed up. I just wanted to put this all behind me. Yesterday's argument, the mess in the common room, the way I'd actually sunk to going through Lydia's stuff—Oh! Of course I couldn't find her pin. I'm such an idiot. She's *wearing* the damn thing. I checked her out surreptitiously, but if there was a society pin on her person, she kept it as hidden as I did.

Well, good. At least we weren't shoving our society memberships in each other's faces then refusing to spill details. We had been putting the society stuff before each other. "Let's not do that anymore, okay?" I suggested, trying *not* to get a better look at a flash of shine I saw above her jeans pocket. It was probably her pin, but I wasn't going to be tempted. See? I could do this. "Let's just...not talk about it."

Lydia surveyed the mess, then eyed me carefully. "You know that's going to be tough, right?"

I nodded. I knew. It would be the elephant-shaped puddle of blood in the room. I loved my relationship with Lydia, but now everything would change. Like us disappearing every Thursday evening instead of hanging out to do Gumdrop Drops. Like spending the night in a bed with your gay society big sib and not being able to dish to your roommate afterward. Like leaving your best friend out of what was about to become the most important part of your Eli career.

The phone rang and I picked it up without answering Lydia. "Hello?"

"Good morning!" my mother exclaimed. "You must have been sleeping pretty deeply not to have heard me before."

My mother likes to play this game where she calls me early on Saturday and Sunday mornings, trying to catch me being not in my bed. You wouldn't believe how many early breakfast meetings I've had in the last three years.

"Hey, Mom," I said. "When did you call? Lydia and I were out shopping." Lydia smiled indulgently.

"Oh. Well, that explains it." My mother doesn't press to uncover obvious lies. I bet she called at eight, before we could even be expected to be at the 24-hour pharmacy. She really doesn't want to know the truth, she just can't prevent herself from confirming her obscene fears. After all, I'm her baby girl. "So, are you studying hard?"

"You know it." This is the Number Two thing she always asks. Sometimes I can follow a script for the conversation. I was so tempted to reply, *No, but that's okay, because my posh secret society guarantees me that I'll ace my exams with the help of their decades' worth of cheat sheets.* But I couldn't tell her anything about that. Not even my mom. Which meant that her Number Three standard question was going to be a bust as well.

And here it was, Number Three: "That's good, sweetie. Have you been up to anything interesting lately?"

Does drinking pomegranate juice out of a human skull and swearing undying fealty to a shadow organization dressed in outlandish costumes count? "Um...nope. My life's pretty much been the same-old, same-old."

Lydia shook her head as she went back to scrubbing the floor. I tugged the hem of my shirt down over my belt loops, over the tiny gold pin that was already pricking my side.

Like anything would ever be the same again.

———

But we tried. After all, it was Saturday night, and spring, and we were two young, smart, single girls who knew exactly how to have a good time.

Which is how we found ourselves at eight o'clock that evening spread out on the sofa in T-shirts, pajama bottoms, and sweat socks, with a bottle of Finlandia Mango, a set of Eli-official "Harvard sucks, Princeton doesn't matter" shot glasses, a bag of gumdrops, and Lydia's DVD of *Bridget Jones's Diary*. We were debating the rules of the game over the opening credits.

"How about we take a drink every time she lights up?" I suggested.

Lydia set about hogging the red gumdrops. "I don't feel like getting alcohol poisoning tonight." She popped a few in her mouth and chewed thoughtfully. "How about we take a drink every time they do a gratuitous, Hollywood-standards-are-out-of-control camera shot of Renée's extra poundage?"

I shrugged. "That sounds more manageable. But...new rules for the sequel." They really started milking the fat jokes in that one.

"Of course!"

It was a relief to talk about something other than secret societies. As we settled into our usual routine, my curiosity about Lydia's society waned (it helped that, if she was wearing their pin, she kept it well hidden). I was still taken aback by the lengths that her group had gone through in their initiation. I would have thought Rose & Grave had the most elaborate, outlandish ceremonies, but then again, a newer organization might make it a point to take their traditions to new heights, each trying to outdo the ones that came before in a sort of secret-society pissing contest. Maybe I'd ask Malcolm what he knew about other organizations' initiation rites and see if I could suss out who included hamburgers in their ceremonies.

Okay, so I was still wondering. Sue me.

Three shots later, Lydia and I were debating whether or not Bridget was making a fool of herself in those see-through office outfits, when there was a knock at our suite door. Lydia leaned over to open it and Brandon walked in.

"Is that dried blood on your doorknob?" he asked without preamble. Lydia and I exchanged glances and shrugged, while Brandon took in the coffee-table spread. "I don't know if Willy Wonka would approve."

"Nonsense," Lydia slurred, pounding her fourth as Daniel successfully navigated Bridget's oversized granny panties. "Candy is dandy, but liquor is quicker."

I didn't drink. This was about to get very sticky, and I knew I'd need every wit that hadn't ceded to the considerable powers of mango vodka. I telepathed to Brandon my fervent desire that he not ask me what I've been up to this weekend.

"So," he asked, taking a place on the sofa between us. "What have you been up to this weekend?"

Supposedly, you. So much for my psychic powers. Must be dulled by alcohol. "Maybe you can help us solve a debate," I cut in, though Lydia was engrossed in the goings-on of Bridget and didn't even appear to have noticed that the man I'd supposedly spent last night with seemed unaware of that fact.

"Shoot," Brandon said, picking out a handful of green gumdrops from the pile. I watched him, wondering if he also had a thing for black jelly beans. And if so, why wasn't I head over heels for him?

"We're trying to decide if Renée Zellweger looks better as Bridget or as a stick figure."

He glanced at the screen. "What does she usually look like?"

Men! You'd think they never read *People*. "Half of that."

Brandon watched Bridget smile. "I think she looks pretty there." And then he looked at me, his brown eyes very warm. "But, then again, I've got a thing for girls in publishing."

I scooched my feet farther up beneath me and Lydia fired off warning glances from behind Brandon's head.

"Amy, you're falling behind." She waved at me with the shot glass. "Brandon, if you don't mind, we're kind of in the middle of a game here."

But Brandon was clearly in no mood to take a hint. He swiped the vodka and an extra glass and poured himself a drink.

"Be careful," I said as he downed it. "The green ones don't really go with the mango."

"Blecch." He grimaced and stared at the empty glass. "You know, I learned in my White Male Sexuality and U.S. Pop Culture class that one sign of masculinity is to drink only alcoholic beverages that are brown or clear."

"This one's clear . . . except for the gumdrops," I argued.

He laughed. "I don't take it seriously. Besides, I already screwed up. My favorite drink is an amaretto sour. Plus, I'm not entirely a *white* male."

"My dad likes Bloody Marys," Lydia said. "Which are red. Are you saying he's gay?"

"Merely a metrosexual."

"And what about wine?" she said, concealing a burp. "It's purple."

And until yesterday, every Digger in history had been

male, and to the best of my knowledge, their official drink was bright pink pomegranate punch. The Order of Rose & Grave must have been very secure in their masculinity.

Either that or Brandon's White Male Sexuality professor was very *in*secure in his. It was a toss-up.

I wondered what was going on in the tomb right now. Were the other new taps there, learning the ropes and bonding with one another? What was I missing out on?

I looked back at Lydia and Brandon, who were cracking up at Daniel's spill in the lake. *Not a thing.* Just because I was in Rose & Grave did not mean I had to abandon my barbarian friends. Nothing had changed.

"Amy!" Lydia threw a gumdrop at me. "Stop cheating. Drink up."

I returned my attention to my forgotten shot glass, where the orange gumdrop had begun to disintegrate. Nope, nothing had changed. Lydia could still drink me under the table. (Note to self: Never do shots with a girl from western New York. They've been drinking since birth.)

"Oops." I tilted the glass toward my mouth, then dug the gooey gumdrop out with my fingers. Inelegant, perhaps, but judging from the look Brandon was giving me, he didn't mind watching me lick melted candy off my thumb.

"Sidebar!" Lydia popped up from the couch, grabbed my arm, tossed a "We'll be right back" in the general direction of Brandon Weare, and dragged me into her bedroom.

As soon as the door was shut, Lydia turned to me and said, "What do you want to do here? Do you want me to leave so you two can be alone? Do you want to go somewhere with him? It's obvious the man didn't come here to watch chick flicks with the roomie."

No, he hadn't, but if he was having fun doing it, why rock the boat?

I twisted my hair up in a frustrated ponytail and let it fall back to my shoulders. "I don't know. I didn't expect him to come around—"

"Please," Lydia said with disdain. "It's Saturday night and you're sleeping together—regularly. You need to accept this, Amy. You aren't accidentally tripping and falling into his bed. He's not coercing you—"

"Don't even say that!"

"—and after the first time or so, you can't even use the oh-wasn't-this-a-terrible-mistake excuse anymore. You're having a relationship, whether you call it that or not."

"I know." I did know. Hadn't Brandon said very much the same thing a few days ago at the Thai place? I'd listened to him that night about Rose & Grave, and that was working out fine, so maybe actually discussing and establishing parameters for our relationship would be a good idea, too.

And I'd always intended on doing just that, as soon as I reached a firm conclusion about what the parameters of our relationship should be. Because, to be honest, when one has been sleeping with one's close friend on an average of once every ten days for the last two months, it's a bit difficult to pretend that one is starting the relationship at the beginning.

We had a saying at Eli: Couples are either *married* or *hooking up*. Students showed the same intensity toward romantic relationships as they did toward every other facet of their existences. There was virtually no casual dating. If you were looking for sex, you wanted it to be easy and convenient, and not get in the way of your studies, art, or efforts to save the world. And if you were looking for love, you were willing to devote a large proportion of your conscious hours to the cause.

I didn't have time for that. I had a publication to run, a grade-point average to maintain, exams to study for, internships to earn—and now, secret society meetings to attend.

"He's a really great guy, Amy."

She was beginning to sound like a broken record with this.

If I didn't know better, I'd think *Lydia* wanted to date Brandon. But she goes for power types, which Brandon Weare, for all his "greatness," was not. Then again, what did I know? I was not exactly an expert when it came to romantic potential.

"And when it doesn't work out," I said with a sigh, "I'll flake out on finals." Lydia had to remember me after Alan. Had to remember Ben Somebody and how she practically had to coax me down from the ledge last spring. "I can't risk it right now. I have too much on my plate."

"How do you know it won't work out?"

"It never has before." I shrugged. "Besides, you know me. I always do something to—screw it up." I just never knew what that was.

There was a knock on the door, and Brandon popped his head in. "You guys just missed a truly phenomenal scene."

Lydia and I laughed. "Careful with these chick flicks, Brandon," she said, "or your White Male Sexuality in America thingy will have more than amaretto sours to worry about."

He smiled. "Okay. In truth, I was hoping you were doing some sort of girls-in-underwear pillow fight. Hollywood led me to believe that college was crawling with quasi-lesbian bedding battles, but I've had my eyes peeled for three years and I'm still waiting."

That was more like a straight male.

"You're looking in the wrong places," I said without thinking. "You have to get tapped into the Society of Duvet & Sham."

"Is that who tapped you the other night?" he rejoined.

I hesitated just a fraction of a second too long before blurting out a lame, "No."

Uh-oh. Why did I have to open my big mouth? Did I have societies on the brain or something? Why didn't I just laugh and say, "I'd tell you, but then I'd have to smother you"?

Brandon was waiting, Lydia was shaking her head, and I fingered the pin in my belt loop for moral support.

"Um, movie?" I suggested, pushing past him and back into the less complicated common room.

But my issues merely followed me there, then promptly erupted.

"Seriously, Haskel," Brandon continued. "Is that where you've been all weekend? I wondered why you weren't at your usual post at the Lit Mag office this morning."

Lydia lost her grip on the bottle of vodka. It thumped once on the corner of the table and toppled to the floor with a seventeen-dollar-and-ninety-five-cent crash.

Crap. Crap crap crappity crap.

I snatched up a pile of Domino's Pizza napkins from the top of the mini-fridge and tossed them onto the spill. The acrid scent of sublimating alcohol instantly blended with Lydia's pine-fresh cleaning efforts from this afternoon. She wasn't moving to help me and her mouth was set in a tight line, but whether she was angrier about my lie or the loss of her vodka was difficult to ascertain.

And then she snorted, mumbled "I knew it!" under her breath, and stomped back into her bedroom.

Yeah, probably angriest at the betrayal. (But maybe she'd get more paper towels.)

This wasn't going to work. We could make up don't-ask-don't-tell ground rules about discussing our respective societies in the suite, but in the process, we'd be leaving out huge chunks of lives. I'd told her I was at Brandon's because it was easier than invoking the society brush-off. I didn't want her to think I was lording my Rose & Grave status over her, since society prestige had always mattered more to Lydia than to me. And then, when we agreed not to talk about it, there seemed no point in saying, "You know how I said I was at Brandon's? Well, I wasn't, but I'm not allowed to talk about that."

But maybe I should have. It would have been awkward,

but at least it wasn't a lie. How many more lies would we have to tell each other, just to keep to our society oaths? The Connubial Bliss reports seemed like a tell-all to our fellow knights. They may be great ideas for some of them, but I already had my tell-all audience, and she wasn't a Digger.

I wondered what kind of promises Lydia had made about her own loyalties. I wondered what lies she had already planned.

Brandon joined me on the floor and began picking up the largest chunks of glass. "What's the story here, babe?"

Babe. Like I was his girlfriend, and we exchanged endearments all the time. Those brown, puppy-dog eyes of his were searching mine in earnest now.

"Nothing." I tugged down on the hem of my shirt. "I... can't talk about it."

"Not even to me?"

Not to my mom, not to Lydia, not to the boy I was sleeping with... "Not to anyone."

"That's silly. My freshman counselor—he was in Book & Key and he had it on his resume, plain as day. And Glenda told us both when she got into Quill & Ink. You can say if you want."

"That's Quill & Ink." How would I know what the rules were elsewhere? I wasn't even totally clear on mine yet. I just remembered the words of my oath. I had *most solemnly avowed never to reveal, by commission or by omission, the existence of, the knowledge considered sacred by, or the names of the membership of the Order of Rose & Grave.* Pretty much left out resumes.

He paused. "But... you *are* in a secret society."

"I can't tell you that."

"That means you are, otherwise you'd just say no."

"That's not true!" I pushed back on my heels and wadded the soaked napkins into a ball.

"Yes it is. Watch: Ask me." He folded his hands.

I sighed. "Brandon, are you in a secret society?"

"No." He grinned. "See?"

I rolled my eyes.

He took the napkin out of my hands and lobbed it into the trash can. Three points. "Now watch this: Amy, are you in a secret society?"

Just say no.

It shouldn't have been that hard. But I didn't, because the truth of the matter, as I now realize, was that our pat little phrases, our *I can't talk about it*s and our *I'd tell you but I'd have to kill you*s are a society member's way of bragging without breaking the oath of secrecy. I was proud that I was one of the first women ever to be tapped into Rose & Grave. I was bursting at the seams to tell all my friends—only, I wasn't allowed to.

In short, saying "no" meant dismissing it, but saying "I'm not allowed to talk about it" meant...

Nyah, nyah, I know something you don't know!

Only, did that count as omission?

Brandon held out his hands as if in presentation. "See?"

I stood up and said coolly, "Don't be ridiculous." On-screen, Bridget was making a fool of herself over something or other, but I'd lost my taste for her antics. Movie Night was over.

And Brandon and I were left alone. We continued cleaning up the mess, and then Brandon said, "You know, Amy, it's okay if you are. I know all that stuff I said the other night might lead you to believe that I disapprove of societies, but if you want to be in one, I won't be unhappy."

"So glad you approve," I snapped. "I don't need your permission to do something, Weare. Not even if we *were* dating."

The contrary-to-fact construction cut him right to the bone. "No." He threw the last wad of towels into the trash and rubbed his hands together with finality. "Though I'd hoped you'd solicit my opinion." He took one last look at the TV screen. "I think I'm going to take off."

No, Brandon, don't. But I didn't say it out loud. I didn't go over and touch him on the shoulder and turn my face to his and kiss him. Though I should have. Because he'd always been really great to me, and because Lydia was right, I owed him a definition.

And maybe an apology. "Brandon," I began, but got no further, as there was a knock on the door.

Brandon, being the closest, opened it, and there stood George Harrison Prescott in his many-zippered jacket. Unlike me, he'd given his Rose & Grave pin a place of honor amongst the zippers. The gold hexagon shone like a beacon in my eyes, but it might have blended in with the rest of the metal to some-one who wasn't looking for it.

"Hey, Amy!" he said brightly. "I'm glad I found you at home." He looked from me to Brandon and back again, and obviously hadn't gained admittance to Eli entirely on good looks and legacy. "Am I interrupting something?"

Yes, I thought.

"No," Brandon said. "I was just leaving."

"Cool." George stepped aside, as if to give Brandon pas-sage into the hall. "Get your shoes on, babe. I want to show you something."

Brandon noticeably flinched at George's casual "babe." I think I might have, too. My friend-with-benefits (benefits that might be revoked, if this sort of scene kept up) turned to me, but his brown eyes showed no warmth. "Are you going into the office tomorrow?"

I nodded.

"Okay," he said. "See you then." And then he left, trading places in the room with George. I heard the entryway door open and shut behind him. Well, I'd thoroughly screwed that one up, hadn't I?

"Amy," said George Harrison Prescott. "Is that dried blood on your doorknob?"

———

Somehow, I convinced George not to start out for the tomb (since that was his purpose in coming over, to pick me up for a late-night jaunt to Rose & Grave) until after I was sure Brandon had made it home. The path to the Diggers' tomb was identical to the quickest way back to Calvin College, and I didn't think that shadowing his steps would make this whole evening any less awkward. But explaining the situation in language and decibel that would be unidentifiable to Lydia (who was still in a huff and her bedroom) did not prove the easiest prospect.

"I'm not alone," I whispered, after a quick trip into my room to change into an outfit more George-worthy. I crooked a thumb toward Lydia's closed bedroom door.

He nodded. "So let's go over to the tomb," he said loudly, "see what's happening."

My eyes widened. "I'm. Not. Alone," I hissed, gesturing more strongly.

He grinned now, and his eyes sparkled behind the matching copper-rimmed glasses. "Why, Amy Haskel," he said in mock reproof, "I had no idea you were such a wild woman. How many boys do you have hidden in your suite this Saturday night?"

I rolled my eyes and pulled on a pair of shoes. Leave it to George Harrison Prescott to equate everything with sex. "No, you priapic hornball. My roommate. Ixnay on the Iggersday."

Now it was his turn for an eye roll. "Yeah, like Lydia doesn't know Pig Latin." He threw his arm around my shoulders and herded me to the door. "Let's go."

Actually, Lydia knew real Latin, too. She had been a Classics major for three semesters. And "priapic hornball" was a bit redundant, though with George, it wasn't overstating the case. At the entryway door, I stopped him.

"Here's the thing, George. That guy who just left? He's in Calvin College. So we can't just follow him down to Rose & Grave or he'll know what we're up to."

"Please," George scoffed. "Do you really take any of that secrecy stuff seriously? Besides, it's a free campus. You and I can go wherever we'd like."

I planted my feet. "I do take it seriously! We took oaths. Doesn't that mean anything to you?"

He looked at me and blinked. "No," he said at last. "I have to say it doesn't. If there were a train coming and I had the choice to save my mother or some random Digger, I'd pick my mom, no matter what stupid oath of fidelity or fraternity or whatever it was that I took in front of a bunch of jerks in costume."

When put like that, it was hard to disagree. "But there's no train here," I argued. "You're just talking about it to be a punk."

He laughed then, a look that suited him even better than the serious one he'd copped a moment ago. "That's the truth. Okay, we'll wait a minute, since your secret's so precious to you."

The way he said it made me feel childish for obeying the society rules. And then I remembered his antics from last night. The metal and glass, the sulfur. "Look, if you hate all the trappings that come with Rose & Grave, why did you join in the first place?"

He pushed open the entryway door and escaped into the night air. "Didn't really have a choice, there," he said. "My dad was kind of insistent."

I remember what some of the other new taps had said before George's entrance last night, about how he'd been dragged in kicking and screaming. And then I thought about how I'd watched him as he stood there in front of the tomb, lighting matches and struggling with himself. I stopped George under an arch with his last name engraved in huge letters on the cornice.

"Your dad is a Digger."

"You met him. Uncle Tony?" He raised his eyebrows.

"Oh." I hadn't known the identity of the character who'd sworn me in. (Though I'd found out at the mansion last night that "Uncle Tony" was the official title for the parliamentary leader of every meeting. Some organizations have chairpersons; Rose & Grave has uncles—and now maybe aunts as well?) "That's kind of cool, though, that he was the one in the ceremony. Like father, like son, you know?"

He snorted. "Yeah, exactly like that." He kicked at the cornice and stuck his hands in the pockets of his jeans. "Let's go."

A bunch of jerks in costume. Okay, Haskel, swift on the uptake. Apparently, George Harrison Prescott was not a big fan of his father. I followed him through the Prescott Gate and down York Street toward Calvin College, now wildly curious to hear the family dirt. We rounded the corner of Hartford College, and suddenly George yanked me back into a stone alcove and clapped a hand over my mouth.

"Shush!" he whispered in a breath that tickled the nape of my neck. "Your boyfriend stopped for pizza."

The alcove was damp and the stone felt gritty beneath my hands, but, pressed up against George Harrison Prescott, I hardly noticed. He slowly released his grip, sliding his palm down my chin and over my throat and collarbone.

I don't think I need to remind you what a smooth operator this kid is. My legs actually quivered.

"He's not my boyfriend," I whispered over my shoulder.

Glare on George's glasses revealed nothing in his eyes. "Good to know."

At that moment, I was not thinking about Brandon walking home outside. I turned fully to George, reassured by the darkness, and put one hand on his shoulder—low on his shoulder, because he was George Harrison Prescott, and I couldn't help myself. "Tell me why you didn't want to join Rose & Grave."

"Tell me why you *did*."

I shrugged. "It seems like a good idea. Huge network, cool tomb, free champagne."

He pulled away from me and sat on a low stone bench. Beneath his jacket, George was wearing a beat-up oxford dress shirt over a fading, cracked vintage concert T. I couldn't make out the band, but he was working the look like a latter-day James Dean. "My mom and dad are divorced. She went to Eli, too. And she was the last of a dying breed of hippies and old-school feminists."

"She burned her bras?"

"She didn't own any." George crossed his arms. "The seventies might have been over, but she wasn't about to admit that. My dad was in his 'rebel against his upbringing' phase when they met. She was rebelling, too, don't get me wrong. And she and my dad just kind of . . . used each other."

"That's terrible."

"He made her think she could change him, she made his Brahmin parents really angry. They disagreed on everything, which must have meant that the sex was nuclear."

Um, TMI.

"The marriage lasted for about thirty seconds after I was born." George shrugged. "When I was little, I thought they broke up over my name. Isn't that stupid? But it was the only disagreement they ever shared with me. Dad wanted me to be a Third. Mom caved on the George part, but gave him one parting shot with the Harrison. Like the Beatle. Cute, huh?"

I'd always thought so. "Where did you grow up?"

"Split time," he replied. "Mom's a social worker in Connecticut. Dad, of course, stays in Westchester. They think of each other as amusing now. Dad finds it funny that Mom still wants to save the world, Mom thinks it's hilarious that Dad became exactly the kind of man he used to hate his father for being."

"I'm sorry." For lack of anything better to say.

"And I'm a conduit." He laughed without mirth. "They come to drop me off or pick me up at one of our houses, take one look at each other, and *boom*."

Boom?

George filled in the blanks. "Until about five years ago, they used to fuck regularly."

What, and leave little Georgie standing in the kitchen? "What happened five years ago?"

"Dad got married." George stood, checked the street. "Now it's only semi-regularly."

I dropped to the bench, too shocked to speak.

He looked back at me, grimaced, and raked his hand through his hair. "I have no clue why I'm telling you all this. Guess the Digger bonding thing is starting already."

Like Malcolm. "The Digger bonding thing where you tell your brothers all your deep dark secrets?"

"Yeah. Or my sister, in this case. At this rate, I'll have nothing left for my C.B."

I stood. "I have a tough time believing that about you, George." I stood very close to him in the confines of the alcove. Perhaps too close.

His eyes widened behind his glasses, as if he was surprised to hear his reputation thrown back at him. Yep, definitely too close. He put his hand up to mine. *And palm to palm is holy palmer's kiss.* If he were an English major, I would have suspected he'd done it on purpose. Maybe he had. Unlike with Brandon, I couldn't read George at all.

TWO THINGS HE MIGHT BE THINKING

1) Oh, look, it's Amy. She's cute and smart and funny.
2) Oh, look, it's a girl in a dark corner. Haven't done her yet.

I took a breath. "The coast is clear now, right?"

He nodded, slowly, and we spilled out into the relative brightness of sodium streetlights.

As we walked down the slate-lined alley between Hartford and Calvin Colleges, we said very little. George, I think, was still shell-shocked over his own gut-spill and I was busy contemplating if I should reciprocate. But what should I say? My parents were happily married, and rarely fought about anything more serious than whether to hire the kid down the street to cut the lawn or do it themselves. That would go over well. Or should I share something darker? The time last year that I slept with a boy whose name I can't remember? Would that make me sound like a slut?

We hit High Street and turned toward the tomb, still in mutual silence. The gate was closed, and George held it open for me—after we both checked to see that no one stood on the street. "Guess no one is inside," he said, referring to the gate-position code.

We were about to find out why.

He jogged up the front steps to the main entrance and froze. When I arrived a moment later, contemplating how dangerous it would be to hang out inside Rose & Grave alone with George Harrison Prescott, I was similarly struck.

The doors had been chained and padlocked together.

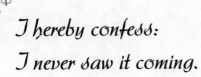 *I hereby confess:*
I never saw it coming.

9.
The Backlash

In retrospect, we should have gone to Malcolm or one of the other seniors right away, but we didn't. After all, we were new at all of this Digger stuff. How were we supposed to know that the padlock was a recent addition to the look of the tomb? I remember reflecting to George at the time that perhaps the caretaker always padlocked it on the days when there were no formal events planned. But when we went around to the side entrance, there was a chain there, too, and neither of us knew where we might obtain the keys.

"We could knock," George suggested, but didn't move to do so. I was relieved to see my hesitation echoed in someone who had been more thoroughly versed in the mores of the society. Even though I'd spent hours inside the tomb yesterday, taking oaths and learning secrets, the same unease about the property that had been cultivated in the last three years still held power over me. I felt, almost, that I didn't belong on the site.

Which, it turns out, is exactly how they wanted me to feel.

Our plans to hang out in the tomb thwarted, we walked

down to Lenny's Lunch, which holds the distinction of having the most batshit hours of any restaurant in New Haven. Really, you never know when it's going to be open. The hours are something like 11 A.M.–3:15 P.M. on Monday, noon–2 P.M. Tuesday, 7–9:30 P.M. Thursday–Friday, and noon–midnight on Saturday. I kid you not (and no, do not hold me responsible for any of these hours. I honestly have no clue when they are open). Plus, there's only one thing on the menu—cheeseburgers on toast with onions and tomato—and the proprietor will kick you out if you ask for ketchup. But if you learn the rules, in a sort of "*Seinfeld* soup-Nazi" way, they make awesome cheeseburgers. (And only cheeseburgers, by the way, not hamburgers. Woe betide the lactose-intolerant.)

We settled into the ancient wooden booths and waited for our food. Over the decades, people had carved encyclopedias' worth of personal histories into the tops and sides of the tables and benches (the bottoms were something you stayed away from if you wanted to keep your appetite). Hearts, crests, quotes from Shakespeare and Stalin—anything goes at Lenny's Lunch. I rubbed the condensation from my bottle of birch beer and polished a carving that read "B + A 1956."

Those are very common initials.

George and I ate our cheeseburgers without ketchup, drank our pops, and talked about movies. We didn't discuss his family, or mine, or the strange locks on the tomb door. The buzz of vodka was finally fading, and I kept my hand over the carving as I ate. George Harrison Prescott was a very attractive man, but I had no interest in contributing to his already stellar track record.

"What are you doing this summer?" George asked.

"I've got an internship at Horton. The publishing company?" A pat of cheese plopped from my burger to the wrapper. Smooth, Amy, smooth.

"In New York? Cool." He twirled his bottle around by the

stem. "I'm going to Europe for a few weeks right after exams, and then I'll probably work for my dad in the city. We should hang out."

"Do you know what you want to do after graduation?"

He shrugged. "One of the three big ones: I-banking, consulting, law school."

"No preference?"

He shrugged. "Not really. Tell me, is this your first publishing internship?"

"In New York, yeah. I worked at the Eli Press a few summers back."

"Well, then you're well positioned to get a job when you graduate. I wish I'd been thinking that far ahead."

See, that's the dirty little secret they never tell anyone. When I first came to Eli, I thought that I'd have employers falling all over me upon graduation, just dying to hire someone with an Ivy League degree. When you're signing your life away to Sallie Mae, the schools stress how fabulous a reputation they have, how it will open all sorts of doors for you. But once you're in the thick of your education, you learn otherwise. You aren't a made man (or woman) just because your diploma bears the Eli seal.

PEOPLE WHO *DO* CARE

1) Investment banking and consulting firms where they can charge their clients through the nose since they're providing Ivy League pedigreed staff (which they proceed to chew up and spit out).

2) Law schools whose rankings are partially based on the credentials of the schools from which they cull their students.

3) Your great-aunt Amelia, who likes to brag to the folks at the VFW.

If you want a job that leads to a career rather than a quick buck, then you'd better have a pretty full resume by the time you get your diploma.

"Don't worry about it," I said. "You'll be making lots more money as a consultant than I will as an editorial assistant. You'll be a better brochure statistic by far."

That's the other kicker. Eli has far more respect for its take-the-money-and-run business consulting graduates, who can turn around and give monetary gifts to the school immediately upon graduation, than for anyone who invests in a long-term career. And looking at the Rose & Grave tap class I'd just joined, I'd say it was a fair bet that the Diggers thought along the same lines. Power and/or wealth seemed to be the order of the day. And again, I was the odd one out.

George snapped his fingers in front of me. "Hey, it's Saturday night. Stop thinking so hard."

I bristled and began peeling the label off my pop bottle. "I'm not." God, he sounded like Brandon.

"Seriously, though, Amy, you have it all planned out. I admire that. You came to Eli knowing exactly what you wanted to do and you're doing it. I came from a double legacy and never once planned for a summer internship."

"You don't need one. You're a Prescott."

"Hmph. Prescott or not, I don't have a clue."

I smiled conspiratorially. "Honestly? Neither do I." But the internship thing I learned early on. I vividly remember sitting in the Lit Mag office one evening freshman year while Glenda tried in vain to soothe an older friend's nerves. The girl had graduated the previous year, and had been looking for a job for the past nine months with no luck, despite her Eli pedigree.

"They don't care," she'd sobbed. "They get a hundred resumes a day, and they don't care how smart I am, or how much

I've read of the Western canon. They just want to know where my internships were!"

"Where were they?" I'd asked, like an idiot frosh.

"Nowhere!" the girl had hissed at me, glaring with baleful red eyes. "I had to work in the summer to pay for this stupid place. Fat lot of good it did me. I'd rather be in more debt now and have a better resume than without a job and up a few thousand dollars."

I took it as my creed. This Horton job was the culmination of everything I'd been working for. It was my ticket to postgrad entry into the world of publishing.

Okay, maybe I did have it all together. Because here I was on a Saturday night, out to eat with the hottest guy in my college (yes, he even paid), a member of the school's most elite secret society, a top student headed off to a glamorous summer job in New York City... from where I stood, the plus column looked pretty good.

He walked me back to my entryway at Prescott College, and I brainstormed ways to leave him at the door that would make me look mysterious, rather than uninterested.

Though if one were to ask Brandon, I apparently always managed the former without breaking a sweat.

I opened the door to the suite carefully, avoiding all contact with the stains still smearing the doorknob, and slipped inside.

"See you tomorrow," he murmured.

I turned back to him. His copper eyes shimmered as if they'd been freshly smelted, and I had to tilt my chin up to look him head-on. Rather nice, actually. "Tomorrow?"

He nodded. "First meeting, remember? Five minutes to six, or VI Diggers-time."

That's right. From now on, the Diggers held the deed to my Sunday and Thursday nights. Missing a meeting was not permitted under any but the most life-threatening circumstances. (As Poe put it, even if you're in the hospital, you'd better be in a coma.) Ditching was viewed as a violation of the oath of fidelity.

I swear to cleave wholly unto the principles of this ancient order, to further its friends and plight its enemies, and place above all others the causes of the Order of Rose & Grave.

Of course, if George didn't put much stock in the secrecy oath, who knew what else about Rose & Grave he'd blow off? Probably skip a meeting the first time it conflicted with getting booty.

"Okay, then," I said, and began to shut the door between us. "Thanks for the burger. Good night, George."

See? See how good I am? I didn't even think about kissing him. Didn't even think about letting him kiss me. I could withstand the charms of even George Harrison Prescott. A veritable pillar of self-control, that's Amy Haskel.

"Good night," he murmured in a voice of unmistakable invitation. The door slid shut. "Good night... *Bugaboo.*"

I melted on the parquet.

———

I might be freely able to commit my entire Sunday and Thursday evenings to Rose & Grave come next fall, but this spring I still had obligations to the facets of my existence that made me worthy of membership in the society in the first place. Not WAP, though. I'd decided it was a lost cause. My Sundays had been seriously proscribed by this new development in my extracurriculars. I had two choices:

1) Wake up at 8 A.M. every Sunday like I'm some sort of science major who has early-morning labs, and read a thousand pages of Tolstoy before any other

college kid could reasonably be expected to be conscious, or
2) Take advantage of Rose & Grave's rumored library
of final exams so that I'd have time in my all-too-
short Sunday afternoons to deal with, I don't know,
everything else in my life? Little things like laundry?

No-brainer.

Today, the top of my To Do list involved finalizing a lineup
for the commencement issue of the Lit Mag. Word had leaked
out about the proposed *Ambition* theme, and, at last check, I
had twenty-three irate e-mails in my in-box from Eli scribblers
about how this development gave them no time to allow their
muses to percolate, ruminate, agitate, and/or commiserate
over the subject. Someone stayed up with a thesaurus, me-
thinks (though "commiserate" was stretching it a bit). But
please. God forbid they actually write from the heart and let us
choose the pieces that best fit the anthology. I foresaw twenty-
three unhappy careers.

Borrowing a trick from my Rose & Grave big sib, I stuck
my society pin through the strap of my Eli-blue messenger
bag, slung it over my shoulder, slipped my feet into a pair of
yellow Chuck Taylors (Prescott College colors), and headed
out the door. In the last week, spring had acquiesced to summer's control, and the student body was out in full force, pasty
white and doing everything they could to counteract the damage of being indoors all winter. Girls lay strewn about the
courtyard in pastel summer skirts as if they were posed for a
campus brochure, while shirtless boys practiced their Frisbee
flicks. Prescott College was not known for its Ultimate team,
but the chests were mostly decent. Eww, except for that one.

Unlike the girls, I was dressed for work rather than sun-
bathing, in another of my ubiquitous pairs of jeans and a

Prescott College T-shirt. (By junior year, the average student amasses about a dozen of those things. They hand them out at will for every college event, from move-in day to the annual spring barbeque. I even have one from a Jell-O wrestling match between the Prescott College dean and master that happened sophomore year, but I don't wear it much. It's still stained blue.)

I arrived at the Literary Magazine's minuscule storefront office and found Brandon already deep in damage control. The floor around his feet was littered with four-fold stingers.

I toed the nearest plane. "You're lucky we never went to electronic submissions."

He didn't look up.

"Ever notice how we get five times the submissions for the commencement issue as we do for every other issue combined?" I placed my bag on my desk. "With the other issues, we're scrambling for stories or reduced to whipping up something at the last minute ourselves so that the layout isn't all ads for Starbucks and stationery shops."

Brandon turned a page and kept reading.

"Of course," I went on, taking my seat and swiveling to face him, "you've always been better than me at that. Writing stories on the fly, I mean."

His eyes paused their back-and-forth scanning, and he blinked. "Thanks."

"I'm better at the scrambling."

"You're certainly demonstrating that now."

I swallowed. Too far.

Brandon nodded his head toward a neat stack of manuscripts at the corner of the desk. "Those four are possibilities."

And the Terse Award goes to...Brandon Weare. "I'm sorry about last night."

He finally looked at me, for all the good it did. I couldn't tell thing one from his expression. "Which part?"

Any part that hurt his feelings.

The door to the office opened and in walked Glenda Foster, bearing a cardboard drinks holder with two Venti iced something-or-others.

I had never been happier to see my mentor, even if she had failed to tap me into her secret society and concealed from me her period of lesbian experimentation. Everyone had her off days. I was sure Glenda still loved me, even if Brandon—

Well, we don't use the L-word in reference to Brandon.

Glenda stopped dead as she caught sight of me. "A-Amy," she said, her voice tinged with nerves. "What are you doing here?"

My brow furrowed. "Excuse me?"

She handed one of the drinks to Brandon. "Okay, B, iced latte for you, caramel frapp for me." Glenda licked a spot of whipped cream off the heel of her palm and avoided meeting my gaze. "Sorry to have skipped you, Amy, but B and I kinda figured you weren't going to show up today."

I flashed a look at Brandon. How dare he? I had just as much right to be here as he did! More even, because I was the editor! We may have argued last night, but he'd have to have a pretty low opinion of me indeed to think I'd abandon my post at the Lit Mag just to avoid him.

"What do you mean?" I asked, turning to him and struggling to keep my voice casual. "I told you I'd be here."

"Right," Glenda said. "It's just...with everything going on..." She waved her hand north by northwest, as if the direction was significant.

"Everything going on?" I prompted.

Brandon cleared his throat. "At Rose & Grave."

I froze, there on the scuffed linoleum. I reached for my belt loop, then remembered I'd put the pin on the handle of my bag.

"*What,*" I whispered, "*is going on at Rose & Grave?*"

Glenda's eyes got wider. "You mean you don't know?"

In one heartbeat, I'd snatched up my bag, and in the next, I was out the door. And as I left, my mind whirling with concerns, there was one that seemed to float to the top.

Great job at secrecy, Amy. This is barely your second day as a Digger, and not a single person of your acquaintance is still in the dark.

———

The "something going on" proved to be a crowd of about fifty people clustered at the apex of High Street. The twenty that stood out were a row of elderly men, all in business suits and sunglasses, in a line that stretched across the front border of the Rose & Grave property like some sort of human shield. Whoever had coordinated their outfits was just a tad too into those agents from *The Matrix*, as far as I was concerned. The tomb itself appeared to have sprouted even more padlocks and chains since my last visit.

Everyone else milled about across the street, trying their best to look as if they hadn't staked out a seat for the showdown.

I spotted Malcolm and Clarissa and sauntered over. "What is this?"

"The backlash," Clarissa sniffed, shooting a glance over her shoulder at the line of men. "Assholes."

Well, that was helpful. I turned my attention to Malcolm, who was in the midst of a heated argument with his cell phone.

"I don't care, just get your ass here—now. I can't believe they went through with their threat. The bastards. No, no, of course not— What, you want me to just go up there and confront them? You aren't hearing me, man, I'm telling you, there's a *crowd*."

"Just as they wanted it, too, no doubt," observed Greg Dorian, sidling up on the other side.

"They're patriarchs?" I said, trying to feel my way through the dark.

Everyone else nodded, leaving me wondering what meeting I'd missed.

"Look. Just get here before the newspapers do, okay?" Malcolm slammed the clamshell phone closed and commenced pacing.

Josh joined the group from where he'd been idling nearby. "Screw the crowd, Cabot. I say, if they don't care to protect their secrecy, then why should we?"

Malcolm shook his head. "Because, newbie, unlike those guys, we actually have a secret to protect." He glared at the shield group. "Very clever composition. I'd bet a hundred dollars that not one of them was tapped after D134—er, that is, the class of 1964."

"What happened in 1964?" one of the other new taps asked.

"Elitist guilt. It was no longer cool to be a Digger, and they went underground."

"Wait a second." I sliced my hand in front of Malcolm to make him hold up. "Are you saying all this secrecy stuff is new?"

Malcolm clucked his tongue. "No respect for history, young'uns. Yes and no. We were never supposed to talk about what we do inside that tomb, or even talk about the membership. It was almost a joke, back in the 19th century when everyone would be wearing full suits everywhere, with their society pins on their suit lapels right at eye level. Insolence. Your pin would be staring everyone right in the face, but they couldn't breathe a word about it, or you'd walk out the door."

Things hadn't changed too much, I reflected.

"But that same membership wasn't a secret," Malcolm went on. "Everyone knew who was in Rose & Grave. Hell, they used to publish the list of Digger taps in the *New York Times* every spring."

"But, the oath..." I stammered. So Lydia had been right. But what kind of crap was that? If it wasn't a secret, why did they call it a *secret* society? They were supposed to kill people who told! Or stick them in a dungeon. Or punish them. Or *something*. (Come on, you thought so, too.) They weren't supposed to publish their names in the frickin' *New York Times*!

Though, I reasoned, that might be a good thing for me. A lot of publishing people read the "paper of record."

I clearly needed to brush up on society lore (as soon as I figured out a way to slip it into my schedule).

"It was a different oath. They didn't talk about what happened behind the closed doors of the tomb, but everyone knew who was in the club. And that was becoming a problem. Diggers were actually getting harassed on campus. Potential taps didn't want to be associated with the organization. We started receiving"—Malcolm shuddered—"rejections from taps. So, to survive, the membership became informally secret. Over the decades, tradition turned it into formality. Times change and so do we." He clenched his fist and I thought he might shake it at the patriarchs. "Don't they get that? Times fucking change!"

Demetria popped up in a patterned scarf and a pair of battered, paint-splattered overalls. "Hey, gang's all here! Some protest, huh? Pretty good for a bunch of old guys."

"I still say we confront them," Josh said.

"That's just what they want," Malcolm argued. "Give them the excuse they need to nail us."

Clarissa seemed to agree. "They didn't take the same oath of secrecy we did. And going up to them in front of all these other people would be a broken oath on a silver platter. Ammunition. Pardon the mixed metaphors."

"Then let's call the police," I suggested. "Don't we have serious pull from them? At the very least, we could make them break up the crowd." I was met with five imperious, incredulous stares.

"Pull?" Clarissa asked. "You're joking, right?"

"Hey, guys, what's up?" Kevin Lee, a.k.a. Frodo, skidded in, arching his neck to see over the heads of the gathered bystanders.

But clearly a group of seven exceeded the limits of Malcolm's plausible deniability and he threw up his hands. "People, people, do none of you understand the value of discretion? Disperse, disperse."

And everyone did, melting into the crowd with such alacrity that I lost track of them (and any chance of getting a straight answer) almost immediately.

I turned around twice, scanning for other Diggers, and finally caught sight of the senior I knew only as Poe. He was sitting on the steps of the English department, a little ways away from everyone else, pretending to read from a volume of Nietzsche while snacking on a bag of Doritos and watching the proceedings with an inscrutable eye.

Poe. Why'd it have to be *Poe*? As I saw it, approaching him already set me up with a handful of problems.

Possible Difficulties

1) I didn't know his real name. Awkward, awkward.
2) He was positioned as far away from the action as one could possibly get.
3) I hate the jerk.

But the pickings were slim. I couldn't even find Clarissa in the crowd anymore, and the blond bitch at least held the distinction of not being a person who had threatened my life recently. I took the stairs two at a time, and came to a halt directly in front of him.

"Ah, Miss Haskel," Poe said, snapping his book shut. "Lovely afternoon, isn't it?"

"Exquisite. I'm looking for a straight answer on what's going on here."

He cocked an eyebrow. "You sound like a member of the fourth estate. Interesting. And here I thought Cabot was prevaricating."

Dude, the SATs were four years ago. Get a life. "Listen, what's the deal with those guys?"

Poe brushed nacho cheese dust off on the leg of his pleated dress pants, which he'd paired with a rather shabby white undershirt. Fashion victim, on top of everything else. "Those guys, as you so eloquently put it, are patriarchs merely acting upon the board of trustees's promise, which most of my club believed to be a bluff."

And Poe hadn't, clearly. "What promise?"

"To close the tomb if we were so bold as to carry through with our intent to tap members of the fairer sex." He nodded in deference to me.

The backlash . . . "What! This is all because of us?"

"You and the other females," he continued as if he hadn't a care in the world. "They refuse to recognize your inclusion."

I tossed my hair. "They need to join the 21st century." Or even the 20th.

"And furthermore, the board and supporting coalition of unwilling patriarchs intend to visit a punishment upon those who acted without their permission. They informed us that they would close the tomb and invalidate the membership of any Digger who supported and/or acted upon the initiation of females."

"You sound like a lawyer," I spluttered through my shock. He sounded so . . . calm!

"Thank you. I'll be attending Eli Law come fall. At least, that's the plan."

(Eli Law, by the way, is rather infamous for *not* turning out lawyers. Supposedly the best law school in the country, but everyone on their roster either becomes professors or politicians.)

"How the hell can you be so blasé about this?" I practically shouted (Malcolm would say I was being indiscreet). "You tapped us, too!"

"Indeed I did," Poe replied, in that infuriatingly unruffled tone.

"Well, aren't you upset about having your—your membership invalidated?"

"I've had a few weeks to get used to the idea." Poe shrugged. "I'm certainly upset about the development. But I can't say I'm surprised. In fact, I was just telling Malcolm a few moments ago—"

"That was you on the cell phone."

"Guilty as charged."

"And you were already here."

"I assure you, as I'm sure you heard me assure him, my presence isn't about to make a modicum of difference at this juncture."

"Dammit, stop talking like that!"

His gray eyes went cold, but he obeyed. "Look, honey, I happen to agree with them. I don't think women should be members of Rose & Grave, and I argued that point as long as my voice held out. I also held no illusions that the TTA board would 'come around' as soon as they saw what a great group of girls we tapped, which was the mistaken hypothesis of the rest of my club. However, when it became obvious that I was the only one of the Diggers who thought so, I decided to support my brothers."

"Why?"

"Because the decision to tap has to be unanimous, and we were at an impasse. From that point on, I didn't say a word. We interviewed girls, we groomed girls, we deliberated about girls, we tapped girls, and we initiated girls, and during the whole process, I never once spoke up about how I thought it was a really bad idea."

He said "girls" like it was a dirty word. I wanted to slap him.

And still, the lecture went on. "What's happening now is exactly what I said would happen, but I'm not going to start throwing 'I told you so's around. We went over the board's head, and acted without the support of the trustees at large. We can't take back the initiation now—you've been inside the tomb, inside the Inner Temple. You've seen everything, know everything. As far as they are concerned, we've committed heresy, and your class's club is an abomination of the Order. Malcolm wants me to go down there and talk to the patriarchs because he thinks that they'll be more likely to listen to someone who's on their side. But because I'm on their side, I have no argument to make."

Forget arguments to *them*—talk about a rimshot! I could make a dozen without breaking a sweat. "Why don't you think women should be allowed in Rose & Grave?"

He looked at me for a long time without blinking, then stood. "Right now, the quickest answer is that tapping you has fucked up my life. They aren't going to stop with the tomb. They'll go after our school records. They'll go after everything. Now, if you'll excuse me, I have a resume to update. If I were you, I'd do the same."

"You're a sexist asshole."

He stopped for a moment. "Maybe I'll put that down under *Skills*."

"And get a job with whom?" I snapped. "The Taliban?"

Emotions flashed so quickly across his face that I had a tough time catching them, but he finally settled on disdain. "I am not implying that women are in any way inferior to men. I am in full support of an elite women's secret society on campus."

I rolled my eyes. "Separate is not equal, buddy. An Eli law student should know that."

"When Wellesley accepts my little brother, I'll revisit the issue." And then he took off down the steps.

At least now I was up to speed. And I also knew that I disliked Poe whatever-his-real-name-was a lot more than even Miss Clarissa "Slumming" Cuthbert. I trudged back down the steps and ran smack into Malcolm, who was redialing his cell phone.

"You can forget it," I said. "He's not coming."

Malcolm looked at me. "Who?"

"Poe."

Malcolm flinched at my use of the society name, but was all business as he grabbed my arm. "How do you know?"

"I just talked to him."

"Here?" Malcolm searched the area with his eyes. "That sneaky bastard!"

"That's not the adjective I'd use."

He frowned. "You don't really know him."

Man, that whole oath of constancy thing really took, didn't it? I wondered if I'd be jumping in to defend Clarissa next. "I know he doesn't want me in the society."

Malcolm sighed. "That's not true. If he truly didn't want it, it wouldn't have happened."

I shook my head. Malcolm might think he knew his society brother, but I'd looked the guy in the eyes. He'd wanted nothing to do with the "fairer sex." Stone Age jerk.

"Okay, then, Amy, we're on our own." His hand slipped down to mine, and he began pulling me forward.

"What are you doing?" I cried as we pushed through the crowd.

"We're going to talk to them."

I started to dig my heels into the asphalt. "But what about... *all that stuff you said*?"

Malcolm looked back and winked. "Loophole, kiddo. We're press."

Ways In Which Amy Haskel And Malcolm Cabot Differ From "Press"

PRESS	AMY HASKEL AND MALCOLM CABOT
✓Is affiliated with the editorial department of a news-producing publication.	✓Are the editor of a journal of literary fiction and the former business manager (i.e., money guy) of a news-producing publication, respectively.
✓Hopes to engage subject in a dialogue that will result in an insightful and informative article printed for public consumption.	✓Have taken oaths of secrecy preventing them from revealing anything of this matter to the public.
✓Has experience with and/or interest in investigative journalism.	✓Have neither.

Considering the above, you can probably guess my reaction.

"The hell I am!" I shouted, drawing the attention of more than a few interested bystanders. "Malcolm, have you ever even *read* the *Eli Literary Magazine*?"

He made a face, as if the very suggestion was anathema to all he found acceptable in his reading material. (Note to self: Include more page-turners in next issue.) "Please, Amy."

Regrouping, he yanked me along. "Look, you've got a media outlet at your disposal. That's all I care about right now."

Well, I thought, as he swung me face-to-face with a silver-haired human shield, at least this fit the theme of "Ambition."

"Mr. Cabot," said one of the patriarchs. "Quite a daring move, I must say. Whatever must your fellows think?"

My society big sib didn't miss a beat. "Malcolm Cabot, *Eli Daily News*. May I ask what brings you to High Street today, sir? It appears you're guarding the entrance to the Rose & Grave tomb. Is this true?" And then, leaning in, he hissed, "I think it would be better if this matter were handled in-house."

"I'm sorry," the patriarch replied. "But I really can't talk about that."

"You're making fools of all of us," Malcolm continued under his breath. "No one wants the society to be a laughing-stock."

"I'm sorry," the patriarch replied. "But I'm really not allowed to talk about that."

"Come on," Malcolm said. "You have to open up a dialogue here. Stop treating me like some kind of bar—" He froze, then straightened, his eyes wide as the rules of the game became clear. "Barbarian. You *prick*."

"You defied us. You pay the price."

"Like hell."

The patriarch went on. "And that's not all. We intend to pursue this to the fullest extent. Good luck with your career, Mr. Cabot."

A frigid cord of fear seemed to band my lungs at the man's oh-so-casual tone, and I felt my blood rush in retaliation. Now it was my turn to be indignant. "Hey! Don't you think that's taking things a little too far?" I caught Malcolm's warning glance. "Um, Amy Haskel, *Eli Lit Mag*." Formalities aside, I continued in a lower voice. "Some stupid undergrad organization is one thing, but you have no right to mess with his future—"

"Amy Haskel," the patriarch said. "Editor of the literary magazine."

I flicked a strand of hair behind my shoulder as if I hadn't a care in the world. "That's what I said."

"Prescott College."

And he could read my T-shirt, too. Big deal.

"Hails from Cleveland, Ohio. Daughter of Carl, an accountant with Simpson Associates, and Mardie, a housewife and former Montessori school teacher. Literature major. Scheduled to begin an editorial internship at Horton Press in Manhattan on June 12."

There seemed to be a sudden blockage in my throat and I fought the urge to swallow convulsively. *Ignore him. It's the stupid Diggers trick. Blah blah blah files on me. Whatever.*

But... my parents' names, my internship start date... Poe had said they'd go after me....

"Nice plan," he sneered. "Good luck with *your* career."

Malcolm had to hold me back.

A scream rose within my chest and somehow, I managed to keep my mouth shut, though I could feel my lungs constrict with the effort of holding it in. *You wouldn't dare!* I thought, staring at the man so intently that even my non-existent powers of telepathy couldn't fail in getting the point across. I'd never once looked at an adult with more concentrated animosity, but then again, I'd never before been in a situation where one had threatened me. No, they usually tried to help me—teach me something, write me recommendations, give me a summer job, tell me how impressed they were with my prodigious achievements and how excited they were to see what I'd be making of my future.

The guy seemed to be intimating he'd like to make sure that I didn't have one.

I couldn't breathe.

And then the cavalry arrived, in the form of the other new taps. Demetria led the charge, followed by half a dozen others. I even saw Jennifer, though George Harrison Prescott was not around.

"No!" Malcolm said. "This is a private interview."

"Right," Demetria said. She puffed her chest out at the head patriarch. "Gonna screw with all of us, dipshit?"

"Let's *go*," Malcolm bellowed. He herded us up and moved us past the shield and the crowd. I saw a few familiar faces at the edge of the rabble. Senior Diggers, waiting in the wings. Malcolm nodded to one as he passed. "Get him," he said, and I had no doubt who it was he meant. "My room. Powwow."

The words galvanized me, and I found my voice at last. Malcolm dragged me away as I raised my fist at the patriarch to deliver a parting shot. "And, by the way, I don't live *in* Cleveland. I'm a suburbs girl. Shaker Heights. Get your facts straight, sucker."

"Amy!" said Malcolm. *"Discretion."*

*I hereby confess:
It did shake me up.*

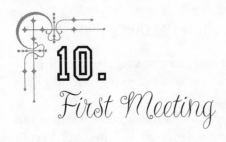

10.
First Meeting

Malcolm hustled us away from the crowd and straight into the side entrance of Calvin College. He handed his set of keys to Greg. "Fourth floor, entryway J. I'll wait for the others."

I leaned heavily against the granite wall. Whatever rush of adrenaline had kept me upright for the last few minutes in front of the tomb had finally worn off. "Are we going to try to get in the back way?"

"What back way?" Malcolm blinked at me.

I waved vaguely toward the wall that separated Calvin College from the Rose & Grave property. "The back way into the tomb. The secret tunnel that the President uses during his clandestine visits."

Malcolm snorted. "Right. Whatever. Not the time for jokes, Amy."

There was no secret back entrance? God, weren't any of the things I'd heard about this society true? Let's see, they weren't always secret, they weren't about to gift me with a million dollars, and they weren't hiding Nazi gold. So, what exactly *were* those idiots protecting with their Y chromosomes? A bunch of decades-old petty thefts from the medical school's skeleton collection?

Still, that ass back there had seemed so...so *sure* of himself. Like he was more than capable of carrying out all of his threats. My legs began to feel a bit weak.

As the Diggers trickled in, Malcolm directed them up to his room. I stood against the weathered granite wall, trying to catch my breath, but my body refused to cooperate. I may not have let the patriarchs see me sweat, but to look at me now, you'd think I was busy making up for it. I tried to chill out, to think of anything but the cold looks I'd received from the men in the human shield. *Okay, Amy, think of...grammar. Foreign grammar.* After a few moments, Malcolm turned in my direction.

"You okay?"

I shrugged. "Sure. What, you think that guy bothered me?" As soon as he turned back to the gate, I held up my hand. It was trembling.

I clamped it into a fist and resumed conjugating irregular Spanish verbs. (Every Lit major has to take a year of literature in a foreign language. Because I'd had a head start in Spanish, I spent a few semesters misunderstanding Borges and Allende. The French people got to breeze through *The Little Prince.* What a gyp.)

Okay, snap out of it, Amy. Tengo, tienes, tiene. Tenemos, teneis, tienen. *If there's one thing I've learned since joining Rose & Grave, it's that half the crap I've heard about it isn't true.* Tuve, tuvisto, tuvo. Tuvimos, tuvisteis, tuvieron. *He's an old man playing a stupid trick.* Tendre, tendras, tendra. Tendremos, tendreis, tendran. *He can't do a thing to me.*

I will have, you will have, he, she, or it will have....

Tapping you has fucked up my life.

Then again, maybe I should reserve final judgment until I

heard what the senior knights of Rose & Grave have to say about the matter.

Malcolm was back to the cell phone, contacting, I assumed, anyone who'd managed to miss our little showdown. I watched him punch out a few urgent text messages.

RG 911. CC 4 J NOW.

"That's the best I can do for now," Malcom said at last, snapping his phone shut. "Come on, Amy. Let's join the others. We'll wait for everybody else upstairs."

"Malcolm," I said, and my voice had, without my permission, gone rather soft and squeaky. "That guy—"

"Is a world-class dick," Malcom said. "And no matter what he says, they don't have the power to kick us out, or do anything else. It's all hot air. But let's not talk about it here, okay? Come on, upstairs."

I followed him into entryway J and we started up the stairs. On the second floor, a suite door opened and the girl with the long brown braid whom I'd first seen when I left Malcolm's room yesterday looked out at us. I imagined she was curious about the rush hour that had so recently passed on the staircase, but she just looked from me to Malcolm, and her eyes narrowed.

With a good look at her, I realized who the girl was. Genevieve Grady, a fellow junior and the *EDN*'s current editor-in-chief. I was surprised that she was even home; the EIC of the school's daily newspaper was a forty-hour-a-week job, whereas mine was relatively cushy—maybe fourteen a month, until we got to publication crunch time. I hadn't seen Genevieve much at all this year, or even last year, which she'd spent churning out stories and networking at a rate carefully calculated to earn her the coveted position.

Perhaps, I wondered, she'd consent to write the foreword to the "Ambition" issue.

"Back for more, huh, Haskel?" she hissed. "That's a new one on the fourth floor."

Malcolm gave her a glance of stone-cold disdain, and ushered me up another flight.

"What's her problem?" I asked.

Malcolm shrugged. "She's a bitch. I imagine that knowledge keeps her in a bad mood most of the time."

He knocked thrice, once, then twice at his own door and it opened to reveal a room in which every flat surface was covered with the behind of a Digger. They clustered on the bed, the futon, the desk, the dresser, and when perches gave out, the floor. I watched Clarissa trying to manipulate her minuscule bottom into an even tinier area of space, and then she waved me over. "Amy, I saved you a seat."

A quick scan of the room showed it was my only option, so I took it, wondering inwardly why Clarissa seemed so damned determined to buddy up at every opportunity. Had I passed some sort of test? I was a Digger, and therefore deemed an acceptable companion in her estimation?

Of course. Ever since I'd been tapped, people had been treating me differently. The workaday Amy Haskel didn't spend her Saturday nights flirting with George Harrison Prescott, wasn't on Clarissa Cuthbert's radar, and didn't hold sleepovers with the likes of Malcolm Cabot—even if there was no sex involved. She didn't engage in shouting matches with distinguished-looking, silver-haired gentlemen who threatened to ruin her life, nor cause older and wiser friends like Glenda Foster to get nervous in her presence.

Some of Rose & Grave's power might be little more than perception, but perception alone seemed to lend quite a bit of clout.

And I still didn't realize how much that meant.

"I don't think we should wait for the others," Malcolm said. "Let's come to order."

The seniors mobilized. Seemingly from nowhere, long black swaths of fabric materialized, and the boys scurried about the room, enshrouding the windows, covering the air vents, and stuffing up the cracks in the door. Soundproofing, though if anyone really wanted to listen in, I doubted that a few pieces of felt would do the trick. Still, in the absence of a real tomb, Diggers couldn't be choosers.

An apartment over Starbucks, however, might have been preferable. I considered Glenda's ubiquitous venti lattes. Did she get special treatment over there because she belonged to the society upstairs? Rose & Grave hadn't even given me a gift card to Cosí.

One of the seniors shrugged. "My turn for Uncle Tony?"

The others nodded and Malcolm grimaced. "Some introduction to the taps, huh?"

"Uncle Tony" picked a paperweight off of Malcolm's desk and rapped it thrice, once, and twice on the desk. "The time is . . . III and 30 minutes, Diggers-time. I call to order this . . ." He looked up. "What meeting is this?" Some of the seniors shrugged.

There was a pattern of three-one-two knocks on the door. Malcolm opened it to reveal Poe, who was scowling and towing along an even more petulant George Harrison Prescott. At once, my heart leapt and sank.

"Seven thousand, one hundred, and twelfth," Poe announced. "Nice soundproofing, by the way." Poe pushed George into the room. "Take a seat, kid."

George plopped down next to Jenny Santos, who made a face and scooted away from him, and he grinned as if he'd just gotten away with something particularly naughty.

The seniors had gone back to padding the entrances to the room, and one was now stuffing throw pillows into the air ducts. When they were satisfied that we'd really blocked out the sound, the one playing "Uncle Tony," the rotating parliamentary head, started up again.

"In the name of Persephone, Keeper of the Flame of Life and the Shadow of Death...I, um, call to order the Knights...." He trailed off, a sheepish shrug in place. "Sorry. I'm helpless without the Black Book."

Another senior waved his hand in dismissal. "Whatever. *Omnis vincit mors, nos cedamus nemini.* Let's get on with it."

Poe practically growled in disapproval. "This is precisely the problem. Our club has been entirely too lax with the traditions of the society, and now we're paying the price for it."

Personally, I couldn't see Poe being relaxed about anything. The colonic flexibility required was beyond his bass-ackwards, chauvinistic sensibilities.

"If you want to Tony, have at it," the senior snapped.

Apparently, one didn't need to ask Poe twice. He stood, cleared his throat, faced the circle, and started to reach for something on his shoulders, almost by reflex.

His non-existent hood. I met Malcolm's eyes and erupted into barely contained giggles. By the time I'd regained control of myself (which involved a lot of red-faced swallowing and four fake coughs), Poe had completed the calling-to-order ritual, which I will not deign to repeat here. If you're looking for the gist, refer to the Initiation chapter of this volume. Suffice it to say that, particularly in the mouth of Poe, it was overlong, needlessly pretentious, relied heavily on Latin-esque gibberish, and possessed far more than its fair share of capital letters. No wonder the rest of the senior knights hadn't bothered memorizing it!

"Okay, we all know what we're here to talk about," began

Malcolm—or, as I suppose I should be calling him now that we were in session, Lancelot.

"Yeah," said my classmate Graverobber, the Greek shipping heir with the unwieldy street handle of Nikolos Dmitri Kandes IV. "Why you never warned us this might happen."

"Basically," said another senior, "the board of the Tobias Trust said that if we initiated women, they'd kick us *all* out. By locking the tomb and speaking to us like barbarians, they've made it clear they've followed through."

"That's outrageous!" Thorndike (Demetria) shouted loud enough to be heard through even the soundproofing. Everyone winced, but I thought it was a predictable reaction from her. Wait until she heard the guy standing at the center of the circle was all for it. He'd be lucky to escape with his genitals intact.

"You bet it is," Graverobber replied. "It's all very well for you, but as I am neither a woman nor a member of the class that tapped them, I am left to question why and whether I should be punished along with the rest."

Naturally, all hell proceeded to break loose.

"We stand together or we fall apart!" Bond, the Englishman Greg Dorian, stated firmly.

"But does it follow that we stand together *in favor* of the females?"

Angel (Clarissa), beside me, gasped, but didn't tag in, either. (You might be wondering why I, never one to keep my comments to myself, wasn't speaking up here. Frankly, I couldn't get a word in edgewise. These people are future professional speakers. Editors—even chatty, outspoken ones—don't have a chance.)

"These girls are our brothers," Keyser Soze argued. (Yay, Josh!)

"For forty-eight hours," Graverobber replied. "And if the

alternative is losing my affiliation, I say *they* should do what's right for *us*, and hit the road."

"Would you kindly desist speaking of me as if I weren't sitting on your lap?" Lil' Demon shot fiery glares at Graverobber from her perch on—well, if not his lap, then damn close.

"It's not you, my dear, it's your entire sex."

Thorndike now visibly trembled with rage, and I figured the Eurotrash Graverobber was lucky she'd have to get past Lil' Demon in order to unleash her fury.

"Look." Soze spread his arms and calm prevailed. (I told you this man could get shit done!) "I want to get a better understanding of what exactly our rights are as opposed to those of the TTA board. It stands to reason that the current club ought to have a fair bit of control over the day-to-day running of the society. Are there specific bylaws or compacts that prohibit the tapping of women?"

"It wasn't thought necessary by the founders." Poe sounded as if he were chewing each word. Bet he thought it would have been a good idea! "And yes, we ought to have sovereignty in our choice of taps, but the Trust holds our purse strings, and by extension, controls everything we do. They own the land, the tomb . . . they pay for all of our benefits."

"And your class has no representation on the board?" Soze asked.

"We do," Poe said. "It's me."

Hooray, we're screwed.

But Soze, always the strategist, didn't miss a beat. "And, um, other avenues?" When Poe understandably failed to respond, he braved on. "Forgive the questions, but I think all of the juniors here feel like we've been thrown into the deep end."

And are drowning in it.

"I want to get a big picture here about what they are trying to do and why they think they have the right to do it. And if they don't, then I think it's a simple matter of bringing the bylaws up for consideration to—"

"To what?" said Lancelot. "The courts? Forget it, pal. That's why we call it a *secret* society. We won't do court cases, where we risk our inner workings becoming public record. We're not a fraternity with a Hellenic organization to turn to in the matter of disputes. Private club. Not subject to any anti-discrimination laws. We don't really have a case."

"You don't need one," Lucky said, shocking the hell out of everyone. "Just the threat of going public might scare your board into backing off."

"P-public?" a senior spluttered. "Are you insane? Do you even know who we are?"

"Better than you think."

"Lady's a shark!" Puck exclaimed, impressed. "Right for the balls." Lucky shot him a withering glance, folded her arms, and sat back in her seat.

"Before we get into all of that," said a new tap whose real name I didn't even know (found out later he was Omar Mathabane, a.k.a. Kismet, the first-ever Diggers tap to hail from the continent of Africa). "I'm interested to see where everyone in this room stands on this issue. *Are* we for the inclusion of women?"

"You're asking *us*?" Demetria hissed, making a fist with one hand and gesturing wildly at the five women in the room. "You're in the country for what, five seconds? And you're all set to join the Establishment!"

The tall basketball player, Big Demon (Benjamin Edwards, for those of you playing the Who's-Who-in-Rose-&-Grave Game), cleared his throat and spoke softly. "At the risk of offending the women and the seniors, I think Graverobber has a point that should be considered, regardless of everything else. The men in D177 did not commit either offense. We didn't tap

women, and we're not women. So, for the purpose of argument, what is the patriarchs' problem with us?"

"Enough!" Lil' Demon detached herself from her ques-
tionable perch and took the floor. "Oh, yes, Kismet, let's vote."
(That Odile managed to keep all the code names straight while
I was lucky to remember half of them convinced me once and
for all that she deserved that Eli diploma.) "Let's find out
where everyone here stands before you all set to talking about
my future. I've had about enough of being talked around and
talked about by men. I spent five years being 'handled'—by my
agent, my stupid father, my record label—and I am so done
with letting any *man* tell me what to do!"

That shut up even Thorndike. Puck seemed to look at
Lil' Demon with newfound appreciation, and I took a deep
breath.

"The way I see it," I said before I could stop myself, "we
have four distinct issues to solve before we can even get a plan
together." I began ticking them off on my fingers:

1) "Have we broken any of the society bylaws?" I
   looked to Poe for confirmation. "Apparently not."
2) "Assuming we have not, what are our rights as active
   members, versus the board's control over the financial aspects of the society?"
3) "On the off chance that they do have a grievance
   against us, what can we do to mitigate the situation
   with the male taps?"
4) I took a deep breath. "And finally, do you guys still
   want the women around at all?"

"Yes," Lancelot said without hesitation. Poe just looked at me
with clear gray eyes. The other seniors were a mess of nods and
thoughtful expressions. Not encouraging.

"Perhaps we should take a vote?" Frodo suggested.

"The problem with that is, they already voted." I said. "They voted the day they agreed to tap us. We're tapped. We're initiated. It's too late. The actions the senior club performed are irrevocable, and that's why the patriarchs waited until now to act. They thought the seniors would come to their senses before this."

"Since when are you such an expert?" Angel asked, finding her tongue at last.

"I'm a quick study." I looked at Poe, who was doing his best to channel Medusa. "And one thing I've learned is that your tapping decisions have to be unanimous. Is the same true for your decision to kick someone out?"

"Yes," Poe grumbled.

"Then I think it's safe to assume that the women aren't going anywhere."

"Woo-hoo!" Angel said softly, pumping her fist in the air. I smiled at her. Yes, I really did. Nothing like a little camaraderie when you learn you have an even bigger enemy out there.

Poe sat back in his seat and folded his arms. "What Bugaboo said isn't entirely accurate."

I turned on him, incredulous. "You told me so, not an hour ago."

Again with the deadpan. This man could give lessons to Bob Newhart. "I did nothing of the sort."

I looked to Lancelot for assistance, but he just appeared confused. All at once, I understood. Poe was so steeped in society mores that the others could afford to be lazy and let him take charge of all the old-fashioned rigmarole. And because they didn't know any better, he was free to manipulate the rules to suit his own agenda.

How in the world had they ever gotten women past him in the first place?

Angel, in the meantime, had skulked back off my soapbox. "Sit down," she whispered, tugging on my sleeve. "He knows a lot more about what's going on in here than you do. You'll end up sounding silly."

I shook her off. "Then maybe he should enlighten us. After all, they're turning the society over to us in a couple of weeks."

"Not you," Poe snapped. "Never really *you*." He cocked his head toward a few of the junior men. "*Them*."

And that was the moment I witnessed some sort of freaky, sci-fi movie of the week telepathy mind trick miracle, as all five women in the room thought the exact same thing. And that thing was: I'm *so* outta here.

In unison we gasped, in unison we stood, and in unison the first female members of Rose & Grave in almost two hundred years turned and walked right out the door.

———

We hit the street fuming.

"I can't believe—those—fucking assholes—who do they think they—*when* do they think they are?" Demetria was choking on her own indignation.

Odile tossed her head. "I'd say about 1831."

Jenny snorted. "Oh, come on, ladies. You really think feminism *won*?"

Clarissa shushed us. "Not in the street, guys. Remember what Malcolm said about discretion."

"Um, were you in the same meeting as the rest of us, *Angel*?" Demetria pointed at the fourth floor. "We're out. If we were ever in."

"Which is debatable," I added, feeling that funny constriction in my chest again. How would I ever face Lydia after all our drama if it turned out that my oh-so-special Rose & Grave tap crashed and burned?

"What is the benefit of keeping quiet now?" Demetria asked. She raised her voice until it echoed around the stone courtyard of Calvin College. "I was a Digger and they done me wrong!"

Clarissa and I tackled her, while Jenny looked on calmly. "The first step is confessing," she said with a wry smile.

"And the next is getting wasted." Odile grabbed me with one hand and Jenny with the other. "Let's go."

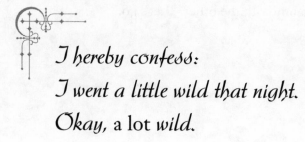

I hereby confess:
I went a little wild that night.
Okay, a lot *wild.*

11.
Powwow

Clarissa steered us away from the nightclub Odile had chosen, into a smaller, more classic Eli bar. It enjoyed a reasonably healthy crowd of Sunday evening drinkers, but not so many that our group couldn't find a nice, out-of-the-way table at which to commiserate. (See? I knew I could come up with a better use for that word!) The bar was split-level, with tables above, and a bar, dance floor, and stage below. We headed up to the top level, where the five of us squeezed into a brown leather booth. I found myself shoved between Demetria and Jennifer, who, with arms folded and a look of supreme disgust on her face, seemed to harbor a desire to be anywhere other than in a pub with the "Brotherhood of Death."

Or Sisterhood of Death, as the case may be.

Curiously, Odile and Clarissa, though thinner than all three of us, seemed to fill the other side of the booth to capacity as well. Must be leaving room for their egos.

"First things first," Demetria announced. "Let's get some alcohol into Madame Tightass over here."

"I don't drink," Jennifer responded, obviously in no doubt as to whom Demetria referred.

"Why ever not?"

"Well, to start with, it's illegal. I'm only twenty."

I ruminated on whether that made her holier-than-thou genius more or less tolerable.

"Never stopped me breaking into Daddy's bourbon," said Clarissa, signaling the barkeep from the lower level.

"Nor me," said Odile. "But then, but the time I was seventeen, I'd already had a stint in rehab. What meth didn't do to me, Miller Lite won't."

"Miller Lite?" I shook my head. "I need something stronger than that tonight."

Clarissa grinned. "You bet." As the barman approached, she laid three twenties on the table. "This is what I want," she said, looking him carefully in the eye and twiddling with something at her collar. "You got pomegranate juice?"

He looked at the money, then at us. "Who are you girls?"

"We're who you think we are," she said simply. "312. Five of them. Straight up, please, and with a twist."

We all stared at her, openmouthed, as the barkeep rushed—actually, jogged—away down the steps.

"How did you know?" I asked.

She smiled again and I noted that the thing on her collar was her Rose & Grave pin. "Membership, girls, has its privileges. And so does legacy. This was my daddy's favorite bar when he was a Knight of D143. Stands to reason that they'd have the society drink."

Now Demetria looked smug. "Fake it till you make it? Is that your strategy?"

"No," said Clarissa. "But I do intend on enjoying the rights I've earned. Like Amy said, we're full-fledged members of Rose & Grave, whether they like it or not. I, for one, am going to act like it."

"Does that include terrorizing bartenders?" I asked.

She fluffed her hair. "That was a simple request, honey. I'd only untuck the terror if we were denied." She settled back in her seat, then tilted her head to the side, studying Demetria as if seeing her for the first time. "You know, Demetria, I never noticed this before in your baggy shirts, but you've got a great rack. Have you ever thought about losing the kente cloth and going for something in a deep V-neck knit? I'm thinking coral, or maybe even peach, with your skin tone. I've got this sweater from BCBG—"

Demetria blinked at her and even Jenny looked shocked. "Let's focus on the issue at hand. Making sure we keep getting the privileges of membership."

"Yes, but do we even want to be members of Rose & Grave anymore?" I fingered the pin on the strap of my bag. Was it only two days ago that I'd received it? Already it seemed to belong to me. "They made it pretty clear that hardly any of them want us there."

"I don't care what they want," Demetria said. "I already heard way too much about that. I'd rather hear about us. I want to know why each of you joined. I think that if we still believe the society can fulfill the reasons we first accepted the tap, then we should fight. If not—"

"Bail?" asked Odile.

Demetria nodded, and since it sounded like a decent plan, we all agreed. Demetria went first. "To me, it was a question of changing society from the inside. There's a certain amount you're going to listen to some black dyke from Pittsburgh, and then there's the amount you'll listen to her if she's waving an Eli diploma in your face, and then, on top of that, there's the amount you'll listen—"

"If she's got a phalanx of powerful Diggers backing her up?" I cut in.

"You got it, sister."

"Do you really think that old-boys' network will back you up, Digger or no?"

Here's where Demetria started looking sheepish. "Not anymore. I'd hoped being tapped meant they were willing to listen to someone like me. Apparently, what it really meant is that they hoped they could make someone like me listen to them."

To my left, Jennifer shuddered.

The drinks arrived in tall, frosted martini glasses and Clarissa slid them along the table. "Just take a sip, Jenny," she instructed.

Odile tasted the concoction, then smiled in appreciation at her seatmate. "Well, I can't say I had any explicit motive for joining like you did, Dee. To me, it's one more exclusive party. If I'm a Digger, I'm a VIP to that many more people." Her tone was completely unapologetic, and so sincere I wasn't even sure if I could feel offended.

Clarissa blinked at her, shocked, I was sure, at being out-snobbed. She turned to the other side of the table. "I'm a legacy," she said. "Of course I was going to join if given the op-portunity. It would be like not attending Eli. I'm a Cuthbert. We're Diggers. Period."

Jennifer traced the rim of her glass, then dipped her pinky in the liquor and sucked on it before responding. "Same as Demetria, I guess. Change the Diggers from the inside out." She looked at me as if satisfied she'd provided a good enough answer. "And you, Amy?"

They all leaned forward. "Yes, what about you?" someone else asked.

Whence the curiosity? My reasons—such as they were—were no better than the rest of theirs, and "My friend-with-benefits told me to stop thinking so hard" didn't seem like particularly strong motivation. I shrugged. "It seemed the right thing to do. It's"—my voice dropped to a whisper—"the most powerful society on campus…in the country. Networking galore. Um, are we sure this place isn't bugged?"

"Bugged?" Clarissa asked. "By whom? The special Digger police you were talking about earlier?"

Don't tell me—another conspiracy theory. "Can someone please provide me with a list of what about Rose & Grave is true and what is false?"

Clarissa laughed. "The second I get one, I'll share it. But you have a point. The walls have ears. Malcolm would be telling us—"

"Discretion!" we all said in unison, lifting our glasses and laughing. I stared down at the 312. It looked like a cosmopolitan that had spent too much time listening to death metal. The bubblegum pink coloration had turned bloodred and almost opaque. I could hardly see the spiral of lemon zest at the bottom. I tasted it. Tart beyond the telling, with a kick of sweetness at the backside that couldn't have been simple syrup. I couldn't detect the alcohol at all. It didn't taste precisely like the "blood" I'd drunk at initiation, but I imagined that for the Digger hoping for a little kick in the faith, it would serve as a reasonable reminder.

"Do you know what they put in this?" I asked Clarissa.

She winked at me. "It's a secret."

Everyone rolled their eyes. I glanced over at Jennifer, who seemed to be making inroads into hers despite her protestations. "So you and Demetria seem to be the only ones with real reasons to be members," I said. "Do you still want to be?"

"My resolve remains as firm as always." Jennifer took another sip.

"My reason doesn't strike you as valid?" Clarissa asked.

"No more than mine does," I replied. "And let's not even talk about Odile."

Odile polished off her drink. "It works for me, which makes it perfectly good. We don't need to get as noble as these two chicks. If we want to be in the"—she lowered her voice— "*thingamajig* for selfish reasons, then who's to tell us we can't? Doesn't mean they won't benefit from the association as well. They help us along, we'll be the best little members they can ask for. That's my philosophy anyway."

And it was tough to have a problem with that.

"Yes. Who cares why we joined?" Clarissa said. "The point is, if we were tapped, then we obviously deserved it, and we should get the rights and privileges associated with it, no matter what kind of genitalia we have. If Odile wants to join merely to get lobster for dinner every Thursday night, then that's her business. Not theirs. What the—*thingamajigs*—get out of it is having the great Odile Dumas as a member."

"And that's pretty freakin' cool," said Odile, signaling the bartender for another 312.

Demetria rolled her eyes.

But I couldn't be so flippant. It was pretty cool. They were lucky to have Odile Dumas as part of their in-crowd. It definitely gave the old-boys' network some 21st century Hollywood cred. And Demetria, who, one step at a time, was going to change the world. I definitely couldn't imagine a cogent argument against Clarissa. Not only was she a legacy, but as soon as she was back on the New York socialite scene, she'd practically run the city. And Jennifer Santos would be the next Bill Gates. That left only . . . me.

Where did Amy Haskel come in?

Clarissa's phone—well, it went off, since "rang" is probably not the appropriate term for the bubbly sound effects issuing from her cell.

She glanced at the display. "Uh-oh, girls, it's George."

Okay, I admit it: pulse sped.

She flipped down the mouthpiece and carried on a quick

conversation. Five minutes later, the rest of the junior taps arrived.

"We've been looking for you everywhere," said George, shoving into the Odile-Clarissa side of the table and winking at me. "The meeting kind of broke up the second you left."

"But I see you didn't leave with us," snapped Demetria, reluctantly scooting over to let Josh and Greg pile in. Kevin took the remaining seat next to George (really not a lot of space on that side) and Benjamin the basketball player (Big Demon, like Little Demon, was a name given to a tap of a particular size) pulled up an end table and a few chairs for himself, Omar, and a very disgruntled-looking Nikolos (a.k.a. Graverobber).

"Well, at first we were all in shock," Benjamin said, settling in and waving at the bartender. "Though not as badly as the seniors. I don't think anyone had ever just walked out of a—"

"*Thingamajig!*" the girls all yelled.

"—meeting before. Nobody knew what to do."

"So we all just sat there, staring at one another," Kevin added.

"Until we realized that we wanted to cast our lot with you all," finished Greg. "Where are the bloody drinks?"

Bloody was right. I slid over the rest of mine and he knocked it back.

"He wanted to 'cast his lot with us,' too?" I asked skeptically, pointing at Nikolos.

The men were saved from answering when the bartender arrived, looking scandalized. He did a quick head count. "Where are the other three?" he asked.

"Abroad." Clarissa handed over a credit card. "Start a tab."

"They know us here?" Josh asked.

"Oh, honey," said Clarissa. "We've even got an official *drink*."

Several hours and at least five rounds of 312s later (perhaps we should have moved to pitchers), the dozen new taps at the table were in possession of darkly stained lips and had proceeded to hammer out a plan of action.

"What I still don't get," Kevin, one of the few naysayers left in the group, said, "is why this is our responsibility rather than the seniors'."

"They're short-timers," Demetria explained. "In a few weeks, they're out of here and the closed tomb will be our problem. It doesn't matter so much to them."

"It does if the patriarchs carry through with their threat," I said. "I heard that guy talk to Malcolm this afternoon. He said they were going to ruin his career." And mine.

Clarissa snorted. "I'd like to see them try. That man is a governor's son. He's plenty well connected without the help of—*thingamajig*. Besides, you really think the patriarchs want to make themselves an enemy like that?"

"They've got plenty of allies without the likes of Governor Cabot," I said, thinking of my pillow talk with Malcolm and his stories of his father's prejudice. To be honest, Malcolm probably *did* need the help of the Diggers if his dad was the only alternative.

And Poe's words wouldn't leave me. *I have a resume to update. If I were you, I'd do the same.* Poe might be a jerk, but he was a smart jerk, and seemed to know more about the Diggers than anyone else. Why shouldn't I trust what he said?

But when I shared my fears with the rest of the group, they just laughed.

"They aren't Big Brother, Amy," Clarissa said. To her credit, Clarissa hadn't made one remark that might be construed to be within the vein of *slumming* all evening. Then again, maybe I was no longer persona non grata now that I had crossed the ranks into Digger. Still, chick was growing on me.

Add it to the list of things I would not be telling Lydia.

"That's not what I'd always heard," I said.

"That's not what you're supposed to hear," said Josh. "Half of the power comes from the mystique. You're told that, um—*thingamajig*—owns half the city, and you look in awe upon any twenty-one-year-old who has managed to join the ranks."

"But what about the Presidents? Why are they always members?"

"Always, or occasionally?" Josh smiled. "Remember, we're culled from the best and brightest at Eli."

"Supposedly," Nikolos added in a growl.

"Why wouldn't some of those people end up being leaders? That's why they were chosen." I sensed a certain personal bias in his tone. "It stands to reason that if there are budding leaders here, the society will sniff them out. But the country's not fixing the vote."

Demetria snorted. "I've seen some stuff that would make you think otherwise."

Josh turned to her. "You and I are going to have to have a conversation about how the electoral college works."

"Later!" cut in Odile. "Right now, we're talking about the patriarchs."

And on it went. We'd move a bit farther into the realm of "getting somewhere," only to be sidetracked by personal differences and petty squabbles. I still wasn't sure we'd sold either Nikolos or Omar on the idea of fighting back, and even Benjamin looked like he could go either way. Nikolos appeared to be remaining with the group only under duress, Omar watched the entire proceedings in stony silence, and Benjamin seemed as if he was waiting to see where the chips landed before making a choice.

George, it should be noted, played footsie with me under the table.

Which wasn't to say he was devoid of input. In fact, it was George who first came up with the idea of approaching the patriarchs on their own turf.

"Where does the board of trustees meet?" he asked, twirling his glass on the tabletop.

"New York Thity," Clarissa said through a mouthful of nachos. (We'd decided to eat. I was pleased to see that the rail-thin Clarissa in fact did.)

"Then let's set up a meeting with them. A real one. Not running up to them in the street in the middle of their demonstration like a couple of schoolkids. They're businessmen. We'll treat them like that. Boardroom, coffee urns, and all."

I excused myself to go to the restroom. A couple of schoolkids? Is that what Malcolm and I had looked like this afternoon? No wonder they'd dismissed us so easily.

In the bathroom, I spent a long time looking in the cracked, rusted-out mirror above the sink. There was probably a line forming outside, but I didn't care. Who was I kidding, in conference with these other Diggers? I was chock-full of outsider conspiracy theories that were beginning to sound increasingly ridiculous every time I uttered them in the company of people who actually had a clue what they were talking about. Line up all of them, all of their astounding accomplishments, and then look at me. What did I have to offer next to these superstars? I belonged in Quill & Ink, not Rose & Grave. If the patriarchs had an argument to make against the female taps, the weakest link to attack was . . . me.

The door burst open, revealing a gang of drunken sophomores. "Omigod," said one, rushing in. "I gotta pee so bad!"

I barely made it out of the way.

Back in the narrow, dark corridor that sloped upward to the split-level body of the bar above, I paused. Maybe I should call it a night. I wasn't adding anything of substance to the proceedings, and I doubted my presence would help them achieve a moment of brilliance. At the phone booth, I stepped up on the stool and peered over the split level through the railing at the booth where the other new taps sat. Josh and Demetria were in a heated debate about something, Benjamin was tapping his feet impatiently on the floorboards (got a perfect view of that from my vantage point), and Odile and Nikolos appeared to be in the midst of a discussion decidedly not about the society—unless there was important Digger lore to be found in her cleavage.

"Hey, boo," said a voice behind me. "What are you doing?"

I started and nearly tottered off the stool. George steadied me with hands on my thighs.

"Careful there," he said as I stepped down onto shaky legs, mindful of the four and a half 312s I'd consumed.

"You shouldn't be using that name," I said, trying to catch my breath and failing. Wasted effort with George Harrison Prescott around. "Not outside the confines of a society function. I'm afraid I'm going to have to fine you two dollars."

"What name?" He stepped a little closer, pinning me between the phone booth and his body.

"You know. My society name."

"Oh," he said softly. "That's not what I said."

"What did you say?" I tilted my chin up in defiance.

"Boo." His eyes glinted copper behind those glasses. "Just 'boo.' It means sweetie, honey, my girl. It's a hip-hop endearment."

I swallowed. *My girl? Play it cool, Amy.* "You're not hip-hop."

"My darling boo," he said, "I'm so very, very hip-hop."

And though I'd been imagining this moment for quite some time, the only thing I could think of as he kissed me was that the Yellow Pages were jabbing me in the spine.

And then, as if he knew it, he slipped his arms around my back and cradled me against him in a manner that chased all thoughts of telephone directories and patriarch battles right out of my head. Oh, yes, the man was hip-hop. "Player" was the term I was looking for, but my mouth was too busy to form the word.

There was a whole mess of reasons I shouldn't have been doing this, but for the life of me they were hard to recall with George Harrison Prescott's tongue in my mouth. He tasted like pomegranate juice and—I finally recognized the other ingredient. Honey.

Okay, Amy, focus. You had a list. What was it?

WHY YOU SHOULDN'T MAKE OUT WITH GEORGE HARRISON PRESCOTT

1) Oh, boy, are you in public right now.
2) George has a list of female conquests as long as the phone book he's protecting you from.
3) I didn't want to have to remind you of this, but you do have a rather unfortunate history with one-night stands.
4) Have you forgotten entirely about a very sweet young man named Brandon?
5) He's now in the same society as— Oh my God, he has his hand up my shirt!

One flick of the wrist and my bra snapped open. In the hallway. Surrounded by drunken sophomores who'd be sure to tattle it around and a few feet away from a whole table full of fellow Diggers. Who knew what would happen if they saw us making out like a couple of—

"Schoolkids," I whispered, pulling away.

"What?" George looked at me, pupils dilated, stained lips wet and inviting.

"You said I acted like a schoolkid when I confronted the patriarchs this afternoon."

He laughed. "That was you? I didn't know. I wasn't there, just heard about it later."

I remembered when he'd shown up at the meeting. He'd probably had his report from Poe. The jerk. Figures we wouldn't have come off in glowing terms.

George traced his hand down my back. "Oh, Amy, that takes balls. Very sexy."

"Balls are sexy?"

"Women who act like they've got them are." He leaned in again, but I stopped him.

"George, what about the meeting?"

"Pretty much over. We're going to New York next Friday to present our case to the patriarchs. Josh et al. are setting up the parley. Benjamin is getting a van."

"And the seniors?"

"We decided to present ourselves as full-fledged Diggers, not the newbie taps who need seniors to babysit us."

That made sense. "Amazing that everything came together the second I left for the bathroom," I said ruefully. See? They didn't need me.

"Why do you think I came to find you? It's no fun up there without you."

"Right, because I'm the joke."

He looked puzzled. "Hardly. You knew everything about the backstory today, understood the whole argument, even before we did. The seven of us are here tonight because we don't want you girls to be second-class citizens. Come on, boo. We need you there, too. You're going to write our manifesto. You're the writer in the club after all."

This time when he tried to kiss me, I let him. Right. The writer of D177. What were a few mistaken beliefs in overblown Digger mythology compared to that?

His whole body was pressed against mine, squishing me into the phone booth. He was standing between my legs, and there were all sorts of things happening below the waist that had no business happening in a bar, even on relatively non-crowded Sunday nights.

Apparently, George thought so, too. "Let's get out of here." His voice was little more than a warm breath in my ear. I nodded and stumbled after him.

"The bill?"

"I think between the heir to Greece, Madame Hollywood, and Miss Park Ave., they've got it covered. We'll get it next time." He grabbed my hand. "Come on."

As the cool air on the street hit my face, my thoughts began to clear. What was I doing? I was leaving a bar with George Harrison Prescott. I was...going home with George Harrison Prescott. And my bra was open under my shirt.

We walked back and he swiped his ID card at the gate to Prescott College while I struggled to put my underclothes back together. My memory banks concocted an elaborate montage of wet-haired breakfast partners I'd seen George saunter into the dining hall with over the past three years. I did *not* want to be one of those chicks.

You don't have to be. Just go back to your room afterward and come down with Lydia.

No! That wasn't the point. I'd done the one-night-stand thing. I hated it. And that was with a stranger. This was George, a person who lived in my building. A person I'd have to see, if not every day, then at least twice a week at society meetings. Society incest. Bad idea.

At the door to my entryway, George started kissing me again. Lord, it was nice. Like a whole piggybank full of copper pennies and sex appeal.

"George." I hated myself at this moment. "I can't."

He took a breath, as if he'd been waiting for this. "Okay."

"Don't you want to know why?"

He stepped back, the smile and shrug slipping into position. "Nope. If it's me, I'm not in the mood to hear it, and if it's you, I'm not going to be the one who helps you figure it out. But, boo," he added, ducking behind me to refasten my bra as easily as he'd undone it at the bar, "I'm not going anywhere, and I like having you around. You know what I mean?"

I nodded, afraid to speak for fear I'd take it back. I pulled the bra down until my breasts popped back into the cups. George watched, clearly amused.

"You're really something else, Amy."

"So are you," I replied. "You act so differently with me than you do when you're with the other Diggers."

He laughed and put his finger to his lips. "Shhh. That's our secret."

And then he hopped down the stairs, strolled over to his entryway, and was gone. For a few seconds, I thought about hurrying after him and throwing myself into his arms, admitting that I'd made a terrible mistake.

I'm lucky I didn't.

Instead, I trudged up to my door, where I noticed that Lydia had cleaned off the last traces of dried whatever-it-was on the doorknob. Finally. And, just think: I had actual classes tomorrow afternoon. Actual reading to do. Actual—I don't know, schoolwork. At college. Imagine that.

Probably a very good thing I wasn't getting laid tonight.

I opened the door to my suite and stepped inside.

Brandon Weare sat on the sofa, his hands full of roses.

I hereby confess:
I am such a slut.

12.
Scandal Sheets

The moment I saw him, I knew exactly what I should say:

1) Brandon, go home. I can't do this tonight.
2) Oh, flowers! How sweet! Golly, I'm wiped. Can we chat tomorrow?
3) Brandon, because I like and respect you so much, I'm going to be honest. This isn't working out. Exhibit A: I've just spent the last half hour making out with another man.

Funny. I knew all of this, and yet the words that tumbled out of my mouth were, "How long have you been sitting here?" In my room? Holding flowers?

"About five minutes?" I saw the notebook in his lap. He was leaving me a message, not sitting around in my room, waiting for me to return. Duh.

"Where's Lydia?" I asked next.

"Not here." He looked at me. "It's Sunday night."

Of course. A time when all the normal society members were happily ensconced in their tombs.

"Come to think, what are you doing here?"

I decided to play coy. "Why wouldn't I be?"

"Oh, Amy..." He sighed, gave up, and held out the roses. "For you."

"Thanks." I gave them an obligatory sniff. Like all roses, the heady scent hit my noggin a full three seconds later. It's almost when you've given them up as merely pretty that a rose wallops you with its perfume.

"Your new favorite." Brandon winked.

I smiled sadly into the blooms. "Yeah, I guess. So, to what do I owe the pleasure?"

"It's an apology. For the way I treated you this morning at the office. I was rude."

"I deserved it." Out loud, too.

He shook his head. "No. Well, okay, maybe a little. But mostly—I'm actually glad you are here tonight, Amy. We need to talk."

"Tonight?" But...I have WAP reading. All of a sudden even Russian literature seemed preferable.

"This second."

Uh-oh. Had Glenda talked him into this? But even as I thought it, I knew I couldn't blame this on a conspiracy. I'd kept Brandon waiting for far too long.

But why had he chosen tonight of all nights to do something about it? Tonight, when I'd been *this* close to hooking up with someone else.

"Okay," I said slowly. "We'll talk."

But now that I'd acquiesced, Brandon seemed in no hurry to get to the point. He stood, stalked to the bookshelves across the common room, and ran his hand through his already shaggy brown hair. It was so very Brandon that I couldn't help but smile. He was so damn cute.

Almost instantly, a hot, horrible wash of guilt quenched that budding tenderness. Yep, cute enough to forget about and go make out with George.

"I'm not saying this isn't my fault, too, Amy," Brandon was saying, and I snapped back to attention.

That sounded promising. "You're not?"

"I mean, I think if I'd been clear from the beginning, we wouldn't have let things go down this ... amorphous path."

"Oh."

"Because that's not how I wanted it. Sure, you weren't ready on Valentine's Day, and I didn't want to push you, but now ..." He returned and sat beside me, pushing the roses aside and taking my hand in his. "After everything we've done together ... God, it's so ironic. Aren't guys supposed to be trying to talk girls into strings-free sexual relationships?"

"Well, times have changed," I said. "It's the 21st century." Although, try to explain that to a hundred years' worth of Diggers....

"But that's not what I want," Brandon went on, then hesitated. "Because ... I'm in love with you, Amy."

PEOPLE WHO HAVE TOLD ME THEY LOVE ME

1) My parents. Duh. Also assorted relatives.
2) Little Stevie Morris, in second grade.
3) Jacob Allbrecker, because you're supposed to say that to a girl when you take her virginity. (I said it, too, to be fair.)
4) Alan Albertson, right before he left for London.
5) Lydia, especially when I bring her late-night snacks.

From the above list, it's easy to discern that Brandon Weare is neither the first nor the most important person in my life who has used the L-word in reference to me. And yet, my familiarity with the concept mattered not one iota in that magical moment when another person comes out and admits that they favor you above anyone else in the world.

Because, let's face it, that's what love—*romantic love*—is, right? Liking that person best?

Here's where I wish I hadn't dropped that Greek philosophy survey right when we got to *Symposium*. (That and the fact that it was way too easy for Malcolm to rag on me about Aristotle.) I remember something about aliens with too many arms and legs, but that's about it. And really, who has a better understanding of love based on extraterrestrial appendages?

"Earth to Amy."

Exactly. How did I miss out on this alien love-fest thingy?

"I'm listening."

He frowned. "Not the reaction I was looking for."

"Dare I ask what it is you were?"

He took a deep breath. "What anyone is who says something like that." But, then, just as quickly, "It's okay. I have no expectations of you saying it, or feeling it."

Just hope. He didn't even have to say it. He never should have had to say any of this.

"But I had to tell you," he went on. "So—I don't know. You'd know why I act the way I do."

"I already know why, Brandon." I put my hand over his, there between us on the sofa.

Another deep breath. "Yeah. I was kind of hoping that you didn't, and that if I told you…" He trailed off and looked down at our clasped hands.

He hoped that if he came right out and said it, I would stop screwing around and fall in love with him, too. I knew this man. Knew him well enough to transcribe the thoughts in his head.

Strange. With most men, admission of unrequited love is a

little wishy-washy. Forget Cyrano de Bergerac, forget Romeo Montague, Act One, Scene One. Girls only go mushy for those men in fiction. In real life, we like a little hard-to-get. Show me a pining man and I'll show you a pussy.

But Brandon continued to break the mold, even here. Beneath the bare bulbs shining harsh, 120-watt light down from the common-room ceiling, seated across from me on a threadbare couch with his hands full of flower-stand roses and his eyes full of expectation, Brandon Weare had never looked more like a man worthy of my love.

And I had never felt like a bigger bitch. Here before me, in splendid, golden reality, sat a kind, brilliant, funny, cute, affectionate lover, the kind of guy that any girl I knew would be happy to not only have in her bed, but also to take home to Mom once school was out. Moreover, he loved me.

And I'd been out with George Harrison Prescott, a player, a ladies' man of the first order. Yes, he was cute, and yes, he was funny, and for all I knew, he might be brilliant as well, but he was *not* and would never be boyfriend material. I'd known that for years.

But, wait a second, who said I wanted a *boyfriend*? I so didn't have time for a boyfriend. Last time I had a boyfriend, I'd been totally burned. I'd told Lydia as much last night. I'd been telling Brandon as much for the past two months.

"Brandon, we've talked about this...."

"Yeah, we have." He made a sound of disgust. "And I think you're full of crap." Mocking me, he began to tick off a list on his fingers. "*We can't be together because, one, I'm not good with boyfriends.* Well, you've never tried it with me. *Two, I'm too busy.* But not too busy to have sex with me every week or so, nor go to dinner with me once a week, nor to call me and see me and hang out half a dozen other times. You think a title change will make a difference in the time commitment? *Three, I don't want to ruin our friendship.* Well, I'm telling you right now, Amy, that it has ruined our friendship. I can't ever go back to the way things were before Valentine's Day. If I'd known it was going to lead to this, I probably—fuck it, I probably would have done it anyway, but I'd have thought about it a lot more seriously. I want to be with you . . . or not. I can't be your booty call anymore."

And there it was. The ultimatum. "So, decide tonight?"

"Yes. No. Yes. Decide tonight." He nodded briskly.

I bit my lip, and tasted pomegranate juice. "Tonight is . . . not the best time."

"You've had two months to think about it."

Yeah, but twenty minutes ago I had another guy's tongue down my throat. I could still taste him. I was surprised Brandon couldn't smell him. "I—I need to go to the bathroom."

Brandon's shoulders dropped. "I'll wait," he said resolutely.

I rushed out of the suite and into the floor bathroom, trying not to hyperventilate. A quick trip into the stall (you do remember the four and a half 312s, right?) and then I checked out my reflection in the mirror above the sink. My mouth was stained a deep purple; it looked like I'd been sucking on pickled beets. My lips were swollen, too, and my cheeks were flushed, still (or maybe again). How could Brandon have missed these signs? I balanced my hands on the porcelain and took several deep, shuddering breaths, until my treacherous heart slowed down to normal measures.

He said he loved me.

I splashed cold water on my face and ran a comb through my hair. I brushed my teeth, concentrating on my stained red gums and scrubbing the hell out of my tongue. Thinking back on it, I should have been a little more self-aware about my actions.

I was getting rid of George.

For Brandon's benefit.

Because Brandon had cared about me for months. Because it had been Brandon who'd sent me funny e-mails, and cards on my birthday, Brandon who had held me the last time I'd cried, Brandon who'd always been there to offer advice, who'd been the one to convince me, however obliquely, to join Rose & Grave in the first place. George was a Johnny-come-lately. I *did* love Brandon. Maybe not yet in a way that Shakespeare would have endorsed, but definitely in a way that probably had its own special name in ancient Greek. *Phileventuallyoksis* or something.

After all, that Roxanne chick went for Cyrano once he finally approached her himself, right? (Or was that just in the Steve Martin version? My literary education is notoriously deficient in Balzac—if it even was Balzac.* It's because the Balzac and Dickens seminar was full last semester, further proving my theory that students will study anything if it has a cool enough title.) Try someone else. Jane Austen. Marianne Dashwood and—well, Colonel Brandon. Now, if that's not a hint, I don't know what is.

I rushed back into my suite, hoping Brandon hadn't misinterpreted my prolonged absence. While I'd been gone, he'd managed to stuff the entire bouquet of roses into a crackled-finish plastic dining-hall glass and had wedged the whole top-heavy shebang between two of Lydia's thick poli-sci textbooks. Now he was back on the couch, fingering the strap on my messenger bag. I froze.

"Nice pin."

"Brandon—"

He stood, his hand out as if to stop me. "Don't leave the room. I'll never mention it again. Tabled forever, if that's what will make you happy."

---

* It's actually not Balzac, but Edmond Rostand. The confessor should really be brushing up. What ever would the Diggers say?

But the thing was, I actually wanted him to ask me about it. I wanted to tell him what was going on, and see if he could parse it any better than the rest of us had. Brandon fixed things. He'd always fixed things for me.

Who wouldn't love a guy like him?

"Should I go?" he asked.

"No."

He blinked, as if surprised. "Really?"

I nodded. "I can't—I can't say what you want me to. I won't say that . . . yet. But I want to be with you. For real."

It was as if Brandon had been strapped to a frame that collapsed at my words. He took two steps forward and enfolded me in his arms. His brown eyes had never seemed so bright, his Amy-smile, the one I knew he reserved just for me, had never seemed so unreserved.

I ran my hands through his hair and cupped his face in my hands. His skin was golden beneath my fingertips. He'd gotten a tan this weekend. Probably out somewhere, playing badminton while I fooled around with boys in black robes. Boys who, as it turned out, never wanted me around in the first place.

Whereas Brandon always had.

I kissed him, and his mouth felt warm and familiar against mine. His breath was not tinged with pomegranate and honey, and our bodies lined up perfectly with no need for me to tilt my chin to meet him. Yet, I sighed, and he smiled, and I took his hand and led him into my bedroom, thankful to whatever it was that had made me hesitate outside with George, and only mildly curious whether a girl who would hook up with two boys in the same night was a totally irredeemable slut or just a person who had managed to come to her senses before she completely screwed up her life.

In retrospect, I probably should have pondered this last part a bit more.

I woke up super-early on Monday morning (okay, more like 9 A.M.—but I *am* a college student) to the phone ringing. As I have already mentioned, my mother has a freaky sixth sense of when her daughter has engaged in illicit sexual activity, even from five states away. She was probably calling to see if she could discern any post-coital qualities to my voice, or perhaps detect the rustlings of a boy in the background, shimmying into his boxer briefs.

I stumbled over a cascade of paper airplanes (don't ask, really) and, hopping into a robe, ran out the door to answer the phone.

"Hello?" *Hello, Mom. No, of course you didn't wake me. Don't you know? I often engage in Monday morning orgies. In fact, as you called, I was just enjoying an especially thorough rogering from two men named Paolo and Butch.* (That would throw her for a loop.)

"Amy?" The voice at the other end of the line was not maternal, yet it did sound worried. "It's Malcolm."

"Oh." Couch. Plop. "Call to apologize?"

Silence. "Right. Yesterday. No, as a matter of fact, I didn't, because I, for one, do not agree with—well, I can't really talk about that right now."

"Figures." I wondered when Brandon's first class was.

"That's actually not why I'm calling. I need to see you, ASAP. Do you have any classes this morning?"

"Don't you already know that, with your awesome Digger mind tricks? Oh, wait, I forgot, there *are* no mind tricks. No special powers, no secret shadow government, no 'we'll cut out your tongue if you talk'—it's all a big smoke screen designed to make your dicks look bigg—"

"Amy, I need to see you right away. It's important. Barbarian matters."

Barbarian? I stole another look into my bedroom, where Brandon, still dead to the world (lucky guy), was making my lumpy duvet look even lumpier. Did Malcolm know about that? And how? Maybe it wasn't all a trick. I looked around the room. Nah. That whole bugging thing was just another one of the conspiracy theories.

And yet... "What is it?" I asked.

"Not on the phone." Oh, right, and I'm not supposed to buy into the bugging thing when he says stuff like that? "Can you meet me in half an hour?" He named a campus coffee shop.

"Well, I kind of have some work—" Like a kilo of WAP.

"It's an emergency."

I grunted. "Fine. You're buying the mochas."

Having agreed to the rendezvous, I rushed off to the shower for a quick eradication of last night and then back to my room to dry off and dress in a manner that wouldn't disturb my—my boyfriend. The pristine term fairly crackled in my head.

I ran a comb through freshly shampooed hair and glanced over at Brandon, who lay twisted in my sheets. Blue morning light from the small window above my bed cast a pale glow over his golden skin, and his hair stood up in all directions. Even in sleep, he was smiling.

I twisted my hair into an impromptu updo, leaned over the bed, and deposited a light kiss on his cheek. "I'll be back soon," I whispered to his sleeping form.

First, I had to get some things straight with Malcolm.

———

A very weary Malcolm looked as if he'd been waiting at the coffee shop for a while, but the paper cup of mocha he slid at me the second I arrived was still scorching hot. I softened slightly. He still owed me an explanation for what had gone down at the meeting yesterday, but at least he was picking up the tab.

"Right on time," he said. "Promptness is much admired by Diggers."

"So I was told at my interview." I slugged back a draught of the coffee. "But let's get a couple things straight here, *Lancelot*." He flinched at the name, but I ignored him. "The ladies of D177 are not going to roll over to some outdated Neanderthal ideas of a 'woman's role.' So if that was your plan, you can drop it right now."

"That was never *my* plan," Malcolm stated. "Though I apparently can't speak for all my brothers."

Frickin' Poe.

"In fact," he went on, "I want to apologize for the way the meeting went yesterday. If it's any consolation, most of the seniors went and found the taps at the bar last night. We heard about the New York scheme and we're willing to do whatever it takes to help."

"I'll believe that when I see it." After all, when the girls had stormed out yesterday, Malcolm hadn't moved a muscle. And I wanted to know why.

"You would have seen it last night. But I think you'd already left." He tilted his head and looked at me curiously. "With ... George?"

Oh, yeah. That reminded me. "And another thing, I will date whoever I want to, and sleep with them, too, and there's not a thing you society people can say about it."

Malcolm stared at me with his mouth open. "Excuse me?"

"Come on, Malcolm. 'Barbarian matters'? Please."

He laughed out loud then, the creases between his eyes momentarily fading. "Yes, Amy, you can sleep with whomever you want. But that's not why I called you this morning. I don't care what you and George do, and none of the other Diggers do, either."

"I did *not* sleep with George!" I cried, indignant. No, I

turned *him* down, and really, how many women can say that? "I slept with...someone else."

Malcolm blinked. "Um, okaaaay. Whatever. I don't have time for a rundown of your obviously very busy social life."

Hey! It wasn't all that busy!

"And honestly, I don't really care. Save it for your C.B."

Those Connubial Bliss reports he'd told me about after the initiation, where we spill the history of our sex lives. "Right. As if we're ever going to see the inside of that tomb again."

"I think you will. The taps I talked to last night seemed pretty determined." He shook his head. "But I digress. Amy, I need your help. It's an emergency."

"The 'barbarian matters' of which you spoke?"

"Exactly." He took a deep breath. "Remember that girl you saw on the stairs yesterday?"

"The one from the *EDN*? Genevieve Grady? Yeah." After all, we both ran in the same English Lit circles. I think I even had a lecture or two with her freshman year.

"Well, she's my ex-girlfriend."

Does not compute. Though it explained her hostility. "How long ago was this?"

"Would it surprise you if I said six weeks?"

"Recalling our conversation in your bed not two days ago, yes."

He took a sip of his drink, as if for fortification. "Are you familiar with the term 'beard'?"

I furrowed my brow. "Not the facial hair?"

"No. The fake lover."

"Not really." But then it hit me. "So you were dating Genevieve in order to throw off—"

"My dad, other suspicious individuals, anyone who might rat me out." He toyed with the corrugated cardboard ring on his cup. "Anyway, Genevieve didn't really get it, though after a while, she kind of figured out the score when I didn't ..." He gestured weakly. "The problem is, she sort of fell for me. I liked her a lot, she was a really great girl. But not like that. I couldn't give her what she wanted."

But he hadn't bothered to tell her beforehand! Even I hadn't been that cruel to Brandon. At least he'd known where I stood all these months. "And she resents that? Gotta tell you, buddy, so far I'm on her side."

"Just wait." He looked down at the table, as if bracing himself for the next part of his story. "When we broke up, it was . . . really bad. I wanted to stay friends. I wanted it to be what it has always been, but she was . . . *vicious*. She said the most awful things to me, and we didn't speak for weeks. You have to understand, I *had* thought very highly of her. But not after the way she treated me when we broke up."

My sympathy meter hovered in the negatives. "Well, yeah, but she was the victim here. You made it out as if you wanted to be her boyfriend, but you were just using her."

"I'm not saying it wasn't wrong," Malcolm replied. "I know I shouldn't have done it. At least, not without her understanding what was really going on."

"Did you tell her that?"

Malcolm shrugged. "Do you think it made her feel better?"

He had me there. If she had truly been in love with him, hearing that he'd thought she'd be cool with using her wouldn't have mollified her in the slightest. But what was the point? "So what does this have to do with me?"

He took a deep breath. "Actually, Amy, it has everything to do with you."

"You lost me," I said, shaking my head.

"I really cared about Genevieve. She was so smart, so talented, so accomplished. The editor of the *Eli Daily News*. Pretty. Well connected, going places. She'd be the type of girl my father would be proud to see me dating."

I circled my hand in the air. "Yeah? And?"

"A model woman." He looked at me meaningfully.

Where had I heard that phrase recently? Someone had said it to me, like a command, almost. Like an expectation to live up to...

Oh. My. God. He was *not* telling me this. I might not be the genius that Jennifer Santos or Joshua Silver was, but this Digger tap was not a complete fool. And she'd just figured out the score.

Malcolm, like a runaway train speeding toward a cliff, went on. "But after we broke up, she was so wretched and mean-spirited, I just couldn't bring myself to—"

"Tap her."

He let out the breath. "Yeah."

"So," I said, pushing forward to the excruciating finish, "you tapped me instead."

"Yeah."

I spilled my mocha right then. The hot liquid splattered all over the table, soaking our napkins, drowning his weird combo bagel, staining the sleeve of his stylish denim jacket, and making a glorious little puddle in my lap.

"Fuck." Malcolm grabbed a handful of napkins and started tossing them around to mop up the worst of the spill. I took another handful to dab at my lap.

"Amy, are you all right?"

When I looked up, it was through a veil of hot tears.

"Oh, I'm *fine*," I hissed at him. "Everything makes sense now."

"What do you mean?"

"I've been asking myself why the hell Rose & Grave would ever be interested in a person like me. Now I know. *They weren't.*"

"That's not completely accurate, Amy."

And now he was channeling Poe! "I know what I'm talking about! At least in this, I know I do. I was sitting there, wondering why all the other taps seemed to already understand so much about the Diggers and know each other so well. It's not like Clarissa and Demetria run in the same social circles. You had a grooming period, didn't you?" Poe had even said as much to me yesterday, but it had been tough to hang on to every detail in his sexist diatribe. "They all knew, unlike me, exactly who was coming for them on Tap Night."

He nodded, still not looking at me.

"That's why Clarissa was so surprised to see me with that letter in the library! That's why they all rushed me in the Grand Library after I was initiated."

Again, a pitiful little nod.

"See?" I tapped my temple with my free hand. "Not so clueless as I seem! And you—I thought you were my champion! You stood up for me back at the interview, you watched over me during the initiation. You were just trying to ensure that I made the cut."

"Well, yeah, but that's a standard thing for big sibs to do."

"But it was more important for me than for the others. I was a last-minute substitute. All those other taps were known quantities. You had to make sure I worked out."

"Amy, that doesn't really matter now."

"Clearly, it does. Because I can tell that I'm different from the others. And they can tell, too. The rest of the taps look at me and ask themselves what I'm doing here. I know they do."

"I think you're being paranoid."

I gave him a look. Get in line. The other Digger taps looked at me as if I were about to fit us all for aluminum sombreros.

He quickly backtracked. "Okay, if they were acting weird at first, it's just because they were expecting Genevieve. But you were the one who, as you said yesterday, got tapped, got initiated. *You're* the member now. You're their fellow."

I twirled my finger in the air. "Whoopee. A year spent

knowing I'm not really good enough to be there. At least it explains the real reason behind the society name you picked out for me. Bugaboo. Pretentious-speak for pain in the ass. Is that what your expectation was? That I'd constantly be trailing behind the others?"

"Good job with the dictionary." He rolled his eyes. (Excuse me? Now he doesn't even have faith in my standing vocabulary. I don't look *everything* up.)

"You didn't want me."

"Now, that's not true. You may not have been my original choice—note that I'm not saying *first*—but we wouldn't have tapped you at all if we didn't think you belonged. We only have fifteen slots."

I was . . . *wait-listed*. At Rose & Grave. I've *never* been wait-listed. I even got into Eli through Early Decision. Amy Haskel is not wait-list material.

"Now, where have I heard you say that before?" I asked facetiously. "Oh, that's right, when you were talking about how much everyone wanted women in the group. Well, we disproved that little theory yesterday, didn't we? How many of your brothers will I have to survey before I get to the truth about this one?" Probably only one: Poe.

"Enough!" Malcolm banged his hands down on the sticky, mochafied table. "You know, this is exactly why we burn the records of our delibs. People's feelings get hurt. I want you, and they want you, and what happened before doesn't matter. You're in; she's not. I never would have told you at all if I'd known you'd take it so poorly."

"News flash, honey," I shot back. "Women don't like being used."

Malcolm stared at me for one long, silent moment. Then he stood up, threw his wad of towels down on the table, and walked out. Through the pane of glass in the front of the shop,

I watched him cross the street and pause on the opposite corner, covering his face with his hands and taking several deep breaths.

Good riddance. After all, it's not as if the jerk had done me any favors recently. Well, he'd washed my clothes and bought me two breakfasts (like a Hobbit). There was that. But he'd also dragged me into a Battle of the Sexes that should have been over and done with a good thirty years ago, all because he needed a warm body to fill a slot.

I didn't belong in Rose & Grave, and that was that. There. Easy. Over. No more rubbing elbows with Clarissa Cuthbert and trying to keep the peace between Odile and Demetria. No more putting up with the condescension of that wretched Poe. Just leave them all to their little games and get back to the life I had before this mess started. Who needed a secret society anyway? I'd only joined because Rose & Grave was supposed to be so all-powerful and scary. But in truth, they were exactly like Brandon had characterized them: Paleolithic, in both outlook and influence. Hardly anything I'd heard about them was true, and on top of their utter lack of omnipotence, they had a seriously backwards perspective on gender equality.

So, who needed them? Who needed rich old men trying to tell me who I was and could be? Who needed rich, young, gay—if closeted—men measuring my worth on a scale? Who needed any of them threatening my future? I had good grades, good friends, a great—if new—boyfriend, and a prestigious-sounding—if boring—summer job.

Screw 'em.

I dumped the mess of napkins and soggy breakfast in the nearest trash can and marched out of the shop, head held high. I was going to go straight home and tell Brandon he was right all along.

But when I arrived back at the suite, the whiteboard

hanging from our door had a note scrawled across it. "Call Horton, 911" with a number, and Lydia's scrawled "L" beneath. Puzzled, I skipped waking up the boy in my bedroom and went straight for the phone.

An assistant, sounding nervous, put me right through.

"Oh, Amy," said my future boss, her tone boding ill. "I thought your roommate left you a message."

"She left me a message to call you."

"Yes, well..." The woman trailed off, seeming to grow more uncomfortable with each passing second. "The thing is, Amy, we're going to have to cancel your internship with us this summer."

The bottom dropped out of my stomach. "What? Why?"

My future boss (No! No, *not* my boss now! My ex–future boss? My future contrary-to-fact boss?) hesitated. "Well, I'm not really at liberty to get into company policy right now, Amy. I can't apologize enough for putting you in this difficult situation. I feel terrible, really—"

"Tell me why." You know how in books, they say, 'Her blood ran cold'? *So* not just an expression.

Good luck with your career.

"I'm sorry. I'm not at liber—"

"Give me a satellite view," I insisted. "Budget cuts? Departmental shifts? Decided I'm not qualified to run the Xerox machine? Tell me. I need to know."

"Amy, I can't—"

"No!" I cried into the phone, probably shocking myself more than her. "You *have* to tell me why."

"I *can't* tell you why." Or she'd have to kill me, no doubt.

"Does it ..." I swallowed, composed myself, and began again, softly. "Does it have anything to do with Rose & Gr—"

"I need to go now, Amy. Good-bye." And she hung up.

I was still staring at the phone, mouth agape, when

Brandon, my sweet barbarian boyfriend, came out of my bedroom, rubbing his eyes. I must have awakened him with my screaming.

"Hey," he said. "Anything wrong?"

Yes. Everything.

I hereby confess:
I almost gave up.

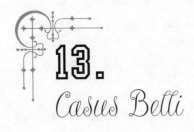

13.

Casus Belli

Malcolm answered his door and I pushed past him, still snif-
fling underneath the hood of my Eli crest sweatshirt (gotta do
something to hide the red nose). He handed me a box of tissues.

"You were almost unintelligible over the phone," he said in
a flat voice.

Tough luck for him. I hadn't improved in the ensuing ten
minutes. In fact, I hadn't even been able to tell Brandon what
had happened to me. It was as if there'd been some sort of
post-hypnotic Diggers suggestion to keep me from talking of
my plight to barbarians. (Really, at this point, maybe we could
all start thinking that these conspiracy theories actually had
some merit?) I'd abandoned him there, utterly oblivious about
what had happened to me in the hour since I'd left him alone in
bed that had the power to turn me into such a shocked, snivel-
ing mess. I'd put the call in to Malcolm then ran out with little
more than a choking good-bye.

"They—they—took my—job!" I managed to get out.
"The patriarchs canceled my summer internship!"

"Yeah." Malcolm sat down on his desk chair. "And you're not the only one. The phone's been ringing off the hook all morning. I've heard from half of the club."

"You told me they couldn't do that! You told me it was a bluff!"

"I was wrong. Not unlike I was about what they'd do if we tapped women. Sorry."

"You're sorry?" I spluttered. "My life is ruined and you're *sorry*?!"

He shot me a look of disgust. "Ruined? Come on, Amy. No hysterics, please."

"There are no decent internships still open this late in the spring. I'm going to spend the summer waiting tables somewhere and then I'll never get a job at *Glamour*. That's even assuming that Condé Nast isn't a Digger."

"As far as I know, Condé Nast isn't even a person."

"Good. At least I won't have that hurdle to leap as well."

"Okay." He put out his hands, palms down. "Just take a couple of deep breaths and let's talk reasonably about this."

Ha! Reasonable had left the building round about the time Big Brother brought down the ax. "How do we know they won't start in on the next of their threats? How do we know I won't suddenly find out I have a D average and a drained bank account?"

"Now, Amy—"

"It was all true, wasn't it? All those things you kept laughing about whenever I brought them up. The cops, the power—"

"The Nazi gold?" he added in a mocking tone. "No. That's all in Switzerland."

I gave him a withering stare. "Laugh it up. I'm the one who's jobless."

"Okay, yes," he amended. "In retrospect, maybe some of it is true. Some. If only because the patriarchs are very powerful people, and powerful people tend to have some...leverage."

I crossed my arms. "I want an apology for all that snickering." And, while we were at it, for not standing up for me yesterday at the meeting. But I didn't even give him the chance to formulate a response. I was too worked up. "And what about your job? Aren't you being punished, too, same as the rest of us?"

"I was supposed to be working with my dad, so no. But now that's in jeopardy, too, for other reasons. That's what I first called you about this morn—"

"When you told me I was your second choice." I threw my hands in the air. "My life is ruined and I'm not even supposed to be here!"

"Oh, puh-lease. Your life is not ruined. At the very worst, you spend a month not seated behind a desk for once."

"Shows how little you know!" I snapped. "Without the proper undergrad internships, employers will throw my resume right in the circular file."

"The Diggers can giveth and the Diggers can taketh away," Malcolm intoned. "Once we get this mess with the TTA board sorted out, everything will get back to normal. You'll be fine, trust me."

"I don't trust you. Not after what you told me this morning."

Malcolm shot out of his chair so fast that it slammed back against his desk. "Would you shut up for one second? I'm in real trouble here, Amy. Not some little society snafu. *Real* trouble."

I silenced, shaken out of my solipsism somewhat by the fact that my big sib could dismiss so lightly anything having to do with his society. He looked like he was about to cry.

"Good lord, Malcolm, what's wrong?"

"I've been trying to tell you all morning. Genevieve Grady is out for my blood. I don't know if it's because I broke her heart or because I didn't tap her into Rose & Grave."

"Maybe a little bit of both?"

"She wants me annihilated."

"And how does she plan to bring about this apocalypse?"

He dropped his head in his hands. "I got home late last night, and when I came in, she was waiting for me in the stairwell. Lurking! Obviously, when she saw you, she put it all together."

Ah, so that's why he'd told me the supposedly secret story behind my tap. Because of this—feud, or whatever.

"And then she dropped the bombshell." Malcolm's voice grew shaky. "She's going to write an exposé in the *EDN* about being 'Closeted at Eli,'" he made quote marks in the air and rolled his eyes, "and she's going to make me Exhibit A."

I made a face. "That's so sleazy. Does she think she's going to get into Columbia J-school by muckraking?"

"If my father reads it, I'm dead."

I reached out and patted his arm. "Come on, what's the chance that your dad or anyone he knows is going to read the college paper?" But even as I said it, I knew that wouldn't be much comfort. The wire services watched our paper carefully, waiting for news of the children of the rich and powerful. If the article came out, it would be splashed all over.

Still, I wasn't prepared for Genevieve's coup de grâce.

"Pretty high." Malcolm snorted. "She's putting it in the commencement issue."

And Malcolm was graduating. Ouch. "And you're sure your dad would flip?"

"Like a gymnast." He shuddered. "I know what he'd do to start. Kick me out, disown me, never speak to me again. What I'm more scared of is what he'd do next. The wrath of the patriarchs would be nothing by comparison."

Now who was getting hysterical? "Okay. But you knew this had to happen eventually, right? I mean, maybe not in so splashy a way, but still. I thought you were just keeping it a secret so he didn't pull you out of Eli before you could get your degree."

Malcolm, however, said nothing, so I pressed. "How long were you planning on staying in the closet?"

"To be honest," he replied in a voice saturated with sarcasm, "I've been so busy with keeping up my grade-point average, I hadn't given it a lot of thought."

"Well, start now. You can't live a lie forever."

"Yeah, but I can't kiss my family good-bye, either. You don't understand what it would be like, Amy. There's nothing you want that would make your parents hate you."

He had me there, I'll admit. "So, what are we going to do?"

Malcolm took a deep breath, as if preparing himself for what came next. "She gave me an alternative."

"Marry her?"

"If only it were that easy." (Honestly, I wasn't sure if he was joking.) "She says that she'll drop the article on me if I provide her full access to the secrets of Rose & Grave."

I let out a short bark of laughter. "Did you tell her that we can't even get ourselves into the tomb at present?"

"Of course not!" He looked offended. "That's not for barbarians to know."

I considered bringing up the several dozen barbarians in the audience milling around High Street yesterday. Plenty of people already knew it. In fact, I'd be surprised if there wasn't an article about the commotion in the *Eli Daily News* right now.

"I told her that Diggers don't stoop to blackmail."

"Oh, no?" I mocked. "That's exactly what the patriarchs are doing to us!"

"Okay, fine. *I* don't stoop to blackmail." Malcolm lifted his chin momentarily, then slumped back in his seat. "But that doesn't mean I could sleep last night. Oh, God, Amy, what am I going to do?"

Why was he asking me? Go ask one of the *real* taps. The smart ones. Josh or something. Or one of the seniors. I'm sure Poe could think up some way to have Genevieve *disappeared* for threatening a Digger.

Of course, since even the Diggers' governing body had Malcolm on their shit list right now, that quarter was probably not going to be the most helpful providing means-by-which-to-threaten. Those resources were all tied up in making sure I had no summer job. "Who else have you told?"

"No one. I didn't want to worry them right now, when we've got all this other stuff to deal with."

"Then why come to me? Why tell me all of these things— some of which you've already said are supposed to be a secret."

Malcolm looked down at his hands. "Well, I was kind of wondering if... *you'd* go out with me."

"What!"

Malcolm rolled his chair forward and clasped my hands in his. "Amy, don't you see, that would solve everything! If we told everyone you're my girlfriend, then her article would come off as just her bitterness over our breakup. I could tell my dad that's why she did it—which is kind of the truth anyway—and also that she's all upset because I didn't tap her. My dad would buy that. He totally would. Hell hath no fury like a woman scorned and all that."

I looked at him in shock. "He wouldn't think you were just pulling the same mustache trick or whatever?"

"Beard. And no. We'd make sure he didn't. I can be very affectionate, and very convincing."

Yeah. He'd been doing it for years.

"He'd have her silly article," Malcolm went on, "but also have us in front of him. He'd see me being straight with his own eyes. My dad's really into personal verification."

"Eww," I said. "I sincerely hope you don't mean what I think you mean." Like, letting him find us in bed. Gross.

"Not unless it's unavoidable." He noted my stricken face. "Amy, that was a joke!"

I whipped my hands away. "No!" I stood up, tried to put as much personal space between us as possible. "Absolutely not."

His face fell. "Amy, please. You don't understand. If this happens, then my life is over."

Or it was started. "Maybe this is a blessing in disguise? You won't have to pretend any longer that you believe all your dad's conservative Republican crap."

Malcolm blinked. "But Amy, I do believe it. You know that, right?" (I *so* didn't know that.) "Well, not the part about homosexuals and minorities, but the rest of the party platform. I am a Republican. Small government, free trade, go Army. I'm in the NRA, for crying out loud."

"Oh." Well, that put a different spin on it all. "You know, there's a name for people like you."

"Pink elephant?" He gave me a wry, lopsided smile. "Come on, Amy, please."

"I can't, Malcolm."

"Please. I know you don't think I deserve any favors right now. I mean, I brought you into Rose & Grave, and you lost your job. But things will get better, I promise. We'll figure out this stuff with the patriarchs and then, well, you'll be surprised at the kind of opportunities you'll get out of this. Isn't that why you joined?"

"You're saying I *owe* you this for making me a Digger?"

"I'm saying you owe me this because of your oath." He stood a little straighter. "*I do hereby most solemnly avow, within the Flame of Life and beneath the Shadow of Death, to bear the confidence and the confessions of my brothers, to support them in all their endeavors, and to keep forever sacred,* et cetera? Have you forgotten already?"

"No. And when the society starts treating me like a member, I'll go back to keeping my promises." Of course, even I knew that's not really how it worked. At least, not if the new taps' argument was going to be: *We're the society. We're the active members. The current students. You're just alums.*

"*I'm* treating you like a member," Malcolm said. "I've never done anything else. I'm your *brother.*"

"Malcolm, even if I wanted to, I couldn't. I have a boyfriend."

He gave me a look of disbelief. "What? Since when?"

"Last night." I toed the throw rug with the edge of my sneaker, wondering exactly how much he knew about my interlude with George.

"So, clearly a very committed relationship," he mocked.

I swallowed. "It's not like that. We are committed, it's just been a long time in coming. It's—Brandon."

"Ah." He nodded in recognition. "Well, good for him for finally tying you down. You're quite a catch."

"Don't be mean."

"I'm not." His expression softened. "You are. Why else would I want to date you?"

"Because the fact that I'm female makes me better fit for presentation than most of your lovers?" I scoffed. "Sorry, Malcolm. But I don't buy that you have any great preference for me. I'm a woman, and I'm available. Same as the reason you put me in Rose & Grave."

He sighed. "What will make you believe that I want you there, Amy?" He pointed toward the tomb that stood beyond the slate of the Calvin College wall. "Not as a warm body, but for what you have to offer?"

"What is that?" I raised my hands in supplication. "I fit a slot you desperately needed to fill."

"Sometimes that's how belonging works."

"Not good enough."

Malcolm was silent for several seconds. When he finally spoke, it was in a voice of despair. "So that's just it, then? You're quitting?"

"Going to cut my losses, yes."

He turned away from me. "Then I really did make a mistake."*

Since there wasn't much to say after that little judgment, I left. Heading back to my room for the second time that morning, I wished (and this one's a first, let me tell you!) that I could turn my brain off. Just for half an hour. My whole body seemed to buzz with thoughts. Every step brought with it increasingly gruesome forecasts of the consequences of my actions and bleaker visions of my future, which had heretofore seemed so 78 degrees and sunny, with a chance of perfection.

By now, Brandon would have hied himself off to class and I had a little over two hours to do my homework before section. But if you think I was actually going to get a crack at schoolwork, then you haven't been paying attention. Apparently, one of the reasons societies tap folks with good GPAs is that once you're in, school is the last thing on your mind.

Waiting for me in the veritable Grand Central Station of my common room sat Clarissa Cuthbert, in white Capri pants and a shimmery pink halter top. Silver hoops dangled from her ears and a pair of sunglasses the size of a small nation (and likely costing as much as said small nation's GNP) perched on top of her smooth blond hair.

We really needed to start locking this door.

"Hi," I said flatly. "Lost any jobs today?"

"You, too?" Clarissa asked. "Isn't this ridiculous? I've been trying to get my dad on the phone all morning. His company does a lot of business with the marketing firm I'm supposed to intern at this summer. It's how I got the job in the first place. I know he'll figure it out. They can't get away with this." She

---

* Though at the time rather cutting, what the confessor didn't know was that the instances of attrition in the Diggers' entire two-century history could probably be counted on one hand.

took her cell phone out of her pocket, shook it, and checked the reception. "I wish he'd get out of this meeting, already."

"Bully for you." I sank into our weathered armchair. "How nice it must be to have strings to pull. I'm still screwed."

Clarissa clasped her knees. "We'll work it out," she said, a determined gleam in her eyes.

"You might," I corrected. "I'm out."

She gasped. "But—but, Amy! You can't quit!"

"Watch me. I don't belong there, Clarissa. Malcolm told me how—how I got tapped."

She gasped—again. "You mean, he revealed the substance of the deliberations?"

But I was through taking note of Clarissa's freaky Digger know-how. Her father, clearly, had not been entirely discreet. "More like how they came about in the first place."

And now she sat back against the chair and rolled her eyes. "Don't tell me you're getting all huffy about that student-paper chick."

That "student-paper chick" had a circulation a thousand times mine. "Look, my very presence wrecks the argument that the seniors tapped 'the best and the brightest' in our class. 'The model women.' I'm not like the rest of you all. Don't you get that? You, of all people?" I gestured weakly around our Goodwill-furnished suite. "In my dorm room."

Clarissa laughed weakly and picked at our shoddy slip-cover. "Oh, yeah, about that. Have you ever thought of subscribing to *Martha Stewart Living*?"

Ugh. Get out! What the hell was she thinking, just waltzing into my suite and making herself at home? Commenting on our furniture? Lord only knew what Lydia would say if she came in and saw us.

Right on cue, Lydia strolled in carrying a laundry basket. She reached inside and tossed a bottle of pop to Clarissa.

"Sorry. They didn't have diet ginger ale. I hope Diet Coke's okay."

Clarissa shrugged and handed my roommate a dollar. "Better than regular."

I had my hands full trying to keep my eyes from gogging out of my head. Lydia opened her bottle of root beer, took a swig, and turned to me. "Want half?"

"What? Too early for vodka?" I asked, holding my hand out for the proffered pop.

Clarissa turned her attention back to me. "Did you know that *I* got into Eli off the wait list?"

"No!" Lydia exclaimed, looking up from the counter, where she was matching socks.

"Yep." Clarissa lifted her chin. "And I'm a three-time legacy. My dad about flipped his lid. And then—oh, God, this is so embarrassing—he donated a Monet to the Eli Art Gallery."

"That worked?" Lydia asked.

"I'm here, aren't I?" Clarissa spared a look for the bringer of the Diet Coke. "I got in." And now she turned back to me. "Off the wait list. Now three years later, it doesn't matter."

"To the person who didn't get in because your dad worked his bigwig magic, it does," I said.

Clarissa shrugged. "That's not the point. I'm just trying to say that I've been an excellent student and in general a credit to the university. They're glad I'm here. So I belong. Wait list or not, I belong now, and have since the moment I stepped on campus freshman year."

I was beginning to grok Clarissa—she didn't have the slightest clue how elitist her statements sounded, and she didn't feel embarrassed about the silver spoon dangling between her lips, either. The wealthy kids could never win. They were either rich bitches who flaunted their money or trustafarian types who wore hand-me-downs and pretended they didn't have any. Either way was abhorrent to the eyes of those whose wallets weren't as fat. At least Clarissa was open about it. Tactless? Maybe, but definitely truthful. And less mean-spirited than I'd spent the last two and a half years believing.

"You don't see anything wrong with manipulating the wait list through a timely application of priceless art?" I asked. Which, as it turns out, had a very particular and definable price. It was worth admission.

"Not really," she replied. "It's entirely possible that the donation did nothing, and I would have gotten in anyway. Besides, the ends in this case justify the means. I wanted to get into Eli, and I did. And once I was in, I showed them what I could do." She leveled a meaningful look at me. "So there."

" 'So there'?" Lydia asked. She'd stopped folding. "You're going to sit here in the suite of two people who got into Eli on our own merits—who might not have gotten in had there been more Monets to dispose of, and say, 'So there'?"

"Would you drop it about the frickin' painting?" Clarissa snapped, whirling to look at Lydia. "It's got nothing to do with my performance since. And no, since you asked, I'm not going to apologize for doing what I could to get in. You can't tell me that every hour you spent candy-striping at your local hospital or whatever other volunteer work you did to pad your application was given out of the kindness of your heart."

Lydia bit her lip and looked down.

"I thought not." Clarissa flicked back a strand of her hair. "I'm just more honest about what I'm going after. You may have liked changing bedpans, but that's not *why* you did it. My father may have been glad to add to Eli's art collection, but he had other motives as well." And she looked at me. "I said it last night at the bar and I'll say it again. Intentions are nothing. Methods are nothing. Results are what matter. Now, are you in or out?"

Lydia gathered up her laundry. "You guys just went way over my head," she said hurriedly. "And, if you don't mind, I think it's best that you stay there. I'll be in my room, rereading Kant. To, um, cleanse my thoughts." A second after the door closed behind her, I heard the not-so-muffled strains of rock music emanating from her stereo. She was even doing her best not to listen in. *Now* she decided to respect the bounds of society secrecy. Now, when I was ready to forget the whole mess.

I dropped my head into my hands. "We don't all think like you, Clarissa. In fact, I think it's safe to say that most liberal arts students have been taught Machiavelli with a decidedly negative slant."

"I must have missed that lecture." And still, the same penetrating stare. No wonder I'd thought she was an unmitigated bitch. She was aggressive, outspoken, ambitious....

"They're fools for denying you, Angel," I said, and the invocation of her society name didn't even make her flinch. "You're a Digger to the core."

"Natch." She winked. "And now, the question remains: Are you?"

I didn't answer. "Historically, what do they do if people quit?"

Her eyes glinted. "You of all people should know this, Amy. We grind their bones to make our bread."

I smiled in spite of myself and Clarissa leaned forward and covered my hand with her slim, manicured one. "Come on. You know you want to be a part of that."

"I'm sorry," I replied. In this, Brandon had not been correct. "I have to think about it."

———

And think I did. For the next few days, I concentrated on little else. Certainly not the commencement issue of the Lit Mag (even Brandon spent most of our office hours flirting, as if making up for lost time), nor focusing on my classes, though I was once again consuming WAP in earnest. With Reading Week nigh and no access to the tomb's library, I couldn't afford to dawdle.

I was miserable. As I'd expected, there were no fabulous, heretofore unclaimed internships waiting for me to stumble across at the Career Center, and an e-mail to my old supervisor at the Eli University Press went unanswered. In an attempt to circumvent what I suspected might be one of her concerns, I sent the following:

> *Pursuant to last, I wanted to assure you that I am in no way connected to* that *organization nor any activity that might upset aforementioned group. Thanks and look forward to hearing from you.*
>
> —*Amy Haskel*

To which I received:

> *Amy,*
> *I'm sure I have no idea what you're talking about.*
> *(Just drop it, okay?)*
> *Yours, etc.*

You may wonder why I confided none of this madness to Brandon. I have no reasonable excuse. I think, on some level, I still believed in that oath. Besides, who knew if my revelation might drag him into the shitstorm as well? I did tell him that I'd lost my internship, which prompted a brainstorming session resulting in a list of twenty-five new places to query about a summer job and some half-baked notion that I'd follow him to Hong Kong, where he was working as a consultant, live in the garret he was renting, and write.

It's a testament to my low level of rationality that I actually considered this.

Lydia, of course, was no help at all. In fact, I was pretty sure that my so-called best friend, despite her diligent application to Kant, spent much of the week gloating over the way my society experience had obviously gone south. Let's just say that not once during my week of despair did she offer me a gumdrop and a shot.

Thursday night, after dinner, Lydia dressed in faux society wear (the dark hoodie and jeans she'd so roundly ridiculed me for donning the week before) and flounced out our door, waggling her fingers at me with a too-bright "Toodleoo!" (Okay, maybe I'm exaggerating just a bit, but honestly? You couldn't miss the smug.)

I sublimated a pout and settled in with my books. If only I'd been tapped by Quill & Ink, none of this would have happened. My current tragedy was entirely due to Malcolm's mistake. If he hadn't screwed over Genevieve, he'd never have been forced to tap me. And then I'd be in a minor but respectable literary society. And I'd have a job. And I'd be fine.

Of course, I could have declined the Rose & Grave tap. I could have stood there in the bathroom, surrounded by boys in robes, stared into that candle, and told them what they could do with their black-lined envelopes. I could have even left the initiation early, before I'd taken any oaths.

But I hadn't done any of that. Because I wanted to know what it was to be a Digger.

And now, I thought, rousing myself from this short period of self-doubt, I knew that it sucked.

I nodded to my textbook, reassured that my decision was correct, and uncapped my highlighter. Madame Rostov, you've been warned.

The phone rang.

Ever full of distractions, my life. Oh, the agony. Was it any wonder this stupid book had not been read? I lunged for the phone, crossing my fingers that the caller was a) Brandon, and b) bearing pizza.

"Amy Maureen Haskel?"

Uh-oh. "Yes?"

"We're calling to inform you that should you choose to pursue this matter any further, we will be forced to broaden our attack to your parents' employment and/or position in their community."

"Wait!" I said. "I'm not pursuing anything—"

"Good evening." And then, of course, *click*.

Bastards. They wouldn't even let me explain myself. And the killer thing about being harassed by a clandestine cabal is that they aren't even listed in Information. Forget about *69, too. There's no way to get in touch with these guys to tell them that you're no longer part of the rebellion.

And, as long as I was questioning their methods, what was with the whole "parents' employment and/or position" crapola? Was that a scripted call? Were they giving everyone the same line? Making sure their bases were covered just in case our folks were of the leisure class? They should have cast their net wider. "Your parents and/or other familial figures of importance." George, for instance, probably wouldn't be too peeved if his dad was brought down a peg or two.

Seriously, if I were leading an intimidation campaign, I would not slack off with a mail-merge threat. Every single one of the insubordinates would receive their very own, personalized coercion. Amateurs.

I shook my head. I had no experience in this, and yet would have handled the whole situation with far more aplomb.

I was two pages farther along in WAP before the significance of that thought hit me. When it did, my distraction caused me to color an entire page in Day-Glo pink.

I'd make a damn good Digger. A much better Digger than any of these sexist patriarchs. Those qualities I'd been noting in Clarissa? I had them, too. They'd be so lucky to have a girl like me on their side. I'd kick the ass of anyone who got in our way, and I'd do it in 21st century style. They had no idea how much they needed that in their back-assward, stuck-in-the-1830s little organization.

It wasn't like I was asking for so much in return, either. A slight career nudge here and there, a lobster dinner or three, and a grandfather clock. I wouldn't even insist upon atomic.

Anyway, the point was, I deserved my membership in Rose & Grave, and I wasn't going to let a bunch of old-fart octogenarians tell me otherwise.

A few moments later, wearing my own dark hoodie, I marched out into the night. I even knew where I'd find them.

Clarissa's apartment was in the posh building in town. The one with the doorman and the marble foyer. Where other off-campus dwellers scraped by with dorm-rate rents and closet-sized living spaces (that weren't, unfortunately, cleaned by Eli janitorial staff, nor lardered by Dining Services), people of the Cuthberts' ilk kicked back in pricey lofts situated oh-so-conveniently above a chichi bar/restaurant that would not look out of place on the Upper West Side.

I buzzed *C. Cuthbert.*

"Yes?" I heard voices in the background.

"Hey," I said. "It's Amy. Let me in."

Silence, and then: "Password?"

Was she kidding me? But then I realized that she was asking for more than that. She wanted commitment. This time, however, I had coffins full of it.

"Password, boo." George. I imagined all eleven of them all crowded around the intercom, waiting for me.

The image made me smile. "Three, one, two."

The door buzzed open.

I hereby confess:
It hurt like a mother.

14.

The City

At three o'clock on Friday afternoon, Ben Edwards, a.k.a. Big Demon, showed up in front of the tomb in a white passenger van he'd borrowed from the athletic department.

"Oh, the class," Odile remarked dryly as she hefted herself into the back. And you had to admit, it wasn't as nice as the limos we'd been tooling around in before the membership had lost its funding.

We all piled into the van. The party consisted of the twelve new taps and Malcolm (who avoided meeting my eyes). Apparently, another car would be following later with five more D176ers. I sat as far away from George as humanly possible, but it didn't seem as if he even remembered making out with me at the bar, let alone had any interest in picking up where we'd left off with more flirtation.

The two-hour trip down to New York City was as uneventful as one could expect from a clunky passenger van helmed by an inexperienced chauffeur trying to navigate the streets of midtown Manhattan on a Friday afternoon. In other words: an exercise in terror. We passengers were mostly spared, but poor

Ben got the brunt of the stress. I'm sorry to report that he was never quite the same afterward and we were momentarily concerned that he'd spend our entire sojourn at the Eli Club cowering in the bathroom, twitching and calling out for his mommy.

Once we'd parked (and Ben had emptied the contents of his stomach on the parking garage's concrete floor), we made our way to the Eli Club, which is located around the corner from Grand Central Station and shares the same Gilded Age architectural decadence. One by one, we shuffled through the cramped revolving door and were spit out ungracefully into an even smaller entrance foyer.

Elegant crown molding, gilt frames, and a sweeping marble staircase and carved mahogany banister defined the formidable lobby of the Eli Club. I'd heard that the establishment threw parties here for students doing summer internships in Manhattan, angling, no doubt, to gain new members once the interns became graduates. Looking about the premises, breathing in air softly scented with calla lilies, I could understand the draw.

This was the bloody, beating heart of Eli's mystique. Rich, elite, old school. No wonder the Tobias Trust had chosen to house their offices here. This is exactly what they wanted Eli to remain, a nest of decadent gentleman's clubs and all-male secret societies.

I glanced at my compatriots. Old school was out.

"Can I help you?" asked a portly gentleman behind the registration desk. A blue blazer easily two sizes too small strained over his girth. A patch with the Eli crest was sewn crookedly on his lapel. If I were the paranoid type, I would think the whole getup was new.

(The cool thing I've learned about paranoia is, once you've confirmed that they *are* indeed after you, it kind of dissipates.)

"Yes," said Malcolm. "Suite 312. We have an appointment."

The doorman looked blank. "I'm sorry, you must have the wrong building. We don't have a Suite 3—"

Malcolm placed both hands palms-down on the countertop and stared at the man. "Look at my collar," he said calmly. "Do you think I got this out of a cereal box? Do you think we all did?"

The man blanched as he took in our crew and their pins. "Just a moment," he whispered, picking up a receiver on his desk. "Hello, sir. Yes, I understand what you said, but—sir?" He listened for a moment in silence. "Sir, they're wearing *the pins*. I was always told that if they were wearing—that I shouldn't—yes, sir." He put down the receiver and looked in our direction without making eye contact with any of us. "Someone will be out shortly."

And someone was—a slight, silver-haired man in a suit, who came within three feet of us and held out his hand. "Please remove your pins and come this way."

Nobody moved.

"Those pins do not belong to you. They belong to the organization. As you are no longer members of—"

"That's what we're here to discuss," grumbled Josh.

"I'm sorry," the man said. "But I can't let you in with those pins on."

"And we're not taking them off." Demetria stepped forward. "And since I know it's happy hour in the dining room upstairs, I'm sure you don't want us to cause a scene that the barbarians might hear."

As if to illustrate her point, the door revolved and out tumbled a trio of businessmen carrying gym bags and briefcases. Malcolm was giving Demetria the evil eye, but no one else seemed scandalized by her threat. If they were going to play dirty with our lives, we'd play dirty with their precious secrecy.

The man glowered at us, spun on his heel (Are you picturing a Nazi? Because you'd have it about right), and walked toward the elevators. "I'll have to take you up in two groups," he said.

I somehow managed to squeeze in with the first, which consisted of Malcolm, Demetria, Clarissa, Josh, Omar, and myself. Our escort sidled in and inserted a small gold key into an elevator lock beneath the buttons. Then he pressed the button for the top floor (which was not floor three, I'd like to point out).

"Interesting place to put a Suite 312," I said aloud.

"Miss, there is no Suite 312."

Now I did turn to Malcolm, who was clearly trying to hold back a smile. "That's our Amy. Always gets to the bottom of things." Malcolm put his arm around my shoulders. "Let's go meet the firing squad."

The top floor of the Eli Club housed what looked like a series of executive offices. Each one had a plaque indicating what organization was renting the space. The Dartmouth Alumni Club, the Eli Crew Team, the University of Virginia Athletic Endowment Organization. The door we paused at had no plaque, only a small white card affixed to the door that read, "Thursday 7–9 P.M."

The other crew of juniors joined us. Jennifer looked pale, and was clutching her crucifix so tightly that her knuckles had turned white. I was sure that if she opened her hand, there'd be a little imprint of Jesus in her palm.

We opened the door and filed inside. The room was windowless, paneled in dark wood, and the ceiling had intricate gold leafing around the edges, but this hardly occupied my attention. Instead, I was too busy with the following:

1) Clarissa shouting, "Dad!" while Mr. Cuthbert, who
  I remember from that long-ago night at Tory's, ignored her and poured himself another glass of water.
2) Poe, seated at the far end of the conference table,
  hands folded before him, face turned down. Beside
  me, Malcolm stiffened, and I knew that he hadn't
  expected to see Poe there, either. Which meant
  only one thing: He was acting for the opposition. (I
  knew it!)

Mr. Cuthbert spoke. "Little Demon, the door, if you please."
Odile started, but Cuthbert shot her a disdainful look as the short
man who'd worked the elevator moved to close the door behind
us. After performing the task, the old "Little Demon" crossed to
the long conference table before us and took his seat, leaving the
dozen students standing in an awkward huddle by the door.

Step one accomplished. They'd succeeded in making us
wait before them like children called into the principal's office.
But the campaign of intimidation had just started.

"Please sit down," said another gentleman, who looked
ridiculously familiar, though for the life of me, I couldn't place
him. He gestured at the empty seats, and we all exchanged
glances as we saw the offerings. Not only were we being di-
vided, we were being trivialized. The long, burnished wood
conference table was surrounded by mismatched chairs.
Some were leather, high-backed, and ergonomic, others
looked liked they'd been swiped from the dining hall to fill out
the table. The comfy leather ones were all occupied, and it
was obvious we were to take the smaller, wooden ones, which
were scattered amongst the patriarchs' places. We fanned
out and sat down on the low Windsor chairs. The tabletop
reached my chest and I thought I detected a smile on one
of my neighboring patriarchs' face as Odile, on his other

side, practically smacked her chin on the table as she sat down.

"Miss Dumas," said the familiar-looking patriarch. "Do you need a booster seat?"

Odile, to her credit, didn't take the bait. "Oh, no," she said. "From this vantage point, I get a much better look at your boogers."

Josh snickered.

"Do you find this amusing, Mr. Silver?" the man snapped.

"Yes, sir," he replied. "I find it very amusing that you thought this little snafu was important enough to leave the White House for."

Ah, now I recognized him. Kurt Gehry, White House Chief of Staff. He was a Digger? Explained *so* much!

Demetria cleared her throat and stood. "Well, since I don't want to be stuck at the kiddie table for any longer than strictly necessary, let's get to the point. We, the current members of Rose & Grave, are here to argue for reinstated access to the tomb on High Street."

"And as a corollary," Josh added, "we demand that you withdraw any *suggestions* you might have made to our employers about our work ethics, trustworthiness, and any other negative opinions you shared."

There was a long spate of silence. And then Mr. Cuthbert spoke up. "No."

"But you have no right to do this," Demetria said.

"And you, Miss Robinson, have no right to be wearing that pin. You have no right to access to the Rose & Grave tomb, and indeed have no right to be addressing this board. The individuals who tapped and initiated you without the permission of the trustees have been stripped of their alignment with our organization, and therefore your initiation is nullified. Is that not correct, Barebones?"

Gehry nodded.

"You don't have the power to kick us out," Malcolm said quietly. "*We're* the members. We control the choice of taps."

"Interesting theory, but alas, the fact of the matter is that *money* controls the fate of the organization, and we control the money, not the seniors. If those in a position of power refuse to recognize you, you won't be recognized. Your Political Science courses must have taught you that."

"They taught me what became of history's overblown dictators."

Cuthbert chose not to recognize that little jibe, either. And, while he was at it, he also chose not to recognize the fact that his daughter was staring at him, openmouthed. "And where are your so-called brothers now, Mr. Cabot?" he said instead.

"More are coming." (Damn Manhattan traffic!) Malcolm looked at Poe. "What do *you* have to say for yourself?"

Poe spoke at last. "I was always against the inclusion of women without the express permission from the board of trustees."

"Poe informed us of your plan," said Mr. Cuthbert, smugly. Thirteen pairs of eyes shot daggers at the dark-haired senior. No wonder they were using his society name and calling the rest of us Miss This and Mr. That. (Though, in retrospect, they should all be liable for fines for speaking society code names in the presence of people they'd deemed "barbarians." Note to self: See if there's a statute of limitations on those levies.)

"You jerk," Malcolm said, staring at Poe with ice in his eyes. "What are you doing?"

Poe ignored him.

Josh tried to steer the conversation back to the point. "We would like to open a dialogue with you about your difficulties with the seniors' choice of taps." We had, in fact, spent several hours last evening configuring exactly the types of arguments we'd be making and who would be making them. Naturally, we left the bulk of the conversation to be handled by those in the group more used to formal debates—i.e., Josh and Demetria.

"We had no difficulty with the choice of you," Gehry said, nodding at Josh. "It's unfortunate that you were a member of an invalidated class."

"And yet," argued Nikolos, according to our script, "you never gave us the opportunity to denounce the females and pick new men to replace them." He'd been very keen on making that point, if only, he argued, because it would make the patriarchs rethink their hasty plan. I thought it made him sound like a prick, but hey, to each his own.

"Would that have been an option?" another patriarch asked.

Nikolos shot a glance at Odile. "No," he mumbled.

"You may think it's a case of throwing the baby out with the bathwater," said another, "but we feel it is best to start fresh with a class untainted by this…incident. The board has already selected a new list of taps from the remainder of the junior class."

"Oh, that's rich," Malcolm snapped, and even Poe looked surprised to hear the news. "Who the hell are you going to get now, after all the other societies have picked them over?"

"That does not concern you, Mr. Cabot."

I rolled my eyes. Yeah, like all that was left was a bunch of slobs? Come on, Malcolm. This was Eli University. There were plenty of superstars who weren't in societies. They might even be planning to tap Brandon, for all we knew. (And good luck with that endeavor!) Just because you weren't in a secret society didn't mean you weren't worthy. It could mean that you'd gotten into a fight with your ex-boyfriend.

"What's your problem with women?" Demetria cut to the chase. "Rose & Grave has, in the last few decades, opened its tap list to minorities, foreigners, homosexuals, people of different religions, creeds, social standings—why not females?"

"It is no prejudice against women," one of the patriarchs said, and proceeded to neatly sidestep all of our intentions. "We just don't feel as if there is any reason to start tapping them. Rose & Grave is a fraternal organization, just like the pale mockery that is the Greek frat system infesting every campus in the country. The inclusion of females would permanently alter the makeup of the society and the character of its meetings."

"It will turn us into a goddamn dating club," another sniffed.

"I can already foresee the accusations of rape."

"What the hell did you people do in there!" Malcolm blurted out.

"Nothing that would interest *you*, boy," Gehry snapped.

Cuthbert said with finality, "The women can feel free to start any society they so choose. We will not interfere."

Well, there went our script and all the best-laid plans of Josh and Demetria.

"You feel strongly enough about all this to sabotage our lives?" Kevin asked, deviating completely. "I lost my job in L.A. because of you wankers."

"Right," Josh added. You could almost see him trying to wrestle this back into his comfort zone. He'd need to work on his poker face a bit before graduating to televised debates. "Such behavior doesn't indicate a simple disinterest in the fairer sex, boys. You care about this too much."

"You misunderstand," Cuthbert replied. "We merely do what we must to maintain the integrity of the organization. The seniors went behind our backs. They were punished, and the illegitimates warned about what we could do if they fought. If you fought. It's a simple operation that has nothing to do with how the board feels about any policy. We do not tolerate any deviation from the oaths, and we strongly believe that to include women in Rose & Grave goes expressly against the mission of our Order, and therefore, all the seniors have violated the oath of fidelity. QED."

Odile shook her head, and her long hair glistened. "It goes against the oath in *your* opinion. I happen to believe that the only way to make this society viable in the next century is to recognize that this isn't a boys' game anymore."

The man between us began scribbling. I looked down at his legal pad to see a page of hastily scrawled notes. The most recent read: "This is a co-ed world. Why should we not have a co-ed society?"

Did the students have allies among this crowd? And if so, why weren't they speaking up? The man at my side held his jaw tight in check and scribbled away on his notebook, occasionally pressing the pen so hard that the ink made splotches on the page.

I placed my hand near his and he looked up, meeting my eyes for one moment with a look of stern encouragement, then turned back to his scribbles.

Yeah, right, buddy. If you ain't talking, then don't expect me to.

"As I have already mentioned," Cuthbert said with a sigh, "we have nothing against the idea of women organizing a secret society of their own."

"But that won't work," Odile said. "Part of the Digger draw is that it's centuries old. It's impossible for a women's society to compete with that, since women were only admitted to Eli in 1971. Rose & Grave has its enormous network of cronies, its property, its multimillion-dollar endowment. Even if the first women at Eli had started a society, they'd only now, thirty-odd years later, have achieved the type of position in society that would be of benefit to the new taps. There's no tomb, no island."

"No atomic grandfather clocks," I mumbled. The patriarch beside me gave me a curious, sidelong glance.

"Even Rose & Grave had to start somewhere."

"Yes," Clarissa scoffed. "With 19th century railroad barons and plantation kings. Russell Tobias and his cronies poured millions into the endeavor in the first decade, because they had the money to burn and a place in society already secured."

"Then, perhaps, my dear," Mr. Cuthbert said, "you should consider that route for you and your friends. That way, at least, I could be sure that my money was being well spent."

Clarissa clapped her mouth shut.

"No, of course you wouldn't want to go that route," he said, his tone oozing sarcasm. "Because it would put a severe dent in your high-heel budget and your sunglass collection."

Odile cut in again. "As I was saying, the society structure is something that takes years to develop. Eli opened its doors to women three decades ago. Even in the general population, it took a generation, but now we are considered to be equal to men."

"Oh, honey," Demetria muttered. "We need to talk."

Odile ignored her. "Rose & Grave needs to catch up or fall into obscurity. You are shutting yourself off from a large market-growth potential. The people you wish to disenfranchise will be valuable members to this society."

"The seniors made sure of that," Josh said, clearly glad to be getting back on track. "They tapped a class that would appeal to you." He pointed at Demetria. "Leaders." At Jenny. "Captains of industry." At Odile. "The rich and famous." At Clarissa. "And legacies."

Skipped right over me, I see. Poli-freakin'-ticians!

He looked at Mr. Cuthbert. "You're fighting against your own daughter, sir."

"With good reason, son." He pointed at Clarissa. "You want to know my problem with women? This is it. She's sitting

right here. I know those boys didn't make good choices, because look who they picked!"

Nobody moved. Nobody breathed. In fact, I'd wager a
good percentage of our hearts stopped beating. Clarissa stared
at his finger, her wide blue eyes unblinking.

"My daughter," the man spat, growing a bit red in the face,
"is a waste of a good credit line. If you only knew what I've
done for her. If you only knew what I've gone through on her
account..." He shook his head. "But of course you don't. You
wouldn't even have gotten that in your files. We hid it so well.
So goddamned well."

Was he talking about how she'd gotten in off the wait list?
Clarissa didn't seem to think that was much of a secret. She
didn't have the least bit of embarrassment about it. However,
she wouldn't have been the first Digger to share a secret with
me, understanding that I would never tell.

Though, to think of it, Lydia had been in the room, too.

"Daddy..." Clarissa whispered.

"What, Clary? You really think you're capable of the kind
of responsibility it means to be a Digger? You really think you
have the strength, the *mental fortitude*?"

"Daddy, please! That was a long time ago!"

"Not long enough. Not nearly long enough." He whirled
on Malcolm. "You want to know what you thought was good
enough for the Diggers, Mr. Cabot? Let me tell you about my
daughter. Let me tell you all about her." He leveled his gaze
on Clarissa, who might have been made of marble. "She got
into 'trouble' on us when she was fourteen. Fourteen, can you
imagine that?"

I considered everything I'd thought of Clarissa Cuthbert
since freshman year. Yeah, I could imagine that. And the truth
was, a month ago, I'd probably have relished this little tid-
bit of info. But not now. Not now that I understood that her
brusqueness was not snobbery, her style was not elitism, and

her supposedly nasty remarks were just misdirected efforts at advice. I don't know how it happened, but somehow my hatred had morphed into toleration, and thence into grudging respect. And now I realized something more: Clarissa was my sister.

"And that was just the start. Clearly not satisfied with whoring around, her next little trick was to develop a so-called eating disorder to get our attention. She'd binge on junk food then take laxatives. That was a fun six months of my life. Got so bad we had to send her away for a little while. Nice little place in the country that beat it right out of her, didn't it, darling?"

Tears the size of vodka shots were now rolling down Clarissa's cheeks. Demetria's mouth was open. Jennifer was holding her cross so tightly, I expected that any moment she'd be afflicted with stigmata of the palm. Odile looked—bored. The rest were transfixed by Mr. Cuthbert's outburst, with the exception of Poe, who just stared at his hands.

I could only picture what life must have been like for a teenaged Clarissa. Scared, clearly confused, obviously looking for attention. I wondered what it had taken to "beat" Clarissa's brush with bulimia out of her. Judging from the look of malicious glee on Mr. Cuthbert's face, it hadn't been pretty. No one would envy her wealth if they saw the price she'd paid for it.

"And then, of course, the cover-up. We couldn't let the universities know why our precious little girl had missed half a semester of eleventh grade, now, could we? Had to hide it. Had to lie. Had to fake all kinds of documents to make sure her record was spotless. Good thing I was a Digger, or we wouldn't have had the connections we needed to handle it. And even that wasn't enough. The little tramp needed our help again to get into Eli. And you think she's good enough to be a Digger. And she can waltz in here like she has the right to. This organization is better than that. It's better than the likes of her."

Clarissa's head drooped in defeat, and something inside of me snapped.

"Shut up!" I stood up so quickly that the cheap wooden chair went flying. "Shut up, shut up, shut up!" Maybe it was my oath, or maybe it was just my humanity, but I wasn't listening to a second more of it. "What kind of father are you? What kind of *person* are you? You can be disappointed in your daughter, you can be angry with her, but to say such terrible things about your own flesh and blood to a roomful of people? You disgust me, Mr. Cuthbert."

And now everyone was staring at me. Amy Haskel, who didn't have any excuse at all to be in Rose & Grave, except that I had a mouth that wouldn't stay closed if my life depended on it. The man at my side was giving me a look that said, *Finally*.

"She's your daughter. You're supposed to love her. You're supposed to support her. You don't think she deserves to be in your precious little secret society, but the way you just acted proves to me that you have grossly misunderstood what it means to be in Rose & Grave." I took a deep breath. "Because since the second I was tapped, Clarissa has treated me like a sister." I thought it had been elitism, but I'd been wrong. In Clarissa's eyes, we'd just finally had something in common, a wedge to use to get our friendship on a roll. "We may have had our differences in the past, and I'm sure as hell not about to admit I agree with half of what she says, but she's been loyal, and kind, and considerate of me since the second we showed up in the same tomb. *That's* your daughter, Mr. Cuthbert. *That's* the young woman you raised."

I paused, but no one seemed ready to chime in. I looked at Clarissa, who now had her head buried in her arms. Her slim shoulders were shaking with sobs.

"And she really, really loves Rose & Grave. More than any of the other taps in my class, she's understood what it means to be a Digger. Because *you* taught it to her. Aren't you proud of that? And she couldn't wait to show all of us. A few months ago, we'd never even acknowledge one another on the street, but now, in Rose & Grave, we have the chance to get to know one another, and to actually belong to something really big. And Clarissa embraced it. This means the world to her, can't you see that? She worked her butt off in school, and she was tapped by the Diggers, and maybe, just maybe, she finally did something that would make you proud. Something that would make you respect her the way you so clearly don't. Because you give your respect to the Diggers, and not to your daughter. Have you thought of that?"

Mr. Cuthbert swallowed.

"No, you haven't. You've forgotten entirely that the Diggers are supposed to be a family, because you can't even treat your family with the respect you'd give a stranger on the street. That's what being a Digger is? That's the kind of person who 'deserves' to be in the society? That's what you mean by a loyal, fraternal order? That's bullshit. Even Poe"—I pointed at him. Even that double-crossing, two-timing, malicious, sexist pig—"even Poe told me that he'd support his brothers, even if he disliked their decision, because they were his brothers, and Diggers stick together. And you somehow talked him out of that. Talked him into breaking his oath of constancy. So now who is forsworn? I'll give you a hint: It's not us."

Everyone just stared at me. Poe looked—well, if possible, he looked paler than usual. Utterly thunderstruck, in point of fact. Good. After all, for someone so society-obsessed as Poe, it must suck to be forsworn.

I barreled on, ignoring his little revelation and subsequent breakdown. Cry me a river, you arrogant ass-wipe. "And it's not the seniors, either. And it's not the patriarchs who helped them with the initiation. Are you hunting them all down, too? Mr. Prescott? The others? There are patriarchs on our side. You're going to have to overhaul the entire alumni to weed us all out." The patriarch beside me shifted slightly in his seat, and I took a deep breath. "I admit that I don't understand how all of this works," I said, and cast another glance at Poe, who was staring down at his own trembling hands, "but I would like to know how many of the patriarchs actually agree with this board."

"Sit *down*, Miss Haskel," said the Chief of Staff to the President of the United States, and that stopped me cold. I collected my chair and fell into it, breathing hard.

What the fuck had I just done?

Poe looked up, tightening his hands into fists. "She's right," he said simply.

Kurt Gehry placed a reassuring hand on Poe's arm. "Son..."

"No, she's very right." He looked at Malcolm. "I'm so sorry, Lance." He looked near tears. "I *lied* to you. I can't believe I did that. You're my *brother*."

"It's okay," Malcolm said.

But my diarrhea of the mouth was obviously contagious. "No, it's not. Don't you see? You don't even have to be here."

"Poe, shut up," Gehry said, this time with steel behind his words.

"And I should have told you," Poe blabbed on. "But I didn't want to piss them off. And I agreed with them. I thought the girls were such a bad idea. I told you so, too. Girls—well ..." He ducked his head. "It doesn't matter."

"It does," said another patriarch. "It's a date-rape case just waiting to happen." He eyed Odile warily as if she were about to cry sexual assault there at the table. The other patriarchs were still in shock from Mr. Cuthbert's outburst. Mr. Cuthbert himself looked like a deflated red balloon. Clarissa still hadn't lifted her head from the table.

"But I kept you in the dark." Poe's voice trembled, but he pushed through. Every sentence fell like a gavel. To him it must have been more like the blade of a guillotine. "All this week, when you were planning, I've been telling them every-thing, and not telling you the one thing you needed to know—"

"Stop talking." Gehry's voice had gone high-pitched and desperate.

"Because the thing is, this board—"

"Stop. Now."

"They're just the board."

"Stop talking, Poe."

"If you're looking for permission, you don't need theirs. You need the trustees at large. And every single alumnus, every patriarch on the planet, is a trustee of Rose & Grave."

Gehry's face turned a lovely shade of magenta that almost matched Demetria's hair. "Shut up this instant or I swear on Persephone that I'll make you pay."

But Poe's resolve had reached terminal velocity. "And we can ask them directly. Do a mail-in vote. Hell, do a call-in. I have all the info back in my room at Eli. If they vote us in, if they vote in women, there's not a damn thing the board can do about it." Poe paused, looking around the room at the taps gathered there, as if seeing them for the first time. His eyes set-tled on mine for the briefest of instants before turning back to Malcolm. "And Lance, I think they will."

The patriarch beside me slid his legal pad in my direction. I looked down at the message scrawled there.

Good job, Bugaboo. Well played.

From there, the meeting degenerated into chaos. Kurt Gehry went hysterical. He was shaking his fist in the air, swearing on everything that was holy that we "little girls" would rue the day we took him on. His face was the color of a ripe eggplant. I wish CNN had been there to capture it. It was hilarious. At last, three patriarchs had to haul him bodily from the room.

Mr. Cuthbert proceeded to get sick into a large potted ficus plant, and George and Odile decided that it was the perfect time to dance a tarantella on the top of the conference-room table. (I didn't know it was a tarantella at the time. Odile had to explain it to me later. I have no idea how George knew the steps.) Jennifer grabbed a box of tissues from the corner and began comforting Clarissa, who appeared to be making a speedy recovery (especially after watching her dad lose his lunch). Malcolm and Poe hugged for a long time, long enough to make me start wondering what exactly it was that Poe had against girls, and the patriarch Little Demon, wringing his hands and looking quite out of sorts, finally kicked us all out.

We whooped and hollered all the way down to the ground floor of the Eli Club and exploded onto Manhattan en masse.

Malcolm and Poe excused themselves from the group almost immediately and caught a Metro North commuter back to Eli in order to get started on the patriarch vote. "We'll do pro/con arguments," Malcolm said to me, and I had no doubt who'd be providing the "con" perspective. "There are about 800 alums, though, so it might take a bit of time. I'm calling the guys who never did show up and telling them to get their asses back to school to help."

I wondered idly if they'd get the tomb reopened before my Russian Novel final in two weeks.

Clarissa treated us all to a lavish dinner at an uptown steak house on her father's AmEx gold card. "Use it before I lose it," she said, signaling for another bottle of bubbly. It's safe to say that no one felt the least bit guilty ordering the surf n' turf.

"I have to make a phone call," Jennifer blurted out before the sliced tomatoes arrived. She rushed off, and when she returned, ten minutes later, it looked as if she'd been crying. However, no one could get her to open up.

"Tender nerves all around," Demetria said, patting her on the shoulder. Jennifer took a deep breath and actually directed a smile in Demetria's direction.

"It's been a long day," she admitted. "And I feel like... everything's changed."

"I hope it has," Kevin said.

Clarissa clinked her glass with mine. "Thanks so much, Amy." Her smile didn't quite reach her eyes. "I can't tell you how much that meant to me. But, what was that bit about not liking you before you were tapped? I didn't even know you."

I bit my lip. "You knew me well enough to—never mind. It's in the past."

"No, tell me."

"Galen Twilo. Freshman year."

She narrowed her eyes. "That loser? I don't think I've spoken to him in years. Do you know he stole my BlackBerry to buy pot?"

"Do you know he slept with me and never spoke to me again?"

She grinned broadly. "Then you had a lucky escape, my friend. That guy is such a little prick."

"Having seen it, I'm inclined to agree. But at the time, I overheard you say he was 'slumming' with me."

Her mouth turned into a little pink O. "I didn't. Did I? My God, what a bitch move!" She put her drink down, and enveloped me in a hug scented with Chanel and tears. "Now I'm really grateful that you stood up for me. Lord knows I hadn't done anything to deserve it."

"You had." I hugged her back. "You're my sister now. We shouldn't be held responsible for stuff we did as teenagers. We'll just stick that bit in the vault along with all—"

"The other crap my dad was talking about?" She smiled mirthlessly. "I hate the girl I used to be, Amy."

I met her eyes. "Good thing she's not around anymore."

"I don't know about that."

"I do," I replied. "Because I've been looking for her since initiation, and I haven't seen her once." And I had. I'd been so ready to judge Clarissa by everything I knew about her, rather than who she actually was. Maybe, if Clarissa could change, then a centuries-old society could as well.

After dinner, Clarissa paid the check and all the girls, true to form, took to the bathroom as a group. "I can't believe they wanted us to give back the pins," Demetria said, admiring the way hers flashed in the mirror.

"Yeah, but you weren't about to let go," I said. "I think we'd have swallowed them or pinned them straight to our bodies before handing them over to those assholes."

"It's too bad they aren't permanent," Odile said. Four pairs of eyes met in the mirror.

Jennifer exited the stall. "Hey, guys," she said, heading toward the nearest sink. "What's the plan now?"

———

"Absolutely not." Jennifer folded her arms across her chest.

"Come on, Jen," Demetria said, tugging her into the tattoo shop. "I have seven, and they hardly hurt at all."

Jennifer planted her feet on either side of the doorway and resisted the larger girl's efforts. "They aren't safe. You can get hepatitis."

Odile rolled her eyes. "Please. This is where Ani Di Franco goes. You wouldn't believe the strings I had to pull to get us in here. It's perfectly clean, and more important, über hip."

"You know," I said, "if she doesn't want one, she doesn't have to—"

"Oh, no you don't, Amy," said Clarissa. "All for one and all that. We're Diggers forever after tonight."

The much-illustrated tattoo artist eyed us warily. "What are you chicks, some kind of girl gang?"

"Something like that," Odile said, putting the finishing touches on her sketch and sliding the paper to him. "There. In black, red, and green. Put the numbers underneath."

"How big?"

"Small as you can make it," Clarissa said. "As Malcolm says…"

We all punched our fists in the air. "Discretion!"

As it turns out, "small as he could make it" was about an inch square, and despite all of Demetria's reassurances, the damn thing hurt like hell.

"That's because you're getting it on your spine, girlfriend," Demetria called out from her chair, where Manhattan's *second*-hottest tattoo artist was mapping out a small hexagon in between the tribal markings already gracing her upper arm. Apparently, Odile's connections got us double-teamed.

I took a deep breath and looked at Clarissa, who, shirt off, was standing before the mirror and admiring the freshly colored tattoo on her shoulder blade. "Right where my Angel wings would be," she said. Clarissa hadn't moved a muscle as the ink was sliced into her flesh, as if the pain of the needles was nothing compared with what she'd already experienced today.

"Okay, do it again," I said. The infernal buzzing started up and I could feel it in my teeth. A million bee stings formed the shape of the seal of Rose & Grave low on my back, and I squeezed my eyes shut—not that it helped, since I couldn't see what they were doing anyway. "How many of these have you done?" I asked the guy, hoping it wouldn't distract him. Since it wasn't distracting me any, I figured I was safe.

"None so cool as putting a coffin on Odile Dumas's breast," he replied. "I gotta get a picture of that for the website."

I squeezed my eyes shut. "Yeah, well, I don't know if that's a good idea. This is kind of a secret."

"What do you mean?"

Odile leaned in, her scarlet hair arranged to cover her bra-less chest. "Have you ever heard of Rose & Grave?" she asked the guy.

"The secret society?" His eyes widened.

Odile smiled and put her finger to her lips.

The buzzing stopped, and the man pulled the tattoo machine away from my skin. "You guys aren't, like, going to have us killed when we're done here, are you?"

Clarissa tilted her head to the side. "Hmmm, that's probably a good idea. What do you think, Lil' Demon?"

Odile ruffled the man's hair. "No, but we might dictate what it is you're allowed to tell Page Six."

When Demetria was finished, Jennifer asked the artist to take her into the back room, and she returned half an hour later, her eyes watery, and refused to let any of us see her tattoo. "It's um, private," she said, eyes downcast.

"That girl," Demetria whispered, "has more secrets than any five Diggers."

"I bet she's really a big kink," Clarissa added. "These religious chicks often are."

I was twisted, the better to see my new tat, which the artist was smearing with Vitamin E as he explained to me what to expect from my first few days of being inked. I glanced at Jennifer, who was popping M&M's (to restore her blood sugar post inking) and laughing with Odile. I touched my skin, which was swollen and tender where the seal had been embedded in my flesh. "We'll find out when we start the meetings, I guess." Those C.B.s were guaranteed to be a hoot.

Clarissa beamed. "Yes, and I'll finally get the equality of hearing some of your secrets. You already heard all of mine."

Odile joined the group. "Well then, let's even the playing field. We'll all tell a secret. I'll start." She took a deep breath. "I don't want to go back into the industry after graduation. There, I said it."

"Okay, I'll play." Demetria ducked her head. "I'm ... kind of into John McCain."

Jennifer chewed her lip for a few seconds, then whispered, "I don't always agree with my pastor."

I tried to sit up, grimacing when the tattooed area ached with every move. "I'm writing a novel," I admitted.

Clarissa laughed. "And here we all thought you were going to tell us if George is a good kisser!"

I turned as red as the skin around my tattoo. "Since when is that a secret?"

"Just teasing," Clarissa said. "To the Diggerettes!"

Demetria grimaced. "Oh, no, that's wretched. I'd rather all the usual Gothic shit they say. You know, the whole Sacred Seal of the Holy Order of the Knights of Persephone blah blah blah."

"That's not it," Odile said. "It's the Flame of Life—"

Jennifer sighed and flipped her braid back. "And the Shadow of Death," she said, rolling her eyes.

Tonight, however, I could take a few extra capital letters. After all, we'd earned them. We'd taken on powerful, intimidating men, and we'd beaten them. My back stung, and I thought of the ink soaking into my bloodstream, becoming a part of my soul. I lightly traced the numerals that were sketched beneath the seal. "Yours in 312," I murmured. Tonight, we'd become something more, for instead of the ubiquitous 312 inscribed beneath the symbol, the five of us had 177 etched into our skin. The first Rose & Grave class of women. The ones that changed it all.

We were Diggers, and nothing would ever be the same.

I hereby confess:

Every rose has its thorn.

15.
Commencement Issues

When I finally got home that night, Brandon was—wait for it—*not* sitting on my couch. Probably a good thing, too. Though I knew that eventually he'd see my new body décor, I figured it was best to wait until:

1) The onion-peel scabs began to heal.
2) It stopped stinging like a bitch.
3) I figured out a way to explain it without breaking my vows.

My parents were going to have a fit when they saw it. Luckily, I wasn't much for wearing bathing suits. It's not like anyone would get a good view unless they caught me in my skivvies. Which, now that I'd solidified a status with Brandon, really limited the options. (Not that I was complaining.)

I tried to go to bed, but I was way too wired to sleep, and seriously considered skipping down to Calvin College and giving Brandon a midnight wake-up call. Instead, I buckled down and started studying. I'd been neglecting my schoolwork since the day the first letter came from Rose & Grave, and I needed to reverse the trend. Exams were in a week and a half, and I had a slew of papers to write before finals.

I managed sixty-four pages of WAP before I fell asleep. (On my stomach, of course.)

The next morning, I was awakened by the sound of persistent thwapping at my door. I opened it to find Lydia holding a black cardboard coffin sized for a member of the terrier family.

"What died?" I asked, rubbing my eyes.

She turned it in my direction. "For you, Bride of Dracula." Inside the coffin-shaped box lay two dozen phenomenal scarlet roses and a small card in creamy, off-white linen. I opened it.

Good job, Boo.
—Your brother

George. Tiny thrills coursed through my body before my higher brain functions could tamp them down and remind them that my boyfriend's name was Brandon and that he would never send me such a macabre, if perfectly suited, gift.

I looked at Lydia. "Can I borrow your vase?"

She shook her head. "Hon, I'm only going to say this once, and then we can go back to our 'let's not talk about it' treaty, but your *people* have very strange taste." And then she went to fetch the vase. (Like she should talk? It wasn't two weeks ago that there was dried blood on our doorknob. Her society people were, if possible, even stranger.)

When she returned, we took to arranging the flowers together, and wouldn't meet each other's eyes.

"Lydia?" I said, and she glanced at me over the top of a blossom. "Is this going to destroy us?"

She swallowed. "God, I hope not."

"It's not fair, you know," I said. "You at least know the name of my society. I don't know anything about yours."

She smirked. "Yeah, but who said life was fair?"

"Hmph." I swatted her with a piece of greenery.

"Buck up, Amy," she said in consolation. "Who needs revelations when you've got roses?"

Good point. I marveled at the blooming perfection of each gorgeous rose and tried in vain to ignore the stubborn thrills that persisted in tripping down my spine as if I weren't in a committed relationship.

They clearly knew something I didn't.

Brandon didn't show up at the Lit Mag office all afternoon, and three messages on his voice mail failed to produce a single callback. At dinnertime, I finally tracked him down outside his dining hall.

"Where have you been?" I asked as he exited the building with an enormous sandwich clumsily wrapped in napkins. He spared me a glance, then turned toward his entryway. I tried again, hoping he'd just—I don't know—been struck with sudden hysterical blindness? "Brandon?"

He took a closer look at his sandwich (See, maybe he *was* losing his eyesight!), then dumped it in the nearest bin and gestured to me. "Not here."

Oh, God. More secret society crap? How the hell could those bastards have gotten to him, too? Brandon was...untouchable. He didn't give a shit what they said. Right?

I followed him into his room, and he sat down on his high-backed, obviously single-serving-only computer chair and surveyed me carefully. "Where were you yesterday?"

"In New York," I replied. Somehow standing there before him made me feel as if I were reporting to a judge. Even the Diggers had let us sit at our meeting. "Remember how I told you a few days ago that I was going down there on...business."

He nodded, then took a deep breath. "I was talking to some friends, and they said they saw you in a bar on Sunday, making out with some guy."

I dropped to the bed. Crap. Crap crap crappity crap. I knew this was going to happen. I just hoped it would have waited until our relationship had fully gelled.

"The thing is," Brandon said, leaning forward and putting his hands together until all his fingertips lined up exactly, "I think I know what you're going to say."

"That it was before . . . ?"

"Yeah."

See? Told you he was a genius. "It was."

"Hmmm." He studied his hands, made little twisted figures out of his fingers. "I thought so. I wanted to talk to you straightaway, but you weren't around last night, so instead I got to spend the evening thinking about it. A lot."

A strange nausea blossomed in my stomach. "Thinking too much isn't a good idea, though, right?" I laughed, nervously. "That's what you're always telling me."

"Maybe I'm wrong." He looked up. "Because what I finally settled on is that even though I don't really have the right to be upset about it, since it happened *before* we made our agreement to be monogamous, I'm still upset about it. Does that make sense?"

I nodded, since my mouth was too dry to speak. Me, I'd be furious to discover that Brandon had hooked up with someone else milliseconds before sleeping with me. But then, I'm a lot less reasonable than he is. Right?

"And last night, I was hoping that when I asked you about it, you'd say, 'Why, Brandon, that's the stupidest thing I've ever heard. They must be thinking about some other girl. I only have eyes for you.'" He pursed his lips. "But you wouldn't have said that, would you?"

No, because it happened. "I can't lie to you."

He nodded, slowly. "Right. That's what I thought. So, first I was angry, and then I thought that I didn't have any right to be angry, and then I thought that that was stupid, and why do I need to be logical about whether or not I'm going to be angry, and then I was angry at myself for thinking that I had the right to be angry without firm logical footing...as you can see, it was a while before I had it all worked out." He shrugged, sheepish. "So the thing is, I don't think I'm going to get over that. It would be nice to, and that would be the technically correct thing to do, but underneath all this logical applied-math exterior, I'm..." He trailed off. "Even if you hadn't made me any promises, Amy, I still wanted to believe that you were coming around to my way of thinking. Not believe that if you'd gotten just a little bit luckier at that bar, you wouldn't have come home at all."

All these imperfect verbs. As if it was a done deal. I swallowed the enormous lump in my throat. "Would it help to know that's what made me understand that I wanted to be with you?"

"Kissing someone else?" He considered it. "Yes, it makes me feel a little bit better about myself. But, Amy, it's not enough. Because it's not just that, you know? You've been so distant all week. As if now that we could say that we were together, you'd placated me for a while. And I know"—he held up his hand—"you've had stuff going on, and I know that it's not something you're 'allowed to talk about,' but when I woke up in your room that morning, you were crying so hard." His brow furrowed, as if he was remembering it with pain. "And you wouldn't even tell me what had happened. You just disappeared. You lost your job, but it wasn't me that you turned to for comfort. That's not a good sign."

"I wasn't looking for comfort then, Brandon," I tried to explain. "I was looking for action. I did come to you, later. You were wonderful."

"I *really* don't want to be your afterthought."

I closed my eyes, and the tears that had been building up crashed down my cheeks. "Brandon..."

He turned away then, probably because he wasn't willing to let himself see me cry. "Here's the thing, Amy. What all that thinking made me realize was that I'd been kidding myself last weekend in your bedroom. I didn't just want a title slapped on our relationship. I wanted a relationship. I hoped that if we called it one, then you'd start treating it like one. But from that very first morning, you didn't. And maybe you never will. You may not kiss other guys at bars now, but that alone doesn't make you my girlfriend."

And then he told me that he didn't want to see me anymore, and that though he'd always care about me, and hoped that we could someday be friends, he couldn't let our relationship continue in any of the permutations it had enjoyed since February 14th.

Sorry for the summation. His actual words were too brutal to keep in my mind. I excised them that night with large amounts of Finlandia Mango. Lydia held me while I cried, and I believed then that all the secret societies in the world wouldn't really come between us.

The thing is, I think I knew it would come to this. Brandon could only put up with my bullshit for so long.

————

Okay, on to happier things. As it turns out, the seniors managed to mobilize the patriarch population much more swiftly than anyone expected, and by the middle of Reading Week, we had our answer: Girls were in.

Understandably, the new taps spent the rest of the week camped out in the tomb, which helped me put Brandon and the rest of my barbarian life out of my mind. I learned all of the tomb's nooks and crannies, secret rooms and hidden staircases.

I combed through the library, and figured out the exact pattern that would make the "clappers" installed in the second-floor skull sconces flicker. (Diggers have a very bizarre sense of humor.) And of course, I crammed for finals, and found that the exam collection in the Rose & Grave library was as helpful as promised.

A secret society tomb during Reading Week is truly a sight to behold. Everywhere, the Diggers had set up little camps from which to corral their troops and prepare for battle. You'd wander through the rooms on a fifteen-minute break from studying, and see tiny microcosms of academia in every corner. Every flat surface, from an empty teak china cabinet to a glass case holding rusty Civil War swords, seemed to sprout families of spiral-bound notebooks, photocopies, textbooks, and laptops whose endless extension cords snaked through the hallways in search of the elusive unused power outlet. The ground around headquarters would be littered with empty pop bottles and cardboard coffee holders, sandwich wrappers and deflated bags of chips. Nearby would be a student's sleeping-spot, identifiable only because it usually encompassed a slightly more comfortable flat surface and a makeshift pillow (usually a sofa and a balled-up sweater, though Greg Dorian very creatively utilized a stuffed mongoose and a billiard table). My little home was the aforementioned window seat in the Grand Library (no body parts, just books) that looked out onto the well-tended courtyard. The outside yard of Rose & Grave may have looked neglected and uninviting, but the inside was paradise. Funny how so many things worked that way.

A week later, I took my seat in Professor Muravcek's lecture hall, three number-two pencils in my hand, and a fair dose of serenity in my brain. I'd do fine, even though I'd left a good 500 pages of WAP unread.

I didn't yet understand that my position was even better than I'd thought.

The T.A. at the lectern lifted several stacks of exams and started up the steps, handing out a dozen or so at the end of each aisle. I lifted my exam packet from the proffered stack and passed the rest along. Once he had finished handing out the materials, he returned to the front of the hall, wrote the time on the chalkboard, and said, "Begin."

I opened the packet, and a tiny white card fell out.

Dear Initiate,
I sincerely hope you've taken careful note of the 1985 final.
It will probably be coming in handy right about now.
                              Yours in 312,
                              Shandy, D171

I glanced back at the T.A., who was shuffling papers at the lectern and very determinedly not meeting my eyes. Another Shandy, just like Harun. I wondered if someday there would be another Bugaboo. Forty-five minutes later, I finished my exam, packed up my things, and headed toward the front desk.

"Done so soon?" the T.A. asked.

"Nineteen-eighty-five was a very good year," I said. It was the year I was born. Of course I'd pick it out of the Diggers' hefty collection, if only to see what kind of questions they thought were important then.

"I knew you'd think so." He smiled. "We're all very impressed with you, you know."

I blushed. "I didn't do anything."

"Oh, yes you did. You put one of your own first. Next to punctuality, that's the best quality to have." He cleared his throat. "Too bad you weren't in my section. I give all my students a pizza party at my house. You could have seen my, ahem, atomic grandfather clock."

I cannot believe that story got out. "You're teasing, right?"

"I'd tell you," he said with a wink, "but then I'd have to kill you." He pointed at my exam. "You're sure you have nothing more to tell me about Kitty and Levin?"

I shuddered. "No offense, but I don't think Russian lit's my thing. Besides, there's something I need to do." I had one of my own who needed me. "Barbarian matters."

He gave me a mock salute. "Carry on, then, sister."

I made straight for the offices of the *Eli Daily News*. The *EDN*, unlike my own lowly publication, occupied a veritable Gothic castle of a structure on campus. Once upon a time, the building had been home to a rival secret society, which had long ago given up the ghost and relinquished its property to the university, who had added windows and turned it over to their illustrious student media outlet.

Genevieve was at her desk in her tiny private office, and, to her credit, managed to hide the majority of her shock when I barged in. But not all.

"Hi," I said. "We need to talk. May I sit?"

"Wha—what are you doing here?"

"I'll give you one guess."

Her eyes flickered toward the door behind me, as if I were concealing a troupe of hired killers.

Best to nip that fear in the bud. "I'm here to talk about a feature you've proposed for the *EDN*'s commencement issue."

"Oh?" She raised an eyebrow.

"I'd like to offer an alternative." She brightened, but I held up my hand. "Not the one you suggested. I've never been a fan of blackmail. However, I must admit that I'm not entirely insensitive to your situation."

"You have no idea what my situation is," Genevieve snapped.

"On the contrary," I replied calmly. "I think I understand it better than you do. And I don't think he's entirely blameless in this affair."

"Get . . . out . . . of my office."

"Not until you hear me out." I waited, but she made no further objection. "Okay, let's talk. You want to write an excruciating piece of muckraking tabloid fodder about a very dear friend of mine, with the full understanding that the article would do irreparable damage to his interpersonal relationships while not revealing any insufficiency of character. I think this is a Bad Idea." (When needed, I can swing capital letters with the best of them.)

"Like I said, you don't understand my situation."

"I do." I leaned forward. "I think you're holding it over his head because what you really want to do is try for a sharp little piece that will assure you a neat job as an investigative journalist at the *Post* or the *Times* or the *Tribune*."

She was silent.

"And I'm here to tell you that you aren't going to get either. What I can offer you, however, is a source—an anonymous source, it must remain—but one that will happily share with you the real reason behind that little disturbance outside the Rose & Grave tomb on High Street two weeks ago."

A fire lit behind Genevieve's eyes. She was a reporter to the core.

"The name you're looking for is Deep Throat."

"Anything I want?"

I shook my head, ever so slightly. "This story. And I promise you, it's good enough to go on with."

Her mouth became a thin line. "Not enough. It's not enough."

"Very well." I sat back in my seat. "However, I must warn you that if you persist in threatening my friends, I will ditch the short stories I've planned for the Lit Mag's commencement issue and go non-fiction. I promise you that my small-circulation magazine will scoop the hell out of your rag and publish the story instead."

Now her mouth did drop open. "You can't do that."

"I've got the printer lined up." I stood. "Let me know what you decide, Genevieve."

"You think you scare me?" she shot at me as I walked toward the door. "You think I'm frightened of your stupid little frat?"

I paused at the door. "If you aren't, then you should be. I'm a Digger. I don't make promises I can't keep."

And then I left. Two hours later, she e-mailed me that we had a deal.

Damn, that felt good. A girl could get used to this kind of power.

————

Considering everything that had happened, actually assembling the commencement issue of the literary magazine was far easier than I'd ever expected. Brandon and I arranged our schedules with the express purpose of spending as little time in the same room as possible. He took over the artwork, while I focused on the actual submissions and organizing the way the pieces fit together into a meaningful whole (or as meaningful as a bunch of overeducated David Foster Wallace wannabes could get in the middle of exam week). I left a lot of the layout work to the rising sophomores, and, despite the fact that my hours at the Lit Mag office were filled with much less mirth and far fewer paper airplanes, I'd never had a better time there. Perhaps I relished the opportunity so much because I feared it would be my last. After all, I still didn't have a summer job. I was pretty sure the next few months would see me plying khakis at the Shaker Square GAP.

The night before commencement, the first copies of "Ambition" arrived, hot off the press, and I flipped through it, surprised at how foreign each freshly minted page appeared to my eyes. Unlike other issues, I hadn't pored over the font size of every running head, nor labored over the arrangement of the advertisements. Even the cover art had been chosen by Brandon, and, as if sharing some final inside joke, he'd picked a shot of a young man silhouetted against an urban backdrop, looking longingly over the city. It looked, as I'd suspected it would, like a perfume ad. However, I thought it was perfect for the melancholy, stark tone of most of the pieces. Brandon, as always, displayed excellent taste.

I had planned on staying for commencement, both to oversee distribution of the magazine and to attend Glenda Foster's graduation. Since the dorms were closed, I camped out in the tomb, and found that I was not the only Digger who'd had that plan. The night before, no one got any sleep, as a gaggle of patriarchs who'd shown up early for the following day's commencement exercises took the opportunity to teach the Digger students the time-honored tradition of Kaboodle Ball, the rules of which, I'm sorry to say, are far too complicated to relate without the aid of charts, graphs, and small, many-jointed marionettes. It's kind of like hide-and-seek by way of rugby, golf, and Calvinball.

The morning of commencement was clear and surprisingly chilly for the season. I busied myself directing three underclass Lit Mag staffers to the distribution centers, but made sure that I picked up a copy of the *Eli Daily News* as well. Surprisingly, working with Genevieve hadn't been the chore I'd anticipated. I think my original assessment was correct. She wasn't an evil bitch—just ambitious, truly heartbroken, and desperate for payback. I had no expectations that her story would be flattering to the society, but then again, it was a lesser evil.

I was in the third column of the feature when someone cleared his throat in front of me. I looked up to see two figures in black gowns and hats: one tall, slim, and pale, with angry gray eyes; the other tan and blond with an enormous smile he was unable to hide.

"Are you the secret source?" Poe blurted.

I blinked at him. "I assure you, I'm just as shocked to see this piece as you are."

Malcolm bit his lip, but his eyes transmitted gratitude.

"This story is a scandal!" Poe shouted. "It reveals everything about our inner workings!"

"Come on," Malcolm said, finding his tongue at last. "All it really says is that Rose & Grave has finally opened its ranks to women."

"And that there was some inner turmoil about it," Poe snapped.

"A fine piece of investigative journalism," I pointed out. "I think the writer lives below Malcolm. She probably heard us at the meeting that night."

"I wouldn't make a big deal out of it." Malcolm clapped Poe on the shoulder. "It's not the first story that claims to bust open our secrets, and it won't be the last, either."

"It really doesn't get into specifics, either," I added. "Except for this bit about how some of the more age-addled patriarchs staged a little protest outside the tomb. If anything, I think it does a pretty good job of swerving around the real heart of the matter. That source—whoever they are—played this writer like a piano." I looked at Malcolm, whose eyebrows informed me not to press my luck.

The three of us headed back into the throng of graduates and their families. "Malcolm!" a blond woman shouted, pointing a digital camera in our direction. Must be Mrs. Cabot. The two boys leaned close to me and we all smiled for the photo op, but as soon as the flash went off, Poe's expression went dour again. When Malcolm trotted off to see how the snapshot turned out, Poe turned to me.

"I wanted to thank you." No one had ever sounded less grateful.

"For?"

He closed his eyes for a moment, as if steeling himself.

"For speaking up in New York. I don't know what I was thinking. Mr. Gehry just had me convinced..." He trailed off, then shook his head. "I'd forgotten some stuff. You reminded me."

"Oh. You're welcome." We stood in awkward silence for a few more moments, before I came up with a neutral topic. "So, what are you doing this summer?"

"*Not* working for the White House." He smiled mirthlessly.

"I'm sorry," I said. So, maybe not so neutral, but at least it explained why Poe of all people would betray his brothers. Ambition, I thought, can be a dangerous thing.

Maybe I was glad I hadn't yet determined the exact shape of mine.

He shrugged. "It's okay. At least I can look at myself in the mirror every morning. I'll probably be down in D.C., though, doing...something. You?"

I shrugged. "Trying to decide between two brilliant offers, at Starbucks and T.G.I. Friday's." And, because I didn't see a reason for this interview to drag on any longer than necessary, I added, "Well, congratulations on graduating. I wish you the best of luck with Eli Law next year." *And I hope I don't see you any more than strictly necessary.*

"Good luck to you, too," Poe said, looking past me toward the tomb on the corner. "I have a feeling you're going to need it."

He loped off and I rolled my eyes. Good riddance. What the hell did Malcolm see in that guy?

Malcolm returned soon after. "Did you guys have a chance to talk?"

"We exchanged thinly veiled insults, yeah."

He sighed. "You know, Amy, you should really give him a chance. He's not as bad as you think."

I cocked my head at him. "Malcolm, is he ... ?"

He threw back his head and laughed. "No, Amy. He's a little

twisted, but otherwise straight as a rod." Then he tapped the paper in his hand. "Thank you. I can't—I can't ever thank you enough for what you did. I don't know how you did it, how you thought of it, but...you're amazing."

"What are little sibs for?" I nodded toward his parents. "Are you going to tell them?"

Malcolm took a deep breath, and his expression turned somber. "Yes. Sometime. Sometime soon. We go up to a cabin in the mountains every summer. My dad and I like to go hunting. I think I'll tell them then. Away from the press and all."

"Good idea. But if I can make a suggestion? Make sure the guns aren't loaded."

He flashed his pearly whites. "Yeah." Already I could see relief etched on his face. Whatever Malcolm might say, he was tired of lying to his folks. I hoped it all worked out, but I wouldn't hold my breath for a happy Cabot family vacation.

Soon after I left Malcolm, I was met by one more Digger—the man who'd been next to me at the Eli Club, taking notes. His auburn hair, liberally sprinkled with gray, shone in the morning sunlight.

"Amy Haskel!" he said brightly, pumping my hand up and down. "I'm so glad I caught up with you. Gus Kelting." He leaned in. "Horace, D142."

"We meet again," I said. And this time, he was talking to me. Good, because I still had a few questions from that afternoon. "I wanted to ask you, why weren't you standing up for us in New York? I saw the notes you wrote me."

"I'd been outvoted," Kelting admitted. "I wasn't allowed to talk. And believe me, it was one of the hardest things I've ever done. But I think you nailed them. I told all my Digger friends. We were very impressed with you. *I* was very impressed." He pulled out a copy of "Ambition." "I read this last night," he said. "Very impressive...also."

"Thank you, sir."

"And, as you can probably tell by my limited vocabulary, I'm not much of a word guy. I'm into economics."

Okay. "That's nice." Where was he going with this?

"Here's the thing, Miss Haskel. I understand you have a bit of an employment problem, and I know that the Diggers are . . . to blame for it. I want to make it up to you. I do work for a think tank down in D.C., and we've got a project this summer that we need some help on. We're trying to establish a rehabilitation program for exploited women, and as part of our bid for funding, we're putting together a book of narratives. Some of these stories—they'd break your heart. But these ladies aren't writers. Some of them aren't even literate. I think a person with your editorial skills would come in handy."

I stared at him for a moment, incredulous. "You're offering me a job?"

"It doesn't pay much more than a stipend, but we'll find you housing, too. I know this isn't in New York . . ."

"An editorial job?"

"Yes. With a good deal of responsibility attached."

Somehow, I managed not to tackle him. This was way cooler than xeroxing form rejections! And Lydia would be in D.C. this summer. (Also Poe, but really, who cares? It's a big city.) "Wow, Mr. Kelting. Thank you!"

"No, Amy. Thank *you*. Besides, you're a Digger. What, we're going to let you spend the summer pumping gas?" He smiled. "Come here, I want you to meet someone."

He took my hand and led me across the lawn to a young woman with long red curls and post-grad-style robes. "Amy Haskel, this is my daughter, Sarah Kelting. *Dr.* Sarah Kelting. She graduated from med school today."

"So I see," I said.

Sarah laughed, and shook my hand. "Dad, are you going to introduce me like that from now on?"

"You bet!" he said, beaming. "Or at least until I've got it paid for."

"So, in other words, from now on," the woman teased.

"Sarah, Amy has just agreed to come work for my company this summer."

"I'm sorry to hear that." She winked at me. "Do you have a place to live in D.C.? I've got a friend who is trying to sublet her studio in Adams Morgan. You'd love it." She looked at Mr. Kelting. "Your company is paying, right?"

He put his arm around his daughter. "She's such a smart-ass, Amy. Comes from not having anyone else to compete with growing up. It was just the two of us." He leaned in and dropped his voice to a conspiratorial whisper. "Back when she was at Eli undergrad, I wanted her to—you know. But I knew it wasn't going to happen. That's why I was so happy to see you girls. It's about time. And when you stood up in there . . ." He laughed. "You reminded me of my Sarah. I wanted you in, for all the Sarahs."

Sarah rolled her eyes and shrugged Kelting's arm off. "Da-a-ad," she said. "Would you stop talking about the you-know-whoggers?" She looked at me and shook her head in consolation. "Is he boring you with tales of that silly little boys' club?"

But I exchanged glances with Gus Kelting, whose Rose & Grave pin, age-burnished to a deeper gold, glinted from the collar of his shirt. "It's not a boys' club," I said. *Not anymore.* "It's one of the most powerful secret societies in the world."

I should know. I'm a member.

Presenting the Rose & Grave Tap Class of D177

1) Clarissa Cuthbert: *Angel*
2) Gregory Dorian: *Bond*
3) Odile Dumas: *Little Demon*
4) Benjamin Edwards: *Big Demon*
5) Howard First: *Number Two*
6) Amy Haskel: *Bugaboo*
7) Nikolos Dmitri Kandes IV: *Graverobber*
8) Kevin Lee: *Frodo*
9) Omar Mathabane: *Kismet*
10) George Harrison Prescott: *Puck*
11) Demetria Robinson: *Thorndike*
12) Jennifer Santos: *Lucky*
13) Harun Sarmast: *Tristram Shandy*
14) Joshua Silver: *Keyser Soze*
15) Mara Taserati: *Juno*

Acknowledgments

I hereby confess my tremendous gratitude to Bantam Dell: Mr. Irwyn Applebaum, Nita Taublib, Gina Wachtel, Tracy Devine, Paolo Pepe, Kelly Chian, Carol Russo, Pam Feinstein, Shawn O'Gallagher, Rachael Dorman, and especially to my champion and friend, the tireless editorial genius Kerri Buckley, who from the very first moment understood Amy almost better than I did, and who I knew would be the perfect tap. Kerri, if I could order an editor custom-made, I'd ask for someone as extraordinary as you.

I'm blown away by the unfailing judgment and vision of Deidre Knight, who has been with me every step of the way, and whose super secret-agent moves are an asset to any society. I'm so glad you're a knight in mine.

Love and whopping big hugs to my parents, who, despite the decades' worth of ribbing about books at Bucs games, have always encouraged me. Your happiness and enthusiasm are joys to behold. Thank you for all the opportunities you have given me and for your endless dedication to your children and their dreams.

Also, to Luke and Brian, the coolest brothers I've ever had, and the rest of my family and childhood friends who put up with and participated in my stories, thank you. Special recognition to Beth for her spot-on designs and Tara for making my vision a reality. Volumes of thanks to my teachers, who over the years tolerated and even encouraged my scribblings, and trusted that I would become a woman of words.

Three cheers for Marley Gibson, the most loyal friend and outrageous critique partner, who took it upon herself to pitch this manuscript sight unseen and "had a feeling" about it from the start. I owe so much to my writing friends: Lex; CLW; Colleen, Elly, Jana, and Wendy; and above all, TARA. I am especially grateful to Cheryl Wilson, who gave me a home and a sense of my own strengths, and to Julie Leto, who got me into this whole mess and has always provided a shining example of the kind of writer I want to be when I grow up.

I am indebted to Jacki and Bob, who let me live in their house while developing the seed of this story and celebrated my sale as if I was one of their own. And props to the whole D.C. crowd for making me feel so at home.

All my appreciation to fellow Bulldogs Lauren, Nicola, and Mackenzie, and further gratitude and apologies to all my bright college friends and companions, who may or may not see themselves in these pages. Here's a hint: if it's good, it's totally about you. If it's bad, it's about, um . . . someone else. And also, I bow to the loose lips of my secret sources. Thank you for not killing me after telling me.

And, finally, my most ardent admiration and love to my partner, Dan. You're the person who made me believe I'd do it, and you've demonstrated your faith with every step and sacrifice along the way. *Aspiret primo Fortuna labori.*

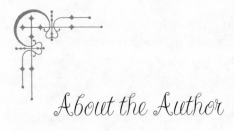

About the Author

DIANA PETERFREUND graduated from Yale University in 2001 with degrees in geology and literature. A former food critic, she now resides in Washington, D.C.; this is her first novel. Bantam Dell will publish the second book in the Secret Society Girl series in Summer 2007.